Tanner was curious about the lawman. His appearance, in conjunction with their own arrival, mocked coincidence. But how could the authorities predict the Haglunds would be in danger? He considered that the marshal, sheriff—whatever he was—might have come to confront Dannell about his wives, but that made no sense. It was obvious the Haglunds had been living here for several years at least. To think the law would only notice them on the same day that Tanner and his men turned up was laughable.

Somehow, someone had connected them to Dannell Haglund's brood. Which meant the lawman was not hunting bigamists. He was hunting Tanner's crew . . .

AVENGING ANGELS

— THE LAWMAN —

LYLE BRANDT

BERKLEY BOOKS, NEW YORK

THE BERKLEY PUBLISHING GROUP
Published by the Penguin Group
Penguin Group (USA) Inc.
375 Hudson Street, New York, New York 10014, USA

Penguin Group (Canada), 90 Eglinton Avenue East, Suite 700, Toronto, Ontario M4P 2Y3, Canada
(a division of Pearson Penguin Canada Inc.)
Penguin Books Ltd., 80 Strand, London WC2R 0RL, England
Penguin Group Ireland, 25 St. Stephen's Green, Dublin 2, Ireland (a division of Penguin Books Ltd.)
Penguin Group (Australia), 250 Camberwell Road, Camberwell, Victoria 3124, Australia
(a division of Pearson Australia Group Pty. Ltd.)
Penguin Books India Pvt. Ltd., 11 Community Centre, Panchsheel Park, New Delhi—110 017, India
Penguin Group (NZ), 67 Apollo Drive, Rosedale, North Shore 0632, New Zealand
(a division of Pearson New Zealand Ltd.)
Penguin Books (South Africa) (Pty.) Ltd., 24 Sturdee Avenue, Rosebank, Johannesburg 2196,
South Africa

Penguin Books Ltd., Registered Offices: 80 Strand, London WC2R 0RL, England

This is a work of fiction. Names, characters, places, and incidents either are the product of the author's imagination or are used fictitiously, and any resemblance to actual persons, living or dead, business establishments, events, or locales is entirely coincidental. The publisher does not have any control over and does not assume any responsibility for author or third-party websites or their content.

AVENGING ANGELS

A Berkley Book / published by arrangement with the author

PRINTING HISTORY
Berkley edition / October 2010

Copyright © 2010 by Michael Newton.
Cover illustration by Bruce Emmett.
Cover design by Steve Ferlauto.

ISBN: 978-0-425-23737-3

BERKLEY®
Berkley Books are published by The Berkley Publishing Group,
a division of Penguin Group (USA) Inc.,
375 Hudson Street, New York, New York 10014.
BERKLEY® is a registered trademark of Penguin Group (USA) Inc.
The "B" design is a trademark of Penguin Group (USA) Inc.

PRINTED IN THE UNITED STATES OF AMERICA

10 9 8 7 6 5 4 3 2 1

Again, and always, for Heather.

PROLOGUE

The killers dressed in black, from high-crowned, flat-brimmed hats to dusty square-toed boots. The only hint of color in their garb came from gray shirts worn beneath their long, black frock coats. Gray concealed more sweat and grime than white did on a long ride, and the killers felt as if they had been on the trail forever.

The Lord's work was never done.

Only the leader's horse was black, but that was pure chance. The animals were not a part of their adopted uniform—nothing but tools, in fact, much like their pistols, worn in black gunbelts. They lived to serve and were expendable.

Like soldiers of the Lord.

There had been seven killers when they had set out on their mission, months beyond remembering gone by. One had been careless in Virginia City and had paid the price. Another had been slow in San Diego, let the mob take him alive, and suffered for it, but there'd been no saving him. Mistakes had consequences.

Five remained, committed to the task they'd been assigned by one who spoke for God on Earth. The Prophet willed them to succeed or die in the attempt, and they could do no less.

Their leader calculated that they had run through half the list of names originally written down in ink the same color as blood. That list was faded now and sweat-stained, nearly separated into quarters on the lines where it'd been folded and unfolded countless times. It did not matter if the letters blurred or if the list itself was lost.

Each of the killers had those names emblazoned on his brain and on his heart. Only when judgment had been executed did they fade and vanish, gone as if the individuals they represented had never been born.

Better for them, in fact, if that were true.

It was an hour short of midday when they smelled the farm. Like predators, their senses were acute, but this required no special talent. They were upwind of the homestead and could plainly smell manure, wood smoke, and something on the fire for dinner.

"Beef," one of the killers said.

"Could be," another granted.

"Reckon it's them?" a third inquired.

Their leader said, "There's only one way to find out."

"Daylight, it's risky," said the one who had spoken of beef.

"It's always risky," their leader reminded him.

"Amen," said the fifth, chiming in since they'd stopped to talk.

"And what if it's *not* them?"

"We're travelers, just passing through," said their leader. "There's no one concerns us who's not on the list and keeps out of our way."

"Stop for dinner, regardless?" asked one.

"Waste of daylight," their leader decreed. "If it's not them, we aren't riding in."

"If it *is* them, we won't be invited to dinner," said one.

"We don't need invitations," the leader replied. "We've been sent to deliver a judgment."

"Amen," said a pair of them, speaking in unison.

"No mercy, then?" asked one who should have known better.

"Only what was shown the Prophet and the Lamb of God." No mercy. No quarter.

The list their leader carried in his pocket, worn along its creases, was not an indictment. Charges had been lodged and judgment rendered long ago and far away. The men in black were simply executioners, dispatched to render punishment decreed by God's spokesman on Earth.

Their own souls might be forfeit if they failed.

"See to your weapons," said their leader, following his own advice. He checked his six-gun first and filled its single empty chamber with a long, bright cartridge. Next, the Henry rifle, primed for firing with a click-clack of its lever action, hammer lowered gently with his thumb before he sheathed it in the saddle boot.

Around him, the metallic sounds of men preparing for a deadly fight were music to his ears. He waited a moment, let them finish, then said, "Let us pray."

They didn't join hands, which would require them to dismount. Contact with one another was unnecessary. Only one hand had the strength to help them now.

"Heavenly Father," he began, "we thank thee for directing us unto your enemies. Give us the strength and fortitude to mete out judgment, blood for blood. In the name of Jesus Christ, amen."

Along the line, four other voices echoed back.

"Amen!"

"That stew smells scrumptious," Bethuel Oman said, smiling across the farmhouse threshold with his hands still dripping wet from the pump outside.

"It's almost ready," Alverice replied, smiling in satisfaction at the compliment. She was a good cook and well conscious of it, but she struggled with the sin of pride.

"You're dripping on the floor," said Zepher, with a prim smile of her own.

"I forgot to leave a towel outside," Bethuel replied.

"You always do," Zepher reminded him, not quite complaining.

"What's a little water on the floor?" asked Ferl.

"A muddy mess from dusty boots," said Alverice.

"I'll use my shirt, then, shall I?" Bethuel teased them.

"No!" Zepher was off to fetch a towel as if the world depended on it, bustling back and pressing it into his hands.

Alverice tasted the stew, closing her eyes in contemplation of its flavor, then announced, "It's done."

"I'll call the young'uns," Bethuel said.

"Do *not* allow them to stampede around this house," Zepher commanded, tacking on a hasty "if you please" that left her cheeks flushed with embarrassment.

"I won't."

Turning, the farmer raised his voice to make it heard behind the barn, beyond the paddock, in the privy—anywhere small ears might be concealed.

"Children!" he called. "Come on to dinner, now. And don't forget to wash your hands!"

It was, in fact, a kind of stampede. The seven of them seemed to come from everywhere at once, as if springing from the ground or dropping from thin air. Bethuel Oman marveled at the energy of youth and often wondered when his own had slipped away, unnoticed in its passing.

Still, he did all right, as witnessed by his crops, both in the field and swarming in his dooryard.

Seven souls for Jesus, and another on the way. The Lord was bountiful, indeed.

And Bethuel was not past it, yet.

Smiling in quiet, not-quite-sinful satisfaction, he stood watch over his brood, ensuring that they all washed up as ordered, before sitting down to dinner. Cleanliness was next to godliness, a touchstone of personal discipline.

The children lined up in reverse order of age, the youngest jostling to be first at the pump. Bethuel left them to it, until a shoving match erupted between two of the boys.

"Chance! Laron! Behave yourselves!" he ordered.

"Yes, Papa," came back, two voices merging as one.

The girls, as usual, were disinclined toward horseplay. Little ladies, even now. It was a fact, Bethuel had noted early on, that even when a man took special pride in sons, a daughter was his weakness.

Something drew Bethuel's gaze up from his children in the yard, away westward, toward a long ridge overlooking his cornfield. A movement of something, perhaps, or—

He spotted the riders, so small they were nearly invisible. Counting their number was out of the question. Say *several* men, and be done with it.

Trouble?

He hurried the children along without sounding alarms, got them into the house in something like passable order. Alverice was dishing out the stew, while seven hungry mouths found seats around the hand-hewn dining table. Ferl and Zepher read his face.

"What is it, Bethuel?" Zepher asked.

"We may have company," he said, and reached up for his shotgun, hanging on the wall.

"It's them," the leader said, still peering through his spyglass toward the distant farmhouse. He had seen one of the targets watching from the doorway, gone now, but presumably alerted.

"Praise the Lord," another said.

The leader folded his telescope and tucked it back into a pocket of his frock coat. "There's a chance that Oman's seen us," he informed the others.

"He can't recognize us this far off," one of them said.

"He ain't a fool, though," added another.

"Fool enough to spurn the Prophet," said a third.

"I mean we need to figure they'll be ready for us."

"They?" The fourth to speak sounded scornful. "Kids and women."

"One boy nearly grown," their leader said. "And don't pretend that women can't use guns. Remember Santa Fe."

That quieted them. They'd be prepared for anything.

"You want to wait for sundown, Amren?" one inquired.

"And give them half a day to fortify the house? No, thank you."

"We're not such easy targets in the dark," another said.

"Neither are they," the leader told him. "And they know the ground. We don't."

"Straight at 'em, then?"

"Not all together," said their leader, Amren Tanner. "Zedek, you and Bliss go south and come around behind them, quiet as you can. Hallace, go north and use the barn for cover, going in. DeLaun, with me."

No one had any further questions. They were used to doing as they're told. They rode off without parting words or backward glances, trailing dust.

"Half done, I reckon, when we finish here," DeLaun Allred remarked.

"Half, or a little better."

He could quote the number with precision, but the leader's mind was focused on the task before him. There were eleven souls inside the farmhouse, some three-quarters of a mile downrange. His enemies had cover and an open field of fire.

But were they schooled to kill without compunction? Without hesitating for a heartbeat?

He presumed to doubt it.

"Shall we go, then?" asked DeLaun.

"We'll let the others have some time. I want them all in place before we reach the house."

DeLaun nodded. "Good idea."

It wouldn't help, if the enemy cut loose from hiding and his aim was true. The love of God was powerful, but anyone who thought that it could ward off bullets was an idiot.

They waited five minutes more, then started the slow ride down to meet their enemies. The leader, having seen them for the first time through his spyglass, moments earlier, had no idea how any of the targets may react. He held the horses to a walk, no rushing, as they passed a field of healthy-looking corn.

Names on a list. Tanner had not been raised to question *why* specific names are listed, what the individuals had done or said to rate his terminal attention. He was not their judge, a function left to higher minds.

He was their executioner.

Three women. Seven children. Killing them wore on a man, but dirty jobs must still be done. His faith demanded obedience to any order issued by the Prophet. He had not failed yet and did not plan to break that record now.

The blood atonement must be made.

"It's nice here," said Allred.

Tanner glanced at him, on the verge of asking if he meant it as a joke, then recollected that Allred had no sense of humor. When he spoke his mind, as limited as it might be, he was saying what he really thought.

"If you like corn," Tanner replied, at last.

"It's green," said Allred. "I miss that at home."

"Well, take advantage of it while you can."

"Amen," said DeLaun.

Bethuel Oman knew they had trouble when the riders separated. Two broke off southward, dropping out of sight behind the skyline, while a third rode north. Bethuel didn't require a West Point military education to recognize a classic pincers movement.

They were trying to surround him.

Not the behavior of passersby stopping for water, directions, or even a meal on the fly. This was mortal danger, and Bethuel didn't know if he was up to racing it.

His shotgun was a lever-action Winchester, twelve gauge, with five rounds in its tubular magazine and one in the chamber. It was advertised as deadly to one hundred yards, but Bethuel figured he'd be lucky to score solid hits at one-third of that range.

He felt the women gathered at his back, peering around him, watching as a pair of horsemen made their slow way to the house.

"Just two?" asked Alverice.

"Five," he replied. "The rest are circling around."

"Oh, God!" Almost a gasp from Zepher.

Bethuel nipped that in the bud. "Zepher, you take the children and go down into the storm cellar."

"But—"

"Do it now, please."

"Yes, Bethuel."

She bustled to it, overriding questions from the youngest ones with stern, brisk orders. Bethuel offered up a silent prayer of thanks that he'd possessed the foresight to construct the cellar with an entry hatch inside the house itself.

Not that a dark hole in the ground would help them, now.

He waited for the hatch to close, until the two riders had covered half the distance from the far ridge to his doorstep, then said, "Alverice, get down the rifle. Ferl, you take the Colt."

Three guns against five. He didn't like the odds, but both women could shoot, although they'd never fired at men before today.

Neither had he.

There'd always been a secret hope that he—they—could avoid this day. Now, Bethuel realized there was no corner of the country, possibly the world, where he could hide.

It wasn't hopeless. They might still survive, defeat their enemies, and bury them in secret. Maybe out behind the barn, where they'd be undisturbed by plowing. But a victory would just mean waiting for the next group to arrive, and then the next one after that, if they survived.

He had endeavored to protect the children from that fear. Adults could bear it, with some practice and a lot of prayer, but children shouldn't have to worry that each day may be their last. They shouldn't have to plan on being killed by strangers, on the orders of a madman they would never meet, who lived eight hundred miles away.

After today, if they were still alive, that fear would never leave them. It infuriated Bethuel, made him clutch the shotgun in a fierce white-knuckled grip. He'd never killed a man before but was prepared to do it now. And relish it.

"Ready," said Alverice, back at his elbow with the rifle. Like his shotgun, it was a repeating Winchester—Model 1873, chambered in .44-40, with fifteen rounds ready to go.

"Ready," Ferl echoed, from his other side. She held the Colt Single-Action Army revolver in her right hand, cradling its long barrel in her left. Mouth set, cheeks pale.

"We've talked about this," Bethuel quietly reminded them. "They won't show any mercy, nor can we. Be mindful of the children and each other. Shoot to kill."

"Five aren't so many," Ferl suggested.

"Less than two to one," said Alverice, forcing a smile.

"Just take one at a time," Bethuel advised them. "Aim and squeeze. Don't jerk the trigger. Make your shots count."

"In the Lord's name," Alverice replied.

"Amen," said Ferl.

We ought to pray, thought Bethuel, but he saw that they were out of time.

• • •

"I'll do the talking," Tanner said, as they entered the dooryard.

Allred did not answer. It was understood between them, hardly needed to be spoken, but the leader's nerves were acting up. He wished, now, that he had been more circumspect, that he had laid back and waited for the sun to set. He felt exposed in the dooryard, facing blind windows and a bolted door.

"Hello, the house!" he called.

"What do you want?" a male voice answered from inside.

"Some water for our horses, friend."

"None for the other three?"

Well, it was worth a gamble. Nothing ventured . . .

"So, you recognize us, then?" he asked the house.

"I've never seen you in my life and never want to," said the disembodied voice.

"You know who sent us?"

"No one we've offended," came the answer. "This is a mistake."

"The Prophet doesn't make mistakes."

"Then *you've* made one."

Tanner hoped that his other men were in position. If they'd lagged, it might cost his life.

"We've come to speak with Bethuel Oman."

"And you've done it. You can leave, now."

"That's your last word?"

"That's my *only* word."

"Well," Tanner said, "in that case—"

Tanner reached up, as if to tip his hat and bid the infidels farewell. It was a signal he'd rehearsed with his companions, but it only worked if they were in position. When the rifles crashed to the left and right of him, he knew they were.

A shotgun blasted at Tanner from a window, as his horse was shying from the rifle fire. The charge of buckshot missed him but struck his stallion's left haunch, causing it to stagger, drop, and roll. Tanner leaped clear, taking the Henry rifle with him as he scurried off in search of cover.

Where to hide?

DeLaun was firing at the house, distracting those inside, or trying to. More guns were firing from the windows. Tanner's ears distinguished a revolver from a rifle, even though they were chambered for the same caliber cartridges. The barrel length determined which shots cracked and which sounded hollow, like a firecracker exploding in a bucket.

He was still running when the shotgun fired again and kicked up dust around his feet. Another missed but was too damned close for comfort. As he dove behind a wooden water trough, he knew it might not save him, but it was all he had available.

His horse squealed pitifully and thrashed in the bloody dust. Tanner would've shot it, but he didn't have rounds to spare just now for wounded animals. Humans demanded his full attention while they were still alive and trying to remain that way.

It would be Tanner's fault if any of his men were killed or injured here. His choice would not be questioned, since the Prophet did not ask for details and it may be months—or years—before they met again, if ever. Should he die here, someone else would come to finish what he'd started. If he was successful, other targets still remained to be located and eliminated.

There was no going home until the list was covered, every name expunged.

But now he was pinned down on a dusty battlefield, baking in the relentless sunshine, sweating through his clothes, and praying for assistance from on high.

No answer.

It remained for Tanner, then, to help himself.

To stay alive, to *win*, he knew that they must breach the house. A standoff worked to the advantage of his enemies. Who knew when neighbors or a passerby might interfere?

He risked a glance toward the barn and saw a wagon standing there. Inside the barn, half masked in shadow, stood a mound of hay.

He had a revelation.

Bethuel Oman hadn't meant to shoot a horse, but any damage that he could inflict upon his enemies was welcome. Closing off his mind and heart to sympathy, ignoring the pathetic sounds of agony, he tracked the unhorsed runner with his shotgun. Fired again. And missed again.

Lord, help me!

Bethuel didn't know if it was sinful, praying for God's help to kill another person, but defense of those he loved took precedence over humanity at large. The Sixth Commandment said, "Thou shalt not kill." But Jesus, in the Book of Matthew, chose another turn of phrase, telling the faithful, "Thou shalt do no murder."

Murder was a killing both illegal under man's law and unjustified. There was no murder on the gallows, on a battlefield in wartime, or when facing gunmen sent to slay the innocent.

Bethuel's ears rang from the echoes of his shotgun blasts and from the shots fired by the women. None of them had scored a hit on any of the black-clad shooters yet, which disappointed him, but they were still secure inside the house. Stout walls absorbed most of the bullets fired in their direction, though a few punched through the thinner window shutters, forcing them to duck and dodge.

"Careful!" he warned, unnecessarily. The women would not risk their lives without good reason.

And the children huddled in the storm cellar with Zepher were the best reason of all.

It struck Bethuel that Zepher had no weapon. If it came down to a last-ditch stand, how would she manage to protect the young ones?

Never mind.

If it came down to that, if any of their adversaries got inside the house, another gun below ground wouldn't matter.

Movement from the barn distracted Bethuel, drawing his attention from the gunman crouched behind the water trough. He tracked a runner with his shotgun, fired in vain, then fell back as a bullet pierced the shutter, just above his firing slit, and stung his face with splinters.

Swallowing a curse, he lunged back to the window, peering toward the barn. What were they doing over there? They might set fire to it, destroy the barn, and roast the animals inside, but that would not defeat him. He had built the farm from nothing and could do the same again. As long as he and his were still alive.

"Bethuel!" Ferl called to him. "They're doing something—"

"In the barn," he interrupted her. "I see."

"What are they up to?"

Bethuel had no breath to waste, confessing ignorance. He tried to watch the two men ducking in and out of cover. Doing . . . what?

They'd made three trips before he understood.

"They're fetching hay," he said. "To fire the wagon."

"What?" asked Alverice. "The *wagon*? Why—"

"To burn the house," he told her.

"Oh, dear Lord!"

"Stop them!" he snapped, but even edging well back to his left, he couldn't bring the scuttling figures under fire from where he stood.

Ferl tried with the revolver, knocking slivers from the near side of the wagon, but their enemies kept busy, bearing armloads of hay to the wagon, returning for more.

How much did they need for a serious fire? Not a full wagonload, but enough that its flames would expand to the house once they'd pushed it up next to a wall. And once the house caught . . .

The faithful weren't supposed to burn. It was a fate reserved for sinners, heretics, and heathens. Never mind that
from the killers' point of view, Bethuel and those he loved
were damned to hellfire. He would take his chances on the
afterlife, but here and now, he still had children to protect.

"I'm going out to stop them," he announced.

"Bethuel, you can't!" said Alverice. Almost a sob.

"There aren't enough of them to cover all the windows,"
he replied. "I'll go out through the girls' room. By the time
they see me coming, it will be too late."

Before the two of them could argue with him any more,
he bolted, running in a crouch across the open family room,
clutching the shotgun to his chest.

Amren Tanner sputtered as a bullet drilled the water trough
and doused him with a jet of tepid water. Thinking of the
animals who'd had their noses in the trough, he spat and
nearly cursed, before remembering his mission and the
strictures of his faith.

A righteous man was godly in all ways and at all times.
No leeway was permitted for transgressions in the heat of
battle, any more than while relaxing peacefully on a ve-
randa in the shade.

And shade was something Tanner would have thanked
his Lord for, as he lay beneath the broiling sun. Even the
water pooling beneath him, turning dust to mud and soiling
his frock coat, provided no relief.

It would be hotter still inside the house, though, if his
plan to rout the infidels succeeded. They would have a taste
of Hell's relentless flames before they died, a preview of
the screaming torment that awaited them for all eternity.

Assuming that Zedek and Bliss could pull it off.

From where he lay, it seemed to Tanner that they had the
wagon nearly filled with hay. Once it was lit, the pair of
them could crouch behind its smoking bulk and use it for

cover as they pushed it toward the house. He and the rest would cover them, but if the home's defenders scored a lucky hit or two, his soldiers had the Prophet's guarantee that they would be rewarded in the afterlife for their valor.

What more could any true believer ask?

He lost sight of his men as they crouched down behind the wagon, out of sight from both the farmhouse and his leaking sanctuary. After several moments, smoke curled upward from the mound of hay that filled the wagon's bed, and finally, he glimpsed a quick, pale tongue of flame.

Ready!

When Bliss and Zedek started pushing, Tanner heard a creaking from the wagon's springs, then it began to move, laboriously creeping toward the house. Tanner reckoned that the wagon had to weigh five hundred pounds, without its burning load. Two horses normally would be required to pull it, so his men weren't doing badly. If they could—

The shotgun blast surprised him, actually made him flinch as dust exploded from the wagon's tailgate, which was pointed toward the house. Where had it come from? Not the windows facing him, which had to mean the shooter was *outside.*

That thought had barely taken form when Bethuel Oman charged the wagon, suddenly emerging from the north side of the house, bellowing curses as he ducked to fire another blast beneath the wagon, angling for the feet and legs of his assailants.

Infidel!

Tanner squeezed off his first shot without aiming, saw the target half turn toward him, and did better with the second, drilling Oman through the chest. The farmer sat down, hard, and blinked at Tanner, sitting with a dazed expression on his face.

No mercy.

Tanner put his third round through the heretic's left eye and slammed him over backward in the dirt. More firing from the house raised dust around him, boring more holes in the nearly empty water trough, but Tanner waited out the storm, then shouted to his men.

"Bliss! Zedek! Move that wagon *now*!"

They did as they were told, putting their backs into it and advancing under fire, while Tanner and DeLaun Allred peppered the windows with their own slugs, spoiling the defenders' aim.

No one remained inside the house but women and their children now. And all of them were doomed. Their fate had been pronounced, judgment delivered. There was no escape.

Tanner was watching when the wagon bumped against the house, Zedek and Bliss retreating toward the barn with pistols blazing. Silence fell, then, but for crackling noises as the hay burned, flames eating their way into the wagon's bed, rising from there to lick the farmhouse wall and leap along its eaves. The roof, covered with hand-hewn wooden shingles, soon began to smoke.

Tanner was cautious about leaving cover. Even when he saw smoke curling from the shuttered windows and beneath the barred front door, he took his time. A sniper in the house could kill him, even if her eyes were teary from the smoke and grief. Bullets did not discriminate by creed.

But when the next shots came, they echoed from inside the house. Whatever lamentations might accompany the gunfire, they were lost within the rushing sound of hungry flames. He counted nine shots, waited, finally picked out the tenth, just as the roof sagged, buckling in.

His soldiers joined him, passing through the smoke like ghosts, until they formed a line outside the farmhouse, fairly baking in its heat. Grim-faced, they stood and watched it burn to crumbling ashes that were scattered by the prairie wind.

1

Jack Slade was down eleven dollars, holding queens and junk, when his turn came to draw. He eyed the dwindling pile of chips in front of him, tried to preserve his poker face, and said, "Two cards."

"Two cards, it is."

The dealer, Arty Chalmers, owned a dry-goods store in Enid, Oklahoma Territory, but he spent at least three afternoons a week in the Landmark Saloon, nursing a beer and playing cards. His wife, Raylene, complained to anyone who'd listen, but if truth be told, Slade thought she liked having the store all to herself.

Slade held a nine of hearts to keep the two queens company, tossing a deuce of diamonds and a five of clubs onto the discard pile. He claimed the new cards, fanned them, and was careful to suppress a grimace as he saw a six and three of hearts.

More junk.

The player on his left—Ed Walker, from the livery—stood pat, and Chalmers drew one card, stifling a smile too late. The dealer had improved his hand, but what had he been holding at the draw?

"Your bet, Tom," Chalmers told the farmer seated on Slade's right. Tom Powell grew corn on ninety acres south of town and was a solid citizen in all respects. He'd drawn three cards and obviously didn't trust them.

"Check," said Powell.

"Same here," Slade said, before the dealer had a chance to ask.

"Well, Ed?"

"I'll bet another dollar," Walker said.

"I'll see that buck and raise you two," said Chalmers. "Tom?"

"Too rich for me," Powell groused. "I fold."

"Marshal?"

Slade knew he ought to let it go, but what would be the sport in that? "I call," he said and put three dollars in the pot.

Chalmers had clearly been expecting Slade to fold. A little frown line formed between his bushy eyebrows, but he kept his lips under control, shooting a glance down toward his hand to verify the cards he held. "Good, good," he said at last. "Let's see 'em, then."

Slade spread his hand faceup, almost embarrassed by the pair of queens with nothing but a lousy nine to back them up. Walker would beat him, now, and then it would be down to Arty Chalmers, facing off against the husky stable hand.

But Walker *didn't* beat him. Going red-faced, muttering a curse, he showed the hand he hadn't bothered trying to improve. A pair of jacks, supported by the ace of spades, a five of diamonds, and a trey of clubs.

Some people.

"Jesus, Ed." Chalmers was trying not to laugh.

"What?" Walker answered. "It's the best damn hand I've had all day."

That set them laughing, Walker joining in at last, belatedly good-natured in defeat. When the amusement ran its course, Chalmers sat back and said, "I guess it's down to me, then, Marshal."

"I guess so," Slade said.

"And this time, I am proud to say . . . the pot is mine."

He faced two pair, kings over eights, and sat there smiling at them for a moment, relishing the victory. Slade saw his money raked away and calculated that he had enough left in his pocket for two, maybe three losing hands.

He knew then it was time to leave: when his mind took a negative turn, expecting defeat. Poker was all about the odds, but while a player couldn't wish good cards into his hand, Slade knew from personal experience that a defeatist attitude spawned reckless betting and increased the likelihood of going broke.

Get out, a voice inside his head advised him.

Slade ignored it and put his dollar ante for the next hand on the table.

Just then, Danny Goodrich, from the courthouse, cleared the Landmark's bat-wing doors and locked eyes with Slade. The gawky seventeen-year-old ran errands for Judge Dennison, his clerk and deputies. The boy took his job seriously, seldom smiling, but today his long freckled face was more somber than usual.

"Um, Marshal Slade?"

"Danny."

"Judge needs to see you right away, sir."

With Danny, it was never *the* judge, always "Judge," treating the title as a name.

Slade knew there was no point asking why. Whoever sent the kid, whether Judge Dennison himself or someone else, wouldn't have confided any details.

"Gentlemen," Slade said, as he retrieved his ante, "it appears you'll have to deal me out."

"Thanks, anyway, for the donation," Chalmers said, raising one hand in a salute.

"Next time," Slade said, "the charity begins at home."

"I'll tell Judge that you're coming," Danny said and left the Landmark at a trot. Slade didn't have to watch to know he would be running full tilt by the time he hit Main Street.

Slade took his time, not dawdling, but refusing to provoke alarm—much less hilarity—by dashing to the courthouse in a breathless rush. If there'd been danger, Danny would have said so. Any shooting, and Slade would've heard it from the Landmark.

Any other urgent matter would be waiting for him when he reached the judge's chambers to receive instructions for his next assignment. Something bloody, he supposed, while hoping that he might be wrong this time.

Just once, Slade thought, it would be nice. Judge Isaac Dennison had briefly moved his chambers to the ground floor of the federal courthouse after he was wounded by assassins trying to resolve a grudge that dated from dark years following the Civil War. It hadn't suited him, conceding even that much to the men who'd failed to kill him with their best shots, and as soon as he could navigate a staircase with the aid of canes, Judge Dennison had gone back to his office on the second floor.

Each morning, he went up the stairs, clumping along, and came back down the same way, in the afternoon. Each day, he was a little lighter on his feet. The past few weeks, he'd used one cane, instead of two, keeping a firm grip on the banister. Before long, Slade supposed, the judge would be himself again.

Or as close to his old self as he could get, anyhow, after he had been kissing-close to death.

The judge was standing when he summoned Slade to enter his private chambers, staring out the same window where shots had struck him barely ten weeks earlier. Below him, in the courtyard, stood a gallows built to handle six men at a time.

Or women, if it ever came to that.

"You sent for me, Judge?"

"Yes, Jack. Have a seat."

Only when Slade was in his chair, facing the judge's desk, did Dennison himself sit down. Slade marked his progress, solid strides with just a hint of limping on the left.

"Jack, I'm afraid there's been some bloody business up along the Kansas border. Have you ever been to Alva?"

"No, sir."

"No. Not many have. It's relatively new. A whistle-stop for the ATSF," Judge Dennison explained, referring to the Atchison, Topeka and Santa Fe Railway. "They've got a depot and a land office for the Cherokee Outlet, trying to build up a town around them."

The Cherokee Outlet was a strip of land sixty miles wide, running more than two hundred miles along the Kansas-Oklahoma border, carved out of Indian Territory in 1866 to punish the Cherokee nation for siding with the Confederacy during the Civil War. A surveyor's error let Kansas cattlemen claim the strip until 1889, when Congress intervened. Four years later, in September 1893, the strip was opened to homesteaders for the largest land run in American—or world—history. More than eight million acres had gone up for grabs, and some of it was still disputed to the point of spilling blood.

"More claim jumping?" asked Slade.

"It isn't clear," Judge Dennison replied. "We've got close to a dozen dead but no details. You'll have to work it out."

Slade didn't like the sound of that. "No details" usually meant the locals were complicit in a crime, or they were sweeping some other dirt under the rug.

"When did the killings start?" he asked.

"Started and ended yesterday, apparently," Judge Dennison replied. "Eleven killed on one spread, all but one of them women and children."

"Only one man?"

"That's the word. They have a sort of constable in Alva, Euliss Drury. I assume he's with the railroad. And the land office is managed by one Garland Brock. He wired about the murders. They're what passes for authority in Alva, but they don't swing any weight."

Slade made a mental note of that and said, "It strikes me as a little odd, Judge."

"What does?"

"Well, sir, in my experience, this kind of killing usually comes from crazy anger, like the Benders, or from calculated greed. A landgrab, say, or tied into a range war. In the second case, there's normally some kind of run-up to the slaughter. Scattered incidents, some other small-scale killing, livestock killed, barn burning. Something."

"It's a good point," Dennison agreed. "The wire I got said nothing about any other crimes, much less a string of murders."

"So, this either blew up out of nowhere," Slade replied, "or—"

"It's the start of something worse," the judge finished his thought. "That's my concern. Along with finding out who killed these folks and bringing him—or them—to justice, of course."

"Yes, sir." Slade cut a sidelong glance toward Dennison's wall clock. "It's getting late," he said. "If I pack up and leave within the hour, I can make a couple miles, then start fresh in the morning."

"That's the spirit," Dennison replied. "Maybe find some accommodating soul who'll put you up tonight and spare you sleeping on the ground."

Was that a smile twitching around the corners of the judge's mouth?

Sees through me like a windowpane, Slade thought, as he rose from his chair, nodding, and said, "Yes, sir."

Dennison's voice caught him with one foot out the door. "Be careful, Jack," he warned. "We don't know what you're riding into, and I can't afford to lose another deputy."

"No, sir," Slade said, and softly closed the office door.

He got the point. A friend and fellow deputy, Hec Daltry, had been murdered recently, as he and Slade had pursued a group of badmen who had sprung a gang member from custody. It wasn't Slade's fault, and he knew Judge Dennison had not intended any finger pointing, but it stung, regardless.

Time to let it go.

Easier said than done.

Slade started back toward his hotel to pack up for the road.

There wasn't much to pack. Before returning to his rented room, Slade stopped at Hazelbaker's general store and bought a week's supply of pemmican, dried beans, and corn dodgers. It didn't qualify as gourmet fare, but it would keep him going, and he'd have no traveling companions to complain about the beans.

Upstairs at the hotel, Slade packed the food in saddlebags, along with ammunition for his Winchester and pistol, a spare shirt and long underwear, two extra pairs of socks, his straight razor, a whetstone for his belt knife, and firearms cleaning tools. A coil of rope was on his saddle at the livery, and he would fill his canteen there before he left town.

But he wasn't going far that afternoon.

Judge Dennison had known it, almost teasing him, the closest that he ever came to joking with his deputies. It stood to reason that the judge would know of his relationship with Faith Connover. They had taken no great pains to hide it, and it figured that her hands were bound to talk.

Gossip be damned.

The circumstances of their meeting were unusual, to say the least. Slade had been gambling his way around the West when his twin brother—Faith's fiancé—had been killed at his ranch, outside Enid, in the kind of landgrab murder Slade had mentioned to Judge Dennison. Time had passed before the news caught up to Slade, then he had come to Oklahoma with his mind fixed on revenge.

Two people had revised that plan. Judge Dennison had offered Slade a badge and license to pursue the killers in a legal manner, promising to hang him if he took them down outside the law. And Faith had given him a glimpse of love's redeeming power.

Not the first-sight kind of love, mind you. Slade was attracted to her instantly—who wouldn't be?—but she was still his brother's fiancée, still grieving for him. Widowed, in effect, before she spoke her wedding vows. Slade couldn't bring himself to voice his feelings for her, growing day by day, until he'd tracked the killers down and finished them, rescuing Faith from death or worse in the process.

And even then, he'd wondered, when it seemed that she might learn to care for him, if Faith saw him or his brother, Jim. His own reflection in the mirror warned him that her grief might lead to serious mistakes, with pain for both of them to follow.

But it seemed, now, that his fear had been unfounded. Worry wasted, as was so often the case. They had been intimate, spoke loving words—though not *the* word, itself—and Slade no longer felt that they were haunted by his brother's ghost.

Their childhood—his and Jim's—had been unusual. Jack had rebelled against his parents, fled the nest as soon as he was able to survive outside it, and became the black sheep of the family, unmentioned at the supper table, birthdays carefully ignored. Jim, on the other hand, had walked the straight and narrow, more or less, and compensated for his twin's failure to toe the line.

Still, twins they were. Identical, in fact, which had provoked a few ghost stories around Enid when Jack came to settle Jim's affairs and find his slayers. Even so, while some twinned siblings talked about a psychic bond transcending time and space, Slade didn't get it. He had never felt Jim's toothaches, heartaches, triumphs, or defeats across the miles that separated them. He'd thought of Jim, and often, but had never seen through Jim's eyes, never felt Faith's touch until her hands were touching him.

And it had been worth waiting for.

Slade walked down to the livery, saddled his roan, and took the highway leading northward out of Enid. Some folks waved as he passed by, but most ignored him. He'd become a fixture of the town, somehow, his coming and going no longer remarkable unless he had a string of prisoners in tow.

It still seemed somewhat odd to Slade that after all his years of drifting he *belonged* somewhere. And that he'd find his calling with a badge pinned to his vest defied the wildest flights of his imagination.

He'd considered bounty hunting once, when times were hard around the poker table, but he'd never followed up on it. It struck him as a fool's game at the time, but here he was, pursuing murderers and every other kind of felon without hope of any payoff other than his monthly salary.

That wasn't strictly true, of course. The first few times he'd caught a bad man on the run—after the business with Jim's killers, anyway—there'd been a feeling of accomplishment that took Slade by surprise. A sense that he'd done something for the people of the territory, maybe for the world at large. Since then, he had been waiting for that feeling to desert him.

But it never had.

Slade didn't buy the notion that a person's occupation came to them by way of Fate or Destiny. In his book, there was no great finger in the sky waiting to touch a man or woman and propel them into medicine, the law, farming, or shopkeeping. But he could say without a moment's hesitation that his time in Enid, all around, had been the happiest he'd ever spent.

And most of that, he knew, came down to Faith.

Two hours after leaving Enid, Slade was on Faith's land. It took another thirty minutes, riding at an easy pace, before he saw her house, barn, and the other outbuildings rise up in front of him. None of her hands were out, that he could see, but with a property that size—her own, combined with Jim's by virtue of his will—the hired men could be mustering Faith's cattle somewhere, far beyond the range of human eyes.

Even when they were close at hand, the hirelings didn't try to intercept him anymore. They all knew Slade by sight, knew that he wore a federal badge, and understood that he had business with the lady of the house that wasn't theirs. As far as Slade knew, all of them respected Faith and treated her like any other boss. If there'd been any problems, Faith had handled them herself, without involving Slade.

At one point, feeling macho, he'd considered rounding up the hands and warning them against the foolishness of spreading tales in town, but Faith had swiftly vetoed it. She'd talked about abusing his authority and set him straight on misplaced notions that she needed Slade or any other man to guard her reputation. Slade was wise enough to listen and obey.

The heart had never been Slade's territory. He had grown up living by his wits and nerve, bending the rules—or breaking them, if they were too much in his way. Wearing a badge had cured that, to some extent, and Slade deferred to Faith on matters of emotion or romance.

But if he ever found that anyone had tried to harm her, they would get a taste of Hell on Earth.

One thing he'd learned about Faith, early on: surprising her was difficult. Not with a compliment that made her blush, or something trivial like that, but actually sneaking up on her. This afternoon, for instance, even though he'd seen no hands around to warn her of a rider coming, she was waiting on the farmhouse porch, all smiles, when Slade arrived.

"You must be some kind of a witch," he said.

"Sweet-talker."

"And I took a bath," he told her, "so I know you didn't *smell* me coming."

"Maybe you should have another one."

"Well, now—"

"With French milled soap."

"You'd smell me then, for sure."

"Only if I was close."

Slade's turn to blush. "I ought to get my mare some feed and water, take her saddle off."

"I'll put the water on to heat."

"Umm."

"Jack, you can't be coming to the supper table filthy from the trail. It isn't civilized."

"I hate to keep you waiting, if you're hungry."

"Then you'd best hop down," she said, "and hurry through those chores."

After Slade's bath, and drying off, and working up another sweat, they got around to eating. Slade was starving by that time, from his exertions, and he tried to help Faith in the kitchen, until she got tired of it and shooed him off.

The meal was steak with baked potatoes, peas, and carrots, fresh-baked bread with apple butter, followed by a pecan pie. Slade had to pace himself, to keep from looking like a total hog, and Faith helped out by asking him about his latest errand for Judge Dennison.

"I don't know much," he told her honestly. "Some killings up by Alva, near the border. First, it sounded like a family, but something's off."

"How so?"

"Well, if the judge has got it right, there's one man dead, three women, and the rest all kids."

"The rest?"

"Seven."

"Oh, Lord."

"Sorry. Let's drop it."

"No! I keep on telling you, I'm not that soft."

"And, yet—"

"Behave!" she cautioned him.

"All right. I just can't figure it, from what the locals wired Judge Dennison. No land wars going on, that he's heard tell of, even with their history of troubles on the Outlet."

"What's that leave?" she asked.

"I'd be inclined to say some kind of grudge against one family, but there should be a couple more dead men, if that's the case."

"Or, it could be some kind of wickedness *within* a family. The missing man—or men—could be the killers."

"You may be right," Slade said. "I have a hunch the Powers That Be in Alva may be holding back the main part of the story."

"All those children. Who'd do such a thing?"

"The Benders would have," Slade reminded her.

"They're dead, thank Heaven."

"But they weren't unique, unfortunately. Children get killed all the time. Even with Indians—"

"You don't think it's another war?"

"No, no. The folks in Alva would've called the army, if they thought that. I'm just saying, when adults start killing one another, sometimes they don't care who's in the middle."

"Jesus. Anyone who'd kill a child . . ."

"Judge Dennison will deal with them, if I can bring them in."

"You always do," she said. "One, you've missed, in all this time. And *he* fell down a well."

"I should've worked it out, before the whole town started drawing water and—"

"Jack, please! You want another piece of pie?"

"I don't know where I'd put it," he admitted.

Smiling impishly, Faith asked him, "Shall I show you?"

"All right, then," Slade grinned. "If you insist."

"Indeed, I do," she said, taking his hand.

Pale daylight woke him, coupled with the scent of coffee brewing. How he'd missed Faith rolling out of bed and getting dressed, Slade couldn't figure. Maybe pure exhaustion had something to do with it.

He felt refreshed, now, though. Ready to go—and wishing he could stay. He wondered if the soft life might agree with him. No more assignments to go out and seek the kind of people sane folks did their utmost to avoid.

It sounded good. But then, he had to stop and think: *farming?* It was a trade that he could learn, Faith teaching him the parts that didn't flow from common sense, but would it suit him?

On the one hand, trail dust, gun smoke, and the gallows. On the other, Faith, a farm . . . and all the headaches that she'd told him came along with it. Even without rustlers and such, she had to fret about the weather, crop blights, market prices, and a list of ailments found in livestock that confused Slade with their names and repulsed him with their symptoms.

Separate lives? Not quite.

He dressed and joined her in the kitchen for a hearty breakfast that included fried eggs and potatoes, bacon, gravy over biscuits, and a steaming mug of coffee.

"Lord, if I lived here—" Slade caught himself, too late.

"What?" Faith asked, casually.

"I believe I'd weigh three hundred pounds within a month," he finished.

"You'd need exercise, it's true."

He changed the subject. "I'm not sure how long this job will take. I'll be in Alva late tomorrow afternoon, if nothing slows me down."

"Then, time to solve your mystery," she said.

"Which may not be a mystery at all."

"And find the man or men responsible for a horrendous crime."

"That's where I hit a snag," Slade said. "Whoever did it knows he's looking at a rope. There's no way he'd just hang around, unless he's dumb as dirt or crazy."

"Crazy like a fox, maybe," said Faith.

"Meaning?"

She shrugged, always worth watching. "If the killer was above suspicion, why run off and draw attention to himself? You'll have to figure out a reason for the killings, first."

"And if it wasn't craziness or family feuding . . ."

"Then you've got a riddle on your hands," she said. "One that it could be dangerous to solve."

"Don't fret," he said. "I never let my guard down on a job."

"Never?"

Slade hoped Kate Bender wasn't on her mind. He'd made a near-fatal mistake that time, which still came back to haunt him on the odd night, in disturbing dreams.

"Okay, I'm working on it."

"See that you do."

"Yes, ma'am."

"They must be monsters, Jack."

Meaning the people who would kill a child, or seven.

"No shortage of monsters, these days," he replied.

"Do you suppose they're getting worse?"

"People, you mean?" Slade shook his head. "I think they've always been like this. Some of them, anyway. I seem to recollect no end of children murdered in the Bible, most of them by orders from on high."

"That's ancient history," said Faith.

"A lot of people never learn from history's mistakes," Slade said.

"I'd hate to think that anyone believed this kind of thing is justified," she said. "Better to think it's just some crazy man, out howling at the moon."

"Well, if that's it, I shouldn't have much trouble spotting him," Slade told her. "Anyone like that will leave a trail blind men could follow."

He refrained from adding that it might turn out to be a trail of bodies. There was no point making matters worse on what had started as a perfect morning.

"God, I wish you didn't have to do this. Hunting lunatics. You've done enough, Jack."

"I'm a bit young to retire," he told her, smiling.

"I'm serious!"

"I know you are. But someone has to do it."

"Someone else," Faith said.

"Not this time, anyway."

She blinked at that, eyes narrowed, maybe looking for a ray of hope behind his words, then let it go.

"Judge Dennison is smart enough to send his best," she said, sounding resigned.

"I wouldn't go that far."

"Because you hide your light under a bushel," Faith replied.

"My light?"

"Your skill, talent—pick any word you like. He saw you coming, Jack. Who knew you'd be a natural?"

"After my wasted youth, you mean?"

"I don't believe that any part of life is wasted," Faith said. "Everything that happens to us, everything we do, moves us along."

"Toward what?" Slade asked.

"The place we need to be."

"Which is?"

"You have to work that out yourself," she said.

"Okay. Right now, the place I need to be is on my horse, headed for Alva."

"Yes."

"I'll help you with the dishes, though."

"You will not. Go and make the world a better place."

"No pressure there," he said, smiling.

"You'll handle it."

"I wish I had your confidence."

"You do," Faith said. "Believe it."

"Will you see me off, then?"

"Absolutely. And I'll see you coming back."

"Before you have a chance to miss me," Slade replied.

"Too late," Faith said. "I miss you now."

2

Alva wasn't much to look at, riding in. Slade had found the railroad tracks at noon, his second day on horseback, and had followed them the last twelve miles or so beneath a sky that threatened rain but never quite delivered. At one point Slade dismounted and walked his roan across a trestle spanning the Salt Fork of the Arkansas River. No trains challenged him, and finally, near suppertime, he saw a town of sorts.

Three buildings caught his eye at once. One, obviously, was a depot for the Atchison, Topeka and Santa Fe Railway, which had given Alva its first lease on life. Another was three stories tall, a box that Slade guessed must be some kind of lodging house. A third, standing between the other two, turned out to be the land office.

As Slade drew closer, say a hundred yards, he noted three apparent shops, a smallish stable, and perhaps a dozen dwellings that put him in mind of shanties on a reservation.

At a glance, he couldn't tell if Alva was about to have a growth spurt or if it was dying young.

More to the point, he didn't care.

Slade had no interest in this whistle-stop, its people, or their future plans. Murder had brought him there, and he'd be pleased to see the last of Alva once he solved that case, when those responsible were under lock and key or in the ground.

Get on with it, Slade thought. And then his stomach growled.

Mindful of his priorities, Slade stopped in at the stable first. It was a humble livery but functional to the extent of having feed, water, and decent stalls available. Slade paid his dollar to a hostler who seemed cheerful, if a bit on the slow side, then walked his saddlebags and rifle down to the hotel.

Whatever happened next, Slade knew that he was bound to stay the night.

The Alva House still had that sawdust smell inside that fades as buildings age. The clerk was twentysomething, ginger-haired, and freckled, focused so completely on Slade's badge that he seemed dumbstruck when Slade asked about a room. A moment later, when the spell broke, he flushed crimson with embarrassment.

"Yes, sir! We have four available. Would you prefer the second floor or third? Facing the street or rear?"

"They all have beds?"

"Of course, sir! We— Ah, yes. A good one, sir. No preference, then?"

Slade asked about the privy situation, learned that Alva House had indoor facilities, and chose the room farthest from them. Better an extra few steps, than a long night of whooshing and rattling pipes.

He got a third-floor room, facing the strip of sparsely populated dirt that Alva called Main Street. Once he had locked his gear inside it, Slade walked down the hall to wash his hands in a newfangled sink. Hot water on his left, cold to his right.

It had begun to sprinkle by the time Slade left the Alva House and crossed Main to the Atchison Café. He half expected decorations from a railroad dining car, but there were checkered tablecloths with candles on the tables and a chandelier made from a wagon wheel with four lamps mounted on its rim.

Unless he'd missed a rush, Slade was their second customer for supper. The other was a portly man who wore a gray suit and a bowler hat. Slade watched him sawing at a steak and made a mental note to order something else.

A young blond waitress came out to meet him, putting on a smile she'd likely practiced with a mirror, leading Slade to a table for two by the window. She pulled out a chair that would place his back to the door, but he circled around to the other and sat, while she seemed to notice his badge for the first time.

"Need some time to decide, sir?" she asked him.

The menu, Slade saw, was written in chalk on a wall-mounted slate, yellow letters some ten inches tall. They had beefsteak, fried chicken, and beef stew on offer, all served with potatoes and greens. Slade went with the chicken, chose coffee to drink, and decided to wait on the pie.

He had a ringside seat for Alva's action, but there didn't seem to be any. Rain pattered on a street with no traffic, and Slade was almost startled when a man walked past the café window, headed for either the dry-goods store or one of Alva's humble houses.

When the waitress brought his chicken, Slade asked, "Is this your normal supper trade?"

She frowned and said, "Oh, no, sir. Most times, we have six or seven in here." Hesitating for a moment, she decided to confide in him. "Trade's off today, 'cause of the funeral."

"Is that a big event, around these parts?"

"*This* one was big, all right. Eleven people, bless their souls."

"I wouldn't think that Alva had a cemetery large enough," Slade said.

"Oh, they're not— What I mean, sir, is they're buried where it happened, more or less."

"Not here, in town."

"No, sir. Not with—"

"Margine!" a gruff voice hailed her, from the kitchen.

"Sorry, sir. I prattle on, sometimes. Pay it no mind."

Slade tucked into his chicken, which was passable. He'd rather have it overdone and crisp than raw inside to keep him in the privy all night long. The high point of the meal was collard greens with bacon and diced onions.

Slade was working on his second drumstick when he saw a short man crossing Main Street from the general direction of the Alva House. The fellow wore a mustache, brown suit dusty at the trouser cuffs, and wide-brimmed hat that seemed too large for him. Slade half expected it to slip over his eyes at any moment, blinding him.

Big Hat came into the café, waved off the nervous-looking blond, and made a beeline for Slade's table by the window. Slade pretended to ignore him, working on his drumstick, but he held it in his left hand, while his right slipped down beneath the table, toward his pistol.

Just in case.

"You'd be the marshal," Big Hat told him, clearing up that mystery.

"And who are you?" Slade asked.

The man drew back his left lapel, showing a round badge with an eagle stamped dead-center on it.

"Euliss Drury, constable," he said.

"Sit down and take a load off," Slade instructed, "while I have a slice of pie."

• • •

The constable sat facing Slade, watched him order dessert, and shook his head when asked if he was dining. "No time for it, Margie," he replied, clearly addressing Slade.

When Margie left to fetch Slade's pie, he told the constable, "There's no rush, here. In fact, from what I hear, you've been a trifle hasty, as it is."

"What's that supposed to mean?" Drury demanded.

"When can I see the victims, Constable?"

"Um . . . well . . . I guess you can't."

"Why's that?"

"Because we buried 'em, this afternoon."

"After the full postmortems, I suppose?"

"Postmortems?"

"Autopsies," Slade clarified.

"No, sir."

"No autopsies?"

"There wasn't any need," Drury replied. "All of 'em shot, and all but one baked in the cellar, when their house burned down."

"So, cause of death was certified by . . . who, again?"

"By me."

"Are you a doctor? Or the coroner?"

"Neither."

"But I'll have to take your word on cause of death, since they're already in the ground."

"You want to dig 'em up?"

"I want to do my job."

"Marshal, I don't know where you think you're at—"

"I'm sitting in a town that's had eleven people murdered," Slade replied, cutting him off. "You asked Judge Dennison for help, and he sent me. Now, I discover that you've screwed things up before I even have a chance to start."

Red-faced, Drury seemed poised to answer back but bit his tongue as Margie brought Slade's pie. She hastily retreated, leaving them alone.

"We're getting off on the wrong foot," said Drury, through clenched teeth.

"They make a fair peach pie," Slade said.

"I guess you'll want to see the Oman place."

"Not in the dark and rain. We'll ride out in the morning."

"We?" Now Drury seemed confused.

"We, as in *you* and *me*," Slade broke it down for him.

"I've got no jurisdiction outside Alva," Drury said.

"No real authority inside it, either," Slade replied. "You're not incorporated as a town, here, and you're not railroad police or one of Pinkerton's. I'll need a guide out to the murder scene tomorrow. That's you."

"Now, look here—"

"Or, I lock you up and find my own way out there. Do my business in however long it takes without your help, then take you back to Enid."

"Enid! Why?"

"On charges of obstructing federal investigations."

"Damn it, man!"

"I'd rather not be burdened with you on the way back, but it's your call."

"What time in the morning?" Drury asked at last, resigned to it.

Slade answered with a question of his own. "How early can you get a plate of eggs around here?"

"At the crack of dawn," Drury replied.

"Half past the crack, then. Meet me at the livery."

"You'll want to meet with Mr. Brock tonight, then."

Slade connected that name to the local land office, from what Judge Dennison had said. "No, thanks," he told the constable. "I won't be buying any property."

"But he's in charge," Drury protested.

"There you go, again, mistaking how things work. This is a U.S. territory, under the direct control of officers appointed by the president of the United States. He put Judge

Dennison in charge. Judge Dennison sent me to represent him here. I hope we're clear on that."

"The railroad—"

"Is a damn fine institution, I've no doubt," Slade interrupted him again. "And if I need a ride somewhere, they'll be the folks I call on. As to law enforcement, they have zero standing anywhere outside their legal right-of-way."

"Well, what am I supposed to say when Mr. Brock asks where you are?"

"Tonight, the Alva House. Tomorrow, riding out with you to look around the murder scene. From there on, I'll be looking for the killers. If I need a posse, and he fits the bill, I'll welcome him to ride along."

"He won't like this," Drury complained.

"We all have disappointments. If he takes it too hard, let him read the Constitution. Section Three, Article Four. Of course, he's free to wire Judge Dennison again. Maybe he'll call me back, and you can deal with this yourself."

"Good Lord! I don't want that!"

"Then ride along with me tomorrow, like I said. We'll make it quick and relatively painless."

"Right. Okay."

"Now, if you don't mind, I'll just finish off this pie."

Dismissed, the constable stood up and left without a parting word. Slade reckoned that he'd made an enemy but didn't mind. He disliked meddling locals who supposed they had authority beyond the letter of the law, simply by virtue of their residence at a particular location. It was natural, he understood, for lawmen to resent outside intrusion in their own backyards, but there was something out of line with what he'd found so far in Alva.

Take the hasty burial, for starters. Slade could understand the urge to get eleven bodies planted in a small town where they didn't even have an ice house to preserve remains, much less a coroner to pass judgment on cause of death.

Slade might have let it go but for the waitress's uneasiness on that score. She'd been on the verge of saying more about it, when the cook or whoever it was had shut her up.

Coincidence?

There hadn't been an order waiting or a customer to claim it. Slade knew that he might be reading too much into it, but he recalled Margine's expression when he'd asked about a funeral in town. Her wide eyes, almost startled, as she said, *"No, sir. Not with—"*

Now, he had Drury trying to insist that Slade sit down to jabber with the local land agent. For what? Even if Brock was the de facto mayor of Alva—which, in truth, had no town government at all—there was no reason to believe that Brock had any knowledge that would help Slade solve the killings.

Was there?

Slade considered asking blond Margine to finish what she'd started telling him before, then changed his mind. He'd gain nothing by making trouble for a woman whom he'd barely met, and if he came up short of leads after tomorrow morning, he could always track her down and talk to her in private. Alva wasn't big enough for anyone to hide in, if Slade wanted to uncover them.

But something smelled.

Slade couldn't place the odor, yet, but he was working on it. Euliss Drury, he was sure, knew more about the killings than he'd shared, so far. There would be time tomorrow, on their ride out to the Oman spread, for Slade to work on him and pry it loose. Failing at that, he might drop by the land office and try another angle of attack.

Leaving the worried waitress with a decent tip, Slade walked down to the livery, checked on his roan, then took a slow stroll back to his hotel. He needed sleep and hoped that if he dreamed, the only face he'd see was Faith's.

• • •

The Atchison Café had just opened for breakfast when Slade arrived the next morning. Margine had been replaced by a redhead who vaguely resembled the clerk at the Alva House, except that her freckles were fetching. The place filled up while Slade was waiting for his ham and eggs, making him wonder if the hour made a difference or if the town had gotten over its brief mourning for a slaughtered family.

Constable Drury beat Slade to the stable and was standing with a saddled piebald gelding when he entered. Slade began to question him again, while saddling his roan.

"How far out is it, to the Oman spread?" he asked.

"I'd call it six or seven miles."

"Neighbors?"

"You've got the Hendershots, a couple miles beyond and farther north. They didn't socialize."

"You know that for a fact?"

"The Omans didn't socialize with *anybody*," Drury said.

"Their choice?"

A lazy shrug. "I'm only saying what I've heard. I never met 'em, personally."

"When you say 'the Omans,' were they all of one name?"

"Well . . ."

"Because I'm wondering about the bodies."

"Bodies?"

"In the wire you sent Judge Dennison, you said one man was killed, three women, seven kids."

"That's right."

"Sounds like they're two men short," Slade said.

"I couldn't speak to that," Drury replied. "As to the names, Bethuel Oman took out the claim, so it's the Oman place. Whether the others had some different names, I couldn't rightly say."

"Because they didn't socialize."

"Or hardly spend no time in town, aside from shopping once a month or so."

When they were mounted, headed out of town, Slade asked, "Who found the bodies?"

"Abel Hendershot. He had some cattle wander off, and he was looking for 'em when he saw the smoke."

"The burning house."

"That's right. He rode on over, even though they weren't real friendly."

"Mighty Christian of him," Slade observed.

"I guess. He found the man shot, off to one side of the house, and no one else in sight, but he could smell 'em . . . you know. Cooking."

Slade knew what he meant. And if he never smelled that stench again, it would be too damned soon.

"So, he alerted you?"

"Not me directly. He rode on to town, told Mr. Brock, and *he* told me."

"Then you went out to look around?"

"The two of us and half a dozen others. Didn't know what we might find, you understand."

"What *did* you find?" Slade asked.

"Just what I said. The man shot, and his house burned down. The fire was mostly out when we got there. Still took a while, though, for the ashes to get cool enough for raking. Trimming off the fat, we found the rest down in the cellar. Shot, they were. Not much by way of burns, but they'd have suffocated down there, with the fire on top of 'em, if they weren't shot first."

"So, was it murder or suicide?"

Drury examined Slade as if he'd lost his mind. "I don't imagine seven children shot themselves, do you?"

"Not likely. How about the women?"

"Um. I couldn't say."

"Did you find weapons in the cellar?"

"Two. A six-gun and a Winchester. Both empty."

"So, the women could've shot the children—as a mercy, say, to keep them from the fire—then shot themselves?"

"I guess it's possible."

"And how'd the fire start? Could you tell?"

"Oh, sure. Somebody lit a wagon full of hay and ran it up against the house."

"Blocking the door?"

"Nope. Over to one side."

"They could've walked right out at any time, then?"

"Unless someone was waiting for 'em in the yard," said Drury.

"Which explains the wagon and the man shot down, outside."

"I'd say so."

Slade spotted the barn, untouched by fire, when they were still the best part of a mile out from the Oman place. He smelled wood ash, but any hint of roasting flesh had been dispersed by wind over the past three days.

Small favors.

Riding in, he saw vultures rise flapping from a horse's carcass, maggot-ridden, swollen in the sun.

"You didn't mention any horses being shot," Slade said.

"It slipped my mind," Drury replied.

Slade scanned the ashes of a former home and saw the skeletal remains of a wagon on his left, where it would once have pressed against a northward-facing wall.

"That was a good-sized wagon," Slade observed.

"I guess so," Drury said.

"You don't suppose they left it parked against the house like that, loaded with hay?"

"It's doubtful."

"So, we have at least three killers. Two pushing the wagon, while a third keeps everyone inside."

"And Mr. Oman?"

"He most likely figured out what they were up to, and he tried to stop them. Didn't make it."

"That makes sense."

"What's missing from the place?" Slade asked.

"Missing?"

"Livestock? Equipment? Weapons? Money?"

"Well, we found two horses in the barn. A little spooked but otherwise all right. They're over at the Hendershots'. The wagon's burned, but there's a plow inside the barn and other tools. We found the guns I mentioned and a shotgun over there, by Oman's body. Money, I can't tell you. If they had some in the house, it's likely smoke and ash."

"So, not a robbery," said Slade.

"I guess not."

"Nor a gang of drifters coming by, spotting the ladies, and deciding they should make themselves at home."

"No?"

"Not unless they changed their minds and thought it would be more fun burning everyone alive."

"I guess not."

"This thing was either random—meaning crazy—or else someone nursed a bitter hatred for the folks who died here."

"Who hates children?" Drury asked him.

"Lots of people. What you need to ask is, who hates kids enough to slaughter them like animals together with their parents." Something hit Slade, then, making him ask, "*Were* these the parents? Of all seven kids?"

Another shrug from Drury. "I already told you, they weren't prone to socializin'. Not neighborly. If anyone in town talked to 'em about anything but buying goods, I couldn't tell you who it was."

"Okay."

"What's on your mind, Marshal?"

Slade's turn to shrug. "Some people take in children. Orphans, runaways, like that. Or kids from relatives who've passed or couldn't handle them."

"You think this was some kind of foundling home?"

"It seems unlikely, I admit."

"You really ought to have a word with Mr. Brock."

"Because . . . ?"

"He might know something useful."

"Such as?"

"It's not for me to say."

"You have a strange idea of where your duty lies," said Slade.

"I'm not obstructing anything, Marshal. Just telling you to speak with Mr. Brock."

"Where are the graves?"

"Around behind the barn."

Slade went to have a look at them, for all the good it did. Low mounds of dirt, one with a plank of wood upstanding, etched with Bethuel Oman's name. The rest unmarked.

Frowning, Slade walked back to his roan.

"All right," he said. "Let's go and see your Mr. Brock."

They rode back to Alva in silence, Slade sifting his thoughts, his companion apparently brooding. The sky overhead was pale blue after yesterday's gray, with no rumor of rain. When they got into town, Slade rode straight for the livery, Drury trailing him at a distance of several yards.

"I don't leave my horse here," he said, while Slade tended the roan. It required no response, and got none.

When he'd finished, Slade found Drury standing beside his horse, more or less where he'd begun the morning. Waiting nervously, shifty eyes sweeping the street. In other circumstances, Slade would have suspected he was being set up for an ambush. As it was, he made his mind up to watch Drury like a hawk and take whatever information he had pried out of the constable with several grams of salt.

"This way," said Drury, leading Slade down dusty Main Street toward the land office. That came as no surprise to Slade, but he still wondered what a clerk who dealt in real estate might know about a massacre outside of town.

Unless he was involved in it, somehow.

Another suspect for his mental list.

The office had seemed larger yesterday, beneath a stormy sky. In full daylight, it wasn't much to look at. Neither was the man who came to greet them as they entered, smiling like a jack-o'-lantern, ruddy-cheeked, with hair slicked back and flattened on his scalp. Slade pegged him somewhere in his forties, maybe ten pounds overweight at five foot eight or nine.

"Marshal," he beamed. "We meet at last. I'm Garland Brock. And your name's Slade, I understand?"

Slade let that pass, saying, "Your constable's hell-bent on having us discuss the Oman killings, but he won't say why. You want to clear that up for me?"

Brock nearly lost his smile at that, but got it back with something of an effort. "Marshal Slade, please join me in my office, won't you? We can speak more privately in there." Spinning around, he called out, "Lottie! Where's that girl?"

"Here, Mr. Brock," replied a mousy woman who'd been standing in the same place since Slade entered.

"Bring some coffee, will you? Make it three."

"Yes, sir."

Slade trailed Brock to his private office, Drury bringing up the rear. When they were all inside, Brock sidestepped to a wall where pencil drawings of a castle had been thumb-tacked.

"Marshal, this is Alva's future," Brock announced, sweeping a hand over the drawings.

"Going back into the Middle Ages?" Slade inquired.

"No, no! These are the plans for our new normal school. When it's completed, it will be the largest and the finest in the territory. Later, after statehood, it will be the first state university."

"A normal school trains teachers?"

"That's exactly right. To educate the children of tomorrow, building Oklahoma from the grass roots up. We're on the ground floor. There are great days coming."

"I'm relieved to hear it. Now, about these murders."

"Marshal, you understand that towns like this—well, *any* towns, in fact—depend in large part on their reputation when it comes to drawing industry. Or students, as the case may be."

"Makes sense," Slade granted.

"And we can't afford to have our sizeable—our *very* sizeable—investment tarnished by unpleasantness."

"Mass murder's just about the most unpleasant thing there is," Slade said.

"Exactly! You'll agree, I'm sure, that it's bad news for Alva."

"Worse news for the victims."

"Certainly! Of course! But should we go out of our way to make it any worse? For Alva *or* the memory of those unfortunates? What's to be gained by raking through the muck?"

"Depends on what turns up," Slade answered. "If I have to rake some muck to find three killers, I don't mind."

"*Three* killers?" Brock's face lost a shade of color. "Who said anything about *three* killers?"

"Maybe more," Slade said. "I'm calling three the bedrock minimum."

"How can you possibly know that?" asked Brock.

"Two men to push the wagon, one to guard the door," said Drury, sounding glum. "I should've worked that out, myself."

"Well, one, three, what's the difference, really?"

"Ask the mathematics teacher from your normal school," Slade said.

"I *mean* to say, if you find one, you'll find the rest, eh, Marshal? Wrap it up as quickly as you can, with no more fuss than absolutely necessary. Let us put our grief behind us and move on."

"I have to say that neither one of you looks all that sad."

"We mourn in different ways," said Brock. "Now, do you think that you can help us? Sort this out and keep it quiet?"

"Mr. Brock," Slade said, "I don't know why in Hell I'm even standing here talking to you."

"Well . . . I asked Euliss here to bring you by so we could get to know each other. Giving me a chance to put this awful business in perspective."

"Lecture me about your town, you mean, and how a little thing like murder's not convenient."

"Hold on, now."

"No, *you* hold on. You've told me why you had your lawman nag me into coming over here. I came. I listened. Now, you need to understand, I'm only wasting time with you because the constable keeps saying you have information that can help me solve these murders. True or false?"

"Solve them? Oh, no. I can't say that."

"Then stop wasting my time."

Slade turned to leave when Brock snaked out a hand and caught hold of his sleeve. He half turned, stared at Brock until the clerk released him, swallowed hard, and said, "There is one thing."

"So, swallow it or spit it out."

"I hate to speak ill of the dead."

"Speak or don't. You've got five seconds."

"The Omans," Brock said. "They were Mormons."

3

"Mormons?"

Brock nodded, eyes downcast. The constable had turned away from Slade, feigning sudden interest in the sketches of the college castle mounted on Brock's wall.

"So all three women—"

"Were his so-called wives," Brock said. "It seems so, Marshal."

"And the children were all his."

"Results of sinful fornication."

"You were planning to conceal this from me," Slade observed, including both of them.

"No, sir!" Brock appeared to take offense at the suggestion. "But we had to break it to you in the right way and at the right time."

"Which was yesterday, first time I met your constable," Slade said.

"We couldn't have you thinking that our town had gone along with this illegal and immoral conduct. Anyway, they

didn't live *in town*, you realize. Why, Euliss had no jurisdiction over—"

"So he keeps on telling me. Was this some kind of secret
kept between the two of you?"

"Secret? No, sir. You can ask anyone in town."

"And do the others share your sense of disapproval?"

"We're as one in opposition to all forms of crime."

Slade didn't let himself get sidetracked into how the giant railroads operated nationwide, the towns and lives they
had destroyed.

"So, none of you took any pains to make the Omans feel
at home? I mean, beyond taking their money when they
came in for supplies?"

"We wouldn't *socialize* with trash, if that's what you're
suggesting," Brock replied.

"I get the picture," Slade replied.

"In which case," Brock pressed on, "you'll certainly agree
that Alva isn't tainted by their sin—or by the crime, however brutal it may be, that wiped the stain away."

"You're all for killing sinners, then, as long as someone
else handles the dirty work?"

"Killing? God, no! Marshal, the Bible says—"

" 'Judge not, lest ye be judged.' " Slade pulled the quote
up from some childhood memory. "As for the law, it leaves
the judging part to Isaac Dennison. Some of the good folks
from your little town may wind up meeting him, before too
long."

"From Alva?" Brock was clearly horrified by the idea.
"Marshal, you can't mean that!"

"Since I first met your lawman, yesterday," Slade said,
"there hasn't been a minute when the two of you weren't
scheming, hiding information, or excusing what was done.
You had the motive and the opportunity."

"For *what*?"

"Mass murder," Slade replied.

Brock looked as if he might faint dead away. Drury supported him, walked Brock around his desk, and sat him down in a tall chair with wheels on its legs.

"Marshal," Drury said, "I swear to you, we had no part in what was done to those . . . the Omans. No one in this town had anything to do with it."

"Am I supposed to trust you now?" asked Slade. "And if I did, in spite of the manure that you've been shoveling my way, you still can't vouch for anybody else in town. You tell me everyone in Alva held the Omans in the same contempt I see from you two, but they must be innocent? I look around and see a town chock-full of suspects."

"No!" Brock fairly gasped. "Please, Marshal—"

"What I need to do, right now, is wire Judge Dennison and tell him everything that you all failed to mention in the first place," Slade informed them. "Then, it looks like I may have to question every mother's son in town. Some of the mothers, too, for all I know."

"Marshal, if word of this gets out—"

"Murder's a funny thing that way," said Slade. "No matter how you try to hide it, it still has a way of coming back to haunt you."

"I promise you," Brock said, braced upright with his elbows planted on the desktop, "no one in this town is capable of murder."

"We're all capable of murder, Mr. Brock. Some folks just never get around to it."

"No one from Alva massacred that family!"

"Well, then, we've got ourselves a mystery," Slade said. "Lord only knows how long I'll be around, if that's the case."

He left them looking green around the gills, brushed past the mousy woman who'd focused on the task of making coffee when she heard the angry voices coming from her boss's office, and stepped out into clean air. Main Street looked just the same as he had left it, but Slade had to ask himself what lies and secrets were concealed behind the storefronts, lurking in the houses.

Slade composed his message to the judge while he was walking from Brock's office to the railway depot. He assumed it would contain the telegraph office. If not, he was prepared to go from door to door until he found what he was looking for.

In fact, the depot had it. Slade passed through its bright façade, emblazoned with the railroad's logogram, and found himself inside an empty waiting room. Off to his left, two separate windows served the same small office, one for TICKETS and the other labeled TELEGRAPH. A bearded man wearing a blue railroad conductor's uniform watched Slade through slim brass bars, like some exotic creature in a zoo.

Slade chose the proper window, let the man stare at his badge a bit, then said, "I need to wire the federal court in Enid."

"Yes, sir," said the beard, seeming a mite reluctant as he pushed a blank telegraph form and pencil toward Slade through a slot in his cage.

Slade wrote: VICTIMS WERE MORMONS STOP FROM ALL APPEARANCES COMMA TOWN HOSTILE STOP PROCEEDING WITH INVESTIGATION STOP WELCOME ADVICE STOP SLADE.

He'd almost written ANY SAGE ADVICE, but didn't trust Judge Dennison to take a joke and caught himself in time. The clerk charged him thirty-eight cents, and Slade waited, watching from outside the cage, until his message had been sent over the wire.

"Any reply," Slade said, "I'm at the Alva House."

"I haven't got a runner, Marshal."

"Right. I'll check back, then."

"There's always someone here."

Back on the street, Slade stood and watched a few townsfolk going about their business, entering and leaving Alva's shops. Hammers were banging at the far end of the street, construction under way. Slade couldn't name the buildings from their wooden skeletons, but Alva lacked a church, saloon, and school to round out its facilities, if it was going to expand.

A church, he thought, which brought him back to Mormons, living on their own away from town, until three killers—maybe more—decided they'd lived long enough. He'd known some kind of special hate or craziness must lie behind a massacre of children, and religion might provide the fuel for both.

Backtracking toward the Atchison Café, Slade racked his brain for any information on the Mormon creed. The basics came to him from childhood lessons, stories heard while he was traveling in later years, and articles in newspapers.

For starters, Slade knew that the church was launched by one man, Joseph Smith, in 1830. At the time, Smith had been living in New York, earning a living as a treasure hunter with a twist. Instead of sweating with a shovel, he would put a stone inside a stovepipe hat and "see" clues to a hidden treasure's whereabouts by peering at the stone, then sell the leads to customers who never struck it rich. When that act started wearing thin, Smith told his neighbors that an angel no one else could see had led him to a buried "holy book" inscribed on golden plates, chock-full of secrets, buried near his home.

Nobody else could see the golden plates, of course. Smith had to read them in a closet, through a "seer stone," while a friend took notes outside the door. Over a period of months, those sessions had produced the Book of Mormon, claiming to describe God's contact with a tribe of Israelites in North America. Established churches ridiculed Smith's "revelations," but he still attracted converts. Slade supposed that some of them were lured by a belated message from on high that told Mormon men to have multiple wives. When that was added to the mix, hostility from neighbors kept Smith's Mormons on the move from state to state.

Slade knew that Smith had faced a charge of bank fraud in Missouri and had fled the state in lieu of standing trial. A couple dozen Mormons had been killed by adversaries in the Show-Me State before the rest packed up and moved to Illinois. A few years later, Smith was jailed there, after Mormons demolished the press of a critical newspaper. He was awaiting trial when lynchers stormed the jail and shot him dead.

Slade found Margine on duty when he entered the café. She looked a little sheepish, but she still dredged up a smile before she led him to the table where he'd eaten supper the day before. Same menu on the wall, so he broke down and ordered stew before returning to his private thoughts.

The violence surrounding Mormonism had not ended with the death of Joseph Smith. His heir, old Brigham Young, had led the faithful on an epic four-year trek across the continent to reach an arid sanctuary they called Deseret. Congress trimmed it down and called it Utah Territory, but left Brigham Young in charge as governor. The march to statehood stumbled on polygamy in 1857, with the church and its militia squaring off against the U.S. Army for a yearlong war that spilled beyond the territory's borders on occasion.

Slade couldn't cite statistics from the final butcher's bill—the war had ended several years before his birth—but he recalled tales of the Mountain Meadows massacre. Mormons and Paiute tribesmen had attacked a wagon train en route from Arkansas to California, killing more than a hundred adult travelers, but spared their children for adoption of a sort by Mormon families. Governor Young "investigated," executed one scapegoat, and left the other killers unidentified.

All ancient history today. Young had been dead for close to twenty years. The church had formally renounced polygamy and excommunicated some who wouldn't let it go. Utah still hadn't been admitted to the Union as a state, so far, but Slade supposed it must be drawing closer to that goal. If asked before today, Slade would've said the days of mayhem had been left behind.

But he would have been wrong.

Margine brought his stew, which exceeded Slade's slim expectations. He ate it with freshly baked bread, enjoying the meal while his thoughts drew him back into darkness, where everything had a foul taste.

There was a chance that Bethuel Oman's faith played no role in the slaughter of his family, but Slade thought it was damned unlikely. Garland Brock and Euliss Drury had already demonstrated animosity enough against the victims to place their names on Slade's list of suspects. And if it was true, as Brock claimed, that Alva's other citizens all shared that animosity, the list had just increased a hundredfold.

Which didn't prove the Omans had been killed by anyone from Alva, even if the whole town had despised them—while, of course, continuing to take and spend their money. That led Slade to wonder how the family had come by any cash, living in isolation as they did, and only spending on the rare occasions when they came to town.

He'd have to ask around, find out if they were selling anything to help ends meet, then backtrack, learn their history, plot out their movements prior to reaching Oklahoma Territory, marking stops along the way. If they had come from Utah, and had troubles there, he'd have to let Judge Dennison contact that territory's U.S. marshal.

And would *he* turn out to be a Mormon, too?

Slade caught himself before his mind could drift into the realm of paranoid conspiracies. He had enough grim work ahead of him, looking for killers made of flesh and blood. Trying to reason out their motive, when it might be jumbled up with talk of angels, golden tablets nobody could see, and the intensity of hatred sometimes spawned by different takes on God and faith.

Slade wasn't a historian, by any means, but he had read enough to know that organized religion was responsible for many of the wars—and all the crazy witch-hunts—suffered by humanity, down through the centuries. The Old Testament was filled with tales of massacres committed under orders from the Lord, and even if you set those tales aside as myths, the real world offered numerous examples of religion run amok.

It went back to the dawn of time, as far as Slade could tell. Crusades and inquisitions. Christians battling Muslims for the Holy Land and burning witches back at home, while everyone ganged up on Jews. If that weren't bad enough, another bloody strain of warfare separated Catholics and Protestants, from Martin Luther's Reformation, down to Know-Nothing riots and burning of convents in major American cities, as late as the 1850s. Lumped together with the Mormon wars, persecution of Quakers, Shakers, and other fringe groups, it wove a tapestry of hate and violence spanning centuries.

To much for me, Slade thought—and knew exactly what he needed.

Make that, *who* he needed.

Leaving money on the table for Margine, he rose and went to find himself a minister.

"Has this town got a preacher?"

The hotel clerk's eyebrows jumped a little at the question, then he said, "Yes, sir. That would be Reverend Pettigrew."

"I haven't seen a church or parsonage," Slade said.

"No, sir. That's in the works. He preaches Sundays at the depot, just for now."

"And this not being Sunday, where might he be found?"

"Across the street, there, at his brother's dry-goods store."

"Thanks."

Slade was standing in the well-appointed store five minutes later. The proprietor had rigged a bell over the door, which jangled to announce the presence of a customer. The owner came out of a back room, smiling through a tidy beard until he saw Slade's badge.

"How may I help you, sir?"

"I'm looking for a Reverend Pettigrew," Slade said. He didn't like the thought of any man being *revered,* but since the hotel clerk had offered no first name, it was the best that he could do.

"My brother," said the shopkeeper, losing the final remnant of his smile. "And may I ask your business?"

"It's official," Slade replied. "And confidential."

"I see." The other Pettigrew turned toward the door he had emerged from moments earlier and called out, "Michael! You have company."

A smaller, somewhat older version of the storekeeper emerged, trailing a broom in one hand. Clean-shaven, with a mass of wavy hair combed down as flat as he could manage, the preacher wore a red-and-black-plaid shirt, blue denim pants, and old brown shoes.

He obviously hadn't known that Slade was coming, but he didn't look surprised.

"How can I help you, Marshal?"

"Is it possible to have a word in private?"

Glowering, the owner said, "I'll leave you two alone, then. Let the inventory wait."

"No need, Robert," the preacher said. "We'll get some air—if that's all right with you, Marshal?"

"Sounds good."

Outside, leaving the shop behind them, Pettigrew said, "Brothers are not always brotherly."

"I've been there," Slade replied.

"You've come to me about the killings, I suppose?"

"How did you figure that?"

Pettigrew smiled. "To the best of my knowledge I've broken no laws. The only incident of any note in this vicinity is the death of Bethuel Oman, with his concubines and offspring. And since that crime has its religious overtones . . ."

"You call the women concubines, not wives?"

"Marshal, you represent the law of man. I'm sure you know that no place in this country lets a man marry a second wife unless the first has died or they have been divorced."

"I do know that," Slade granted. "I'm just curious about your choice of terms."

"It's found in scripture, from the book of Genesis through Daniel. It signifies a mistress or a pros—"

"I get it. Did you know the Omans, personally?"

"It would be too much to say I knew them. I knew *of* them, certainly. And I approached the man, once, when they came to town. I asked him certain questions that appeared to agitate him. He was not amenable to a debate."

"Of what, exactly?"

"Scripture. Do you realize, Marshal, that Mormons—or Latter-Day Saints, as they style themselves—subscribe to *alternate* scriptures? That they exalt a book of fabricated tales concocted by a madman as not only *equal* to the Holy Bible but *superior* to the authentic word of God?"

"You have strong feelings on the subject."

"As a clergyman, how could I not?" asked Pettigrew.

"And which church do you represent, again?"

"My own, sir. I am not affiliated with the usual denominations—Baptist, Methodist, what have you. All are tainted by their commerce with the world of sin."

"As to the Mormons, now, your chief objection is polygamy?" asked Slade.

"One of a thousand, sir. And not the worst, by any means. You may recall that many patriarchs of scripture had multiple wives. Abraham, Jacob, David—why, King Solomon alone had seven hundred wives and three hundred con- cubines."

"He must've been exhausted," Slade observed.

The preacher made a sound resembling laughter, quickly stifled. "Very possibly. But then our savior set the standard for all Christians in his time on Earth."

"Unless they've changed the word since I first learned it, he was never married."

"That's true, but speaking to the Pharisees in Matthew, chapter nineteen, he decreed that a man shall leave his par- ents, cleaving to his wife, 'and they twain shall be one flesh.' *Twain* means *two,* sir. Not three or three dozen."

"But you say that's not the main objection against Mor- monism?"

"Oh, it may well be, for some. But if you're educated in the scriptures, you know where the true danger lies."

"And where's that?"

"In perversion of God's holy word, sir! Mormonism teaches that God the Father started as a mere man on an- other planet, where he attained divinity by following the dictates of *another* god, then came to Earth *with his wife,* to produce spirit offspring in Heaven. Those spawn include not only Christ and Satan, with the angels, but all human souls on Earth today. They *linger* somewhere in the sky and wait to *penetrate* our newborn children. Have you ever heard such blasphemy? Lord Jesus and the Devil, brothers!"

"Well—"

"And that's not all, sir. Mormons claim that you can pray lost souls from Hell back into Heaven, if you're baptized in their name *after they die.* Can you imagine? Granting eter- nal salvation without repentance?"

"It's a stumper," Slade replied. "Do others here in Alva share your knowledge and opinion of the Mormon creed?"

"I've done my best to educate them, Marshal. As to what they think or feel . . . well, I leave divination and mind read- ing to the Devil's children."

"No one's come to you, all pleased as punch for getting rid of such a blight on the community?"

"Certainly not!"

"Because, knowing the way you feel, someone might seek approval from a figure he admires. Seek out your blessing, you might say."

The preacher stopped short, staring hard at Slade. "Marshal, do you believe that I *inspired* these ghastly murders?"

"Nothing that I've seen suggests it," Slade replied. Thinking, *Except your attitude and every word you say.*

"Because I take the Ten Commandments very seriously, sir. And number six declares, 'Thou shalt not kill.'"

"With plenty of exceptions, though."

"I beg your pardon?"

"As I recall, the Bible has a list of people we're *required* to kill. Aside from murderers and witches, there's adulterers, false prophets, sodomites, blasphemers, people who work on the Sabbath, even kids who sass their folks and brides who lie about being virgins. I likely missed a few."

"But, Marshal, those are all *Old Testament* rules. As Paul tells us, in Romans Six:Fourteen, we're not under the law, but under grace."

"Okay, that clears it up," Slade said. "Thanks for your time, Pastor. And if someone *should* get in touch with you about this case . . ."

"You'll be the first to know, of course," said Pettigrew, before he turned back toward the waiting broom.

A younger clerk was in the railroad depot's ticket cage when Slade returned, identified himself, and asked if he had any messages.

"Yes, sir," the clerk replied, declining any vestige of a smile. "If you'll just sign here, for receipt."

Slade scrawled his name and took his telegram. He left the waiting room before he opened it, a waste of time, assuming that the same clerk had received the message and translated it from Morse code into English. It read: PURSUE ALL, REPEAT, ALL AVENUES OF INVESTIGATION STOP INQUIRY WIRED TO MARSHAL UTAH TERRITORY STOP NO STONE UN-TURNED STOP DENNISON.

Slade pocketed the telegram, uncertain what his next move ought to be. Judge Dennison was handling the Utah end of things, but Slade would be surprised if it paid off. Even assuming that the Omans hailed from Utah, would the U.S. marshal there know anything about them? And, if so, would he report it to the judge in Oklahoma? If the Utah marshal happened to be Mormon, would he pass the tele-gram to leaders of the church, instead of making personal inquiries?

Once again, Slade worried that he might be falling prey to notions of conspiracy, influenced by the prejudice he'd found so far in Alva. On the other hand, when two or more killers joined forces to commit a homicide, that *was* the legal definition of conspiracy. As to the rest, whether relig-ion had influenced the attack or not, he'd have to wait and see.

Assuming there was any evidence to find.

Slade wasn't looking forward to the dreary task of grill-ing Alva's citizenry one by one. Unless he missed his guess, Drury and Brock would huddle with their friends, tell those who hadn't guessed about Slade's mission, and advise them that he wasn't falling into line with their attempt to salvage Alva's reputation. Word would spread from there—was likely spreading, even now—and there was every chance he'd meet a wall of stony silence as he went from door to door, watch-ing the townsfolk slam them in his face.

A waste of time, most likely, but he had no other angle of attack. Until he could collect some background informa-tion on the victims, if he ever did, the only course remain-ing to him was a fishing expedition over hostile waters.

And to start it, there was no time like the present.

Slade decided he would start on Main Street's north side, work his way from west to east, then cross and come back westward, trying every home and shop along the way, speaking to anyone he found. If that proved fruitless, as expected, Slade would use whatever daylight still remained to visit homes that stood away from Main Street. There would be some duplication there, no doubt, apologies required for bracing certain people twice, but he would get it done.

No stone unturned.

Slade was approaching the stable, prepared to ask the simpleminded hostler what he knew about the Omans, when a voice was raised behind him, calling out his name. He turned to find the constable approaching, hands in pockets, looking glum.

"Marshal," he said, by way of greeting.

"Constable. What can I do for you?"

"I reckon it's the other way around."

"How's that?"

"Well, sir, there's something Mr. Brock forgot to mention, earlier. About the Omans. When you spoke to him."

When else? Slade thought, but said: "Oh, yes?"

"Yes, sir."

"You want to share that with me, or are you just dropping hints?"

"You see, the thing is . . . well, he didn't mention that there was another Mormon family the Omans kept in touch with."

"Where? Close by?" Slade felt the anger rising in him.

"Not close, exactly," Drury said. "Maybe a half day's ride, off east of town."

"You have a name?"

"Haglund."

"That's it?"

"I haven't made a study of 'em. Never been out to their place. Can't tell you if I ever saw 'em here in town.

One thing for sure, they never came in like the Omans, all the women and their young'uns in a bunch."

"You wouldn't know them if you passed them on the street," Slade said.

"No, sir."

"How did you hear about them, then?"

"Just word of mouth, you know," Drury replied. "I reckon Bethuel must've mentioned them sometime, either to someone here in town or when he thought no one was listening. 'My friends, the Haglunds.' Something in that line."

"And Brock was keeping that a secret from me, as he sees it, to protect the town?"

A shrug. "I guess that's right."

"What made you spill it?" Slade inquired.

"I've just been thinking," Drury said. "If someone wanted Oman and his people dead because they're Mormons—or, they *were*—that someone could be gunning for the Haglunds, too."

"That just occurred to you?"

"No, sir. But like I said, before—"

"It's all outside your jurisdiction. I remember. Tell me, Constable, who pinned that badge on you?"

"The town."

"By which, you mean . . . ?"

"Well, Mr. Brock. The railroad. Take your pick, I guess."

"I'm guessing you weren't chosen for a tendency to rock the boat."

"The boat?"

"Forget it. Can you tell me how to find the Haglund place?"

"It's like I said—"

"You've never been there. But you know they're east of town, about a half day's ride."

"I sorta put that much together, listening to folks."

"And was that all you put together?"

"Someone might've said their spread was near the river, now you mention it."

"Meaning the Salt Fork of the Arkansas?"

"The only river hereabouts."

Slade checked the sky and knew he couldn't make the trip that day. He'd lose daylight before he covered half the necessary distance, which would leave him searching for the river—and an isolated homestead—in the dead of night.

Stone-faced, he told Drury, "You'd better hope I find them, Constable. And that they're still alive."

4

The killers suspected they were lost. It had happened before, more than once, to their leader's chagrin. They told themselves that God provided all things in need, but he had left them roaming in the wilderness on several occasions when a simple nudge in one direction would have helped immensely.

Amren Tanner knew his men were restless, but he had no sympathy. He understood their feelings, and he held them in contempt. The Lord, he was convinced, hated whiners.

Tanner owed his temperament and training to a legendary mentor, Porter Rockwell, gone to his reward these fifteen years and more. At Rockwell's death—against all odds, from illness, while awaiting trial for homicide—the *Salt Lake Tribune* had linked him to "at least a hundred murders."

Murders!

How could any action taken in defense of God's own chosen people be a crime?

Tanner had not tied Rockwell's record, but he was going strong. Perhaps, someday, his name would be remembered and his deeds revered. That some would try to demonize him, Tanner had no doubt.

Above all else, he did not wish to be remembered as a bungler. He abhorred the thought of facing God on Judgment Day and being asked, "Why did you make so many foolish errors?"

He had explanations ready in each case, for all the good that they would do. Killing the wrong man in Nevada had been a fluke. What were the odds that one remote and sparsely settled county would have *two* men named Flavius Romney? And even then, he had atoned by killing both.

Losing his own men was not Tanner's fault. He could defend that view for all eternity, if need be. The responsibility might lie with him, but he couldn't second-guess when one of his companions would get careless, drop his guard, and thus endanger all of them.

In fact, he thought it something of a miracle that only two had fallen on the way to where they stood.

Wherever *that* was.

They were lost, all right, but he would not admit to any weakness. One or two of them, he thought, already doubted his leadership, although they lacked the fortitude to challenge him.

And if they did? What, then?

Would they demand a new leader to see them through the trials ahead, to the completion of their mission? Or would they forsake their orders, scatter to the winds in search of new identities, perhaps with wives and children like the ones they've slain?

Returning to the Prophet's court without complete success was not an option. Neither could they simply lie, claiming they had eradicated all the targets from their list, while some still lived. The Prophet would see through their vain deception and destroy them, then dispatch another team to do their work.

Tanner would not acknowledge failure, even if he had to forge on alone. But at the moment, he wasn't going anywhere.

He was lost.

"We were supposed to go northeast," Bliss Kimball said.

"We've *gone* northeast," Tanner replied. "We're *facing* northeast, as we speak."

"Well, then, where are they?"

Tanner turned toward Kimball, gimlet-eyed. He did not say what should be obvious: that they had received bad information from a trusted source and couldn't go back to punish him without wasting weeks on the trail. And then again, perhaps their source spoke honestly but had himself been misinformed.

"We've found the river," he reminded them, pointing. "There'll be homes along it, either way we turn. First one we find, we'll ask and keep on asking, till one of them knows the name."

Haglund.

A larger family than the Omans, he'd been told, and thus more dangerous. They had more children, steeped in foul apostasy, and might be breeding even as he sat there, straddling a pinto taken from the Oman ranch as reimbursement for his gut-shot stallion. And the *children* would have children, reared in sin, if they were allowed to live.

"We'll look suspicious, ridin' up and down the river, askin' questions," Hallace Pratt suggested.

Or maybe we'll get lucky, Tanner thought, *and find them at the first place we stop.* But what he said was, "Only one of us will go up to a house and ask. The rest stay out of sight and wait."

"What if it's them?" DeLaun Allred inquired.

Tanner swallowed the first retort that came to mind, and

asked forgiveness for the unspoken profanity. "DeLaun," he said, "we'll have a look first, like we always do."

"Oh, right."

Sometimes he wished that the Lord's appointed cutting tools could hold a sharper edge.

"Which way, then?" Zedek Welch askied the question, no defiance in his tone.

"We'll track the river north," Tanner replied, "in case we've drifted too far south."

No intimation that it might be his fault. No concessions between hard men on a killing quest.

As with the others on his list, Tanner had never seen the Haglunds. He had fair descriptions of the adults, but a great deal might depend on hair, weight, clothing. More than anything, he trusted the fact that they should only find one family with four wives underneath one roof.

It was enough to seal their fate.

Slade was the first in line for breakfast at the Atchison Café, wolfing his ham and eggs, washing it down with coffee strong enough to stand and fight a battle on its own. The hostler had a sleepy look about him when Slade reached the livery, but that appeared to be his normal state. He wished Slade well in parting, then lapsed back into a blissful daze.

Slade left town with a half name, vague directions, and a vestige of suspicion that Drury and Brock might be sending him off on a wild-goose chase. If that proved out, he would be back with manacles for both of them, and they could ride his dust to Enid and tell their story to a judge who definitely wouldn't be amused. No one was hanged for filing false reports, but they would see the inside of a cell.

And if the constable had told the truth, at last? What then?

Slade reckoned there were three ways it could go. If the Omans were isolated targets—marked for death by enemies who hated them specifically, instead of for their faith—the Haglunds should be free and clear. If, on the other hand, someone was killing Mormons in the territory, they would clearly be at risk.

A third way it could play was if the constable in Alva had it wrong, concerning Bethuel Oman's friendship with the Haglunds. Gleaned from rumors, picked up secondhand at best, that information might be totally erroneous. In fact, the Haglunds could be *suspects* in the Oman killings.

Life had taught Slade that belonging to the same church didn't make parishioners fast friends. In fact, some of the worst backbiting that he'd ever heard had come from Christian ladies gossiping about their fellow worshipers. It seemed to Slade that human nature trumped religion, every time.

And what *was* it that made religion such a frequent killing issue, anyway? Why were some people moved to violence because their neighbors worshiped on one day and not another? Or because they sprinkled water during baptism, instead of dunking in a river? Nitpicking the Bible to prove points about the afterlife struck Slade as a colossal waste of time and energy, but killing in the name God— whatever he was called—was sacrilege incarnate.

Two miles out of town, with some uncertain distance still ahead of him, Slade wondered how he'd find the Haglunds. Half a day on horseback could be thirty miles or more, depending on how hard he pushed the roan, and even then, the vague directions Drury had provided—"east of town"—might take him miles off course. Worst case, he could spend days roaming the country east of Alva, maybe weeks, with no result.

Half of America lay east of Alva, when he thought about it. Finding one spread in that vast domain, without some kind of landmark, could turn out to be impossible.

Unless the killers made it easy for him, sure. If they showed up ahead of Slade and torched the place, he might be quick enough to see the smoke signals and follow them to find another slaughterhouse. But if he came too late, rode on past the ruins, off by even half a mile . . .

The river still might help him. Following the Salt Fork of the Arkansas eastward would lead him back to Enid, more or less, but the river ran two hundred miles or so from where the Arkansas turned north, toward Wichita. Again, he could waste days just following its course and still not find the Haglunds. Drury claimed they were "near the river," which could mean right on its bank or anywhere within a couple miles.

Slade knew he needed luck or else a helpful neighbor of the Haglunds who could point him toward their spread. The next town east of Alva should be Medford, just another railroad whistle-stop beyond the range of his intended search and on the wrong side of the river.

"At least," Slade told his roan, "I'm doing something." The alternative was killing time in Alva, quizzing everyone he met about the Omans, likely getting nowhere, very slowly.

Slade would use the day in searching. If he hadn't found the Haglund spread by nightfall or some helpful soul to steer him toward it, he would camp and get an early start for Alva in the morning. And he'd be taking back a prisoner to Enid, even if it was only a lying slug who wore a railroad badge.

By then, perhaps, Judge Dennison would have some word from Utah. Slade wasn't convinced there would be any help from that quarter, but they could hardly pass it up without trying.

Now, too late, Slade wished that he had wired the judge about his new lead, on the Haglunds. Then again, if they had enemies out west, raising the name in correspondence might increase their danger. Judges weren't the only ones with access to a telegraph, by any means—though he couldn't have said where the assassins might receive a wire.

Unless, of course, they were in Alva. Left behind, while he went gallivanting off in search of phantoms.

Questioning each mile he covered to the east, Slade forged ahead under an ashen sky whose color matched his mood.

"We're lost, I tell you." Hallace Pratt took care to keep his voice down, even though he trailed the three lead riders by an easy hundred feet.

"So?" Zedek Welch replied. "What are you wantin' me to do about it?"

"Nothing. I'm just saying."

"Well, I *knew* that. Is there something else?"

There was, but Pratt wasn't entirely sure if he could trust Welch with the full range of his private thoughts. He hadn't known the shorter, lazy-tongued gunman before they were picked for this mission. Chosen by Amren Tanner, a mutual . . . what?

Not friend. The leader of their hunting party didn't have friends. He held something back from every other human he encountered, moving through his life. He had the aspect of a solitary wolf, shunning the pack except where it was necessary for survival.

An acquaintance, then. They had done several small jobs for the Prophet, Tanner always in command, before the order came for their far-ranging mission. Killing off a renegade in Provo. Threatening a small apostate group near Cedar City. Hunting down one of the Prophet's enemies at Castle Dale.

Now, they were on a mission that would capture hearts and minds when it was spoken of, but only in the circles of the highly placed and sanctified. Because their actions were illegal, even though heroic, they might not be written down and taught in schools with stories of the Mormon Trail and locust plague of 1848.

It did not bother Pratt that his name would most likely be forgotten when he died. He had no wife or children, no siblings or living parents. He was, it sometimes startled him to realize, cast from Tanner's mold, but on a smaller scale.

His isolation made Pratt perfect for their mission, and he did not flinch from killing—never had—but he'd begun to wonder how much longer it would take to see their work completed. Half a dozen times he'd dreamed of the companions lost on this hunt up to now.

Weldon Killebrew was dead because a sheriff's deputy got nosy in Virginia City. When he had singled Weldon out for questioning, pushing it hard, the youngest member of their group had pulled his gun. Five seconds later, both the deputy and Killebrew were dead.

Pratt remembered riding like a wind from Hades over the Nevada desert, slowing through the mountains, dodging posses for the next week. Finally, when one had come too close, they'd stung the man hunters with rifle fire and sent them home.

It was an omen, Hallace thought. *And not the last.*

In San Diego, near the ocean, Nordell Lambourne had made his last mistake on Earth. Tanner had planned the execution of an aging heretic down to perfection, charting his movements and learning routines, choosing the best location for an ambush after sunset, but Lambourne had been on the prod, eager for a chance to prove himself a warrior for the Lord.

One thing they'd failed to notice, following their target on his rounds for three days running, was the pistol hidden underneath his suit jacket. Only a small one, but its first shot was enough for Nordell Lambourne, putting out his eye and boring through the brain behind it.

There had been no time for funerals, in either case. Now, Pratt wondered if Tanner would have stopped to bury him and read a verse over his grave, if Bethuel Oman's aim had been a little better. Did Tanner possess any human emotions?

There was anger, of course. Pratt and the rest had seen it several times, though Tanner always stopped short of a vulgar display. Frustration showed up, now and then, when it took undue time to locate a new target. More and more of that as time dragged on, drawing them farther from their homes.

And bitter hatred, certainly. Tracking the heretics and renegades was not just Tanner's job. It was his calling. He was born to it, the way some men are born to farming or to politics. The hand of God directed some, while leaving most to find their way alone.

Pratt hoped that wasn't blasphemy, but at the moment he was too saddle weary to care. There would be time enough to ask forgiveness later. Or, at least, he hoped so.

Once they found the Haglunds—*if* they found the Haglunds—there were five more targets on their list, together with assorted wives and children. Tanner had the route all planned, the southern tip of Illinois their farthest eastern stop, then circling back through northern Missouri, Nebraska, and Colorado. When they were done, they would have visited seven of the forty-four states and three territories.

Pratt wondered if someone in Salt Lake City was charting their progress, maybe sticking pins in a map. He assumed the Prophet must keep track of them somehow—Tanner sent telegrams from time to time but wouldn't discuss them afterward—but who else knew about their mission and the blood they'd spilled?

Jesus, of course. It had all been done in his name, after all. How could he fail to notice?

"Catch up, you two," Tanner called out to Pratt and Welch. Welch cut a glance at Pratt, then made a little huffing noise and booted his horse into a trot.

Pratt followed, keeping Jesus foremost in his mind and hoping he would soon provide the guidance they required to see their mission through.

In thy own holy name, amen!

• • •

Most mornings, Dannell Haglund woke up knowing that he was a lucky man. He did not have to count his blessings, since he saw them every day.

Braylyn, his first wife, was the thinker and the best cook of the lot, with hidden depths that still surprised Haglund from time to time. She'd given him two daughters, Wandle and Shaylin.

Second wife Alema had been slow conceiving. By the time she bore a son—named Heber, after Noah's great-grandson in scripture—Dannell already had another boy to carry on his line.

Third wife Vonelle had produced Haglund's first son, Draycen, and a daughter named Posey, second in line among the girls.

Fourth wife Tennys had borne Haglund's youngest son, named after the angel Moroni. She was pregnant again. So was Alema, just starting to show. They were obedient to Haglund, mindful of his needs, and of God's order to be fruitful and multiply. Even the Prophet said—

Haglund froze with his hammer poised, drawn back to strike a nail protruding from a piece of lumber cut to patch the west wall of his barn. His fist tightened around the hammer's handle for a moment, as if strangling it, and then relaxed.

It had been twelve years since his church abandoned him, although he guessed there would be some who thought it was the other way around. Haglund, like his father before him, had chosen to follow the sacred principle of plural marriage as revealed to Joseph Smith. He knew the relevant texts from Smith's Doctrine and Covenants by heart and treasured them as God's holy words.

Haglund despised cowards, although there were some who had called *him* a coward and worse for leaving Utah Territory. Haglund had no time to bandy words with fools. He'd watched the church retreat from pure obedience to God and Prophet Smith, surrendering its land and self-respect to curry favor with a Congress that despised Latter-Day Saints. Did not the First Amendment to the U.S. Constitution guarantee religious freedom, without interference from the government? And yet . . .

Haglund willed himself to relax, finished driving the nail, and took another from a pocket of his denim overalls. One of his horses had been frisky, kicking in its stall, and snapped a couple of two-by-six boards in the process. He'd soon have the damage repaired and get on to more productive tasks.

But still, the anger haunted him. And fear.

Anger, because it galled him to have spokesmen from the latest so-called Prophet tell him that weddings performed in the temple would be disavowed by the church. And for what? The privilege of statehood. Which, as far as Haglund could tell, entitled Utah's citizens to pay more tax than ever before, while heathens on the far side of the continent told them how to live, enforcing the demands with threats of military force.

Given a choice, which he was not, Haglund would have voted for a sovereign and self-sustaining State of Deseret. What had the great United States ever done for Mormons but hound them from one state to another, under constant threat of death and persecution? If America was Hell-bound, why clamber aboard a sinking ship?

Worse yet was the hypocrisy. Even as leaders of the church pressured their flocks to give up plural marriage and make their children bastards to accommodate demands from Washington, Haglund saw some who simply hid their extra wives away, packing them off to smaller towns where they'd subsist on weekend visits in rotation, while their husbands mouthed self-righteous platitudes for public consumption.

Dannell Haglund had refused to knuckle under. He had left the modern Zion with his growing tribe and struck off to build a new life. After a false start in New Mexico, they'd pushed on farther eastward, winding up in Oklahoma Territory. Still not safe, perhaps, but they had room to breathe.

Haglund assumed that he'd been excommunicated from the church by now, cut off in theory from his God and any hope of Heaven. And what of it? Did a church that had surrendered its most sacred principles to Mammon have the ear of God? Would not its leaders be among the first to burn on Judgment Day?

Twelve years, and even now he still expected retribution. Every day, after the first thoughts of how God had blessed his life, Haglund remembered that it might be snuffed out in a heartbeat. There'd been rumors of marauding zealots, silencing defectors from the church, exacting blood atonement for their so-called sins. Haglund still wasn't sure if he believed those tales, but Bethuel Oman did, keeping his weapons handy day and night.

Oman was Haglund's first real friend in ages, met by chance one shopping day in Alva, way off to the west, where Haglund bought essentials twice a year. He had been stunned to see Bethuel parade three wives as if it were acceptable and stole a chance to speak with him in private, while the women were distracted by yard goods.

At first, Oman suspected some cruel joke, but after meeting Braylyn, he'd been grateful to accept the fact that he and his were no longer alone. They could not visit often, both with farms to run and living more than twenty miles apart, but they arranged to meet without fail on each Pioneer Day, July 24, and on May 15—the date in 1829 when John the Baptist called on Joseph Smith. They took turns traveling, and Haglund had begun to take their fellowship for granted, as a blessed constant in his life.

But he had seen and felt the fear that gripped Bethuel Oman at any mention of the Danites. Haglund wasn't sure that he believed in them, but nothing would surprise him in the rotten world today.

So he remained alert, if not exactly on his guard, and

waited for the ax to fall. Each day was God's gift to the ·
faithful. He could give, and he could take away.

Slade found the farm at half past one o'clock. That is to say,
he spied a house, barn, and outbuildings from a distance,
unsure how long he'd been riding on the unseen farmer's
land. He hoped he'd found the Haglunds, but Slade wasn't
taking any bets.

The residents of isolated Oklahoma farms were nervous
folk, and rightly so. Drifters were dangerous, and renegades
still jumped the local reservations now and then. The nearest
law was miles away, too often on a par with Alva's constable.
Homesteaders who intended to survive had to defend themselves, instead of praying for salvation in the nick of time.

It came as no surprise to Slade, then, when a lean man
emerged from the farmhouse with rifle in hand, calling out
from a distance, "That's close enough, stranger!"

"I'm a U.S. marshal," Slade replied. "Just stopping by to
have a word."

"Come on, then," said the farmer. "Nice and easy. Hands
where I can see 'em."

Slade was happy to oblige, taking his time, making no
sudden or suspicious moves. His badge would not be clearly
visible until he'd closed the gap to thirty feet or so, and
even then the farmer might suspect it was a fake. Slade knew
of outlaws who had posed as lawmen to close within striking range of their victims. He didn't blame the farmer for
keeping his guard up, and he didn't want to die from being
careless.

Nice and easy.

"Name's Jack Slade," he said when he was close enough
to speak without shouting. "I work out of Enid, for Judge
Dennison."

"Heard the name," said the farmer, then added, "the
judge's. Not yours."

"Stands to reason. And you are . . . ?"

"Mel Waymire. You wanted a word?"

"Truth be told," Slade replied, "I was hoping your name might be Haglund."

Farmer Waymire made a sour face and said, "Not even close."

"I'm sensing that you know them, though."

"Know *of* 'em," Waymire instantly corrected him. "I never met 'em, and I never hope to."

"Why is that?" Slade asked.

"You're lookin' for 'em, and you don't know?"

"Why don't you enlighten me?"

Seeming confused beneath his anger, Waymire said, "Lord, man. They's *Mormons*."

"That's a bad thing?"

"Well, I hope to shout!" said Waymire, very nearly shouting as he said it. "You must know the sinning they get up to. Six or seven wives for every man. It's damned indecent!"

"I suppose it is, to some," Slade said.

"To anyone with common sense," Waymire insisted. "Say, if you're a lawman, ain't that kinda thing illegal in the territory?"

"I'd have to research it."

"Are you gonna lock 'em up?" The farmer sounded eager, now.

"I'd have to find them, first."

"Well, I can help you, there," said Waymire. "Theirs'll be the next spread over, heading northwest. Eight, nine miles, I'd say it is."

"Appreciate your help," Slade said, already turning from the farmhouse and its guardian.

"Tell 'em I sent you!" Waymire shouted after him. "Wish I could be there when you put the shackles on 'em!"

Slade left the farmer to his bigotry and concentrated on his heading, wondering what he would find as he approached the Haglund farm. Would there be ashes waiting for him, or was he in time to help them? Come to that, did they have anything at all to fear, besides the bias of their neighbors?

Slade was far from working out the details of his case, but it had been an education. Though aware of prejudice between religions, he'd avoided all the worst of it during his drifting, gambling days. Unless hell-bent on saving souls, the strongest church types didn't spend much time around saloons or poker tables. As a lawman, now, he got a glimpse of different sides to people.

Some stood out for kindness, generosity, the traits most commonly describes as virtues. Others wore a righteous mask while wading hip-deep in corruption. Oddly—or, perhaps, predictably—he'd found no steady correlation between Sunday hymn-singing and common decency.

Slade guessed there was a verse from scripture that would cover such hypocrisy. There seemed to be a verse for all occasions, even some that contradicted one another, but he hadn't memorized enough of the Good Book to recollect one.

Never mind.

Slade had his own code, and he meant to honor it.

5

They found the Haglund spread in early afternoon. Concealed within a clump of trees, atop a hill that overlooked the property, the killers waited and watched. Tanner applied his spyglass to the house, the barn, the other rough-hewn buildings, counting children in the yard but seeing no adults at first.

"Well, is it them?" DeLaun Allred inquired.

"Have patience," Tanner said. "I don't know, yet."

"It's been a quarter of an hour."

Tanner turned to him, holding out the spyglass. "Here, then," he replied. "You try it. Maybe it will let *you* see through walls."

"Forget it," Allred said, waving him off. "I'm just itching to get it over with."

"Then scratch without the jabber. Let me watch in peace."

He turned back to the spread below them, scanning with the glass. Children ran in and out of the barn, playing tag or some such, their laughter faint and almost ghostly when it reached Tanner's ears.

Looking at the kids, he almost hoped they'd found the wrong place, but he didn't think so. It was a fact that farmers often had large broods, and yet—

A man emerged from the barn, took off his hat, and sleeved the perspiration from his forehead. When he called out to the running children, message indecipherable from a distance, they reacted with laughter, broke formation, scattered like a swarm of startled mice.

As with the other targets on his list, Tanner had not seen Dannell Haglund in the flesh, nor in a photograph or painted likeness. Studying the farmer, he decided they were a fair match—six feet tall, or thereabouts, broad shoulders, raven-haired. The beard was salt and pepper, but long years in exile, at hard labor, might have sprinkled it with gray.

A strong man, by the look of him. But was he the *right* man?

"Gimme the word," Bliss Kimball offered, almost whispering from Tanner's left. "I'll take him down from here."

Bliss was their marksman, with his .50-90 Sharps rifle that could drop a man—or anything else, for that matter—a thousand yards out. He took pride in his shooting, likewise in the souls he had released to find their just reward.

"And make us ride the whole way down there under fire from anyone inside the house? No, thank you," Tanner said.

"You're the boss."

Tanner considered a response, but let it go. He *was* the boss. The Prophet's chosen voice and strong right hand, in fact. If Bliss or any of the others came to doubt it, Tanner was prepared to set them straight.

And leave them in the dust, if need be.

As he watched, now, a woman stepped out of the house, said something to the children, then exchanged conversation with the man. Tanner wished he was a lip-reader or had some magical device to let him eavesdrop on them from a distance.

I could use a seer stone, he decided, half smiling at the prospect of a miracle squandered on such as him.

If his description of the men he sought was often vague, descriptions of their wives were nonexistent. He supposed there were just too many of them. Someone at the Prophet's court presumed that it would be a waste of time describing all of them. Perhaps the schemers questioned Tanner's memory. Perhaps they'd never seen the women and had no idea what any of them looked like.

Foolish.

Tanner waited and watched. For the longest time—it felt like sweating hours—man and woman gossiped without moving. He stayed in the yard, she on the porch. When he began to close the gap between them, strolling toward the house and trailing children like a thrashing kite's tail, Tanner feared they'd all go back inside the house and disappear.

"Still time for me to drop him," Bliss proposed.

"No."

"We woulda seen another man by now," said Zedek Welch.

"Quiet, the lot of you!" snapped Tanner, and they hushed.

Someone was moving farther back, inside the house. Shadows prevented him verifying sex or age. If he could only reach across the yawning open ground between them, light a lamp inside the house . . .

The figure turned, advanced to the doorway, visible at last. It is another woman, maybe older than the one already on the porch, though Tanner couldn't judge fairly from a distance. Farming-weathered people, just the same as houses, barns, and tools. Some of the oldest-looking women he had ever seen were farmers' wives in Utah, worn out from their endless rounds of bearing children, cooking meals, and scratching lives out of the soil.

"All right," he said at last. "I think it's them."

• • •

"Well," Slade told his gelding, "here we go again."

The roan snorted.

"I know exactly how you feel," Slade said, then urged the horse forward.

He'd spent some time examining the farm, before approaching it. Nothing that he could see distinguished either house or outbuildings from others Slade had seen on this trip or while roaming in the past. Plains farmers, for the most part, didn't paint their homes in garish colors or do anything that might cause passing, hostile eyes to focus and become intrigued. Drab colors were the first line of defense.

For all of that, the farm seemed prosperous enough. Surrounding fields grew corn and wheat. A good-sized kitchen garden sprouted vegetables. Five horses lazed in a spacious corral, some thirty yards west of the house, with a shade tree to offer relief from the sun. Slade saw no cattle, but a distant lowing from the barn told him the settlers kept at least one, probably for milk. Chickens and children scurried in the dooryard.

On his slow approach, Slade marked the farm's surroundings. A long, low rise of hills off to the west was topped by trees, but distance made them useless as a windbreak. Short grass covered most of the landscape, fading from spring green into summer beige. The corn and wheat looked thirsty, but a bank of clouds approaching from the east held out some hope of rain.

Crossing a thousand yards of open ground gave anyone inside the house an ample opportunity to eyeball Slade. That could be good or bad, depending on the occupants. He had already freed the hammer thong that trapped his Colt Peacemaker in its holster, but he made no other moves that might be deemed hostile by any normal mind.

Which was the rub, of course.

Slade didn't know if those inside the farmhouse qualified as *normal*. If in fact he'd found the Haglunds, Slade was dealing with a clan that broke the law by practicing polygamy and might, therefore, resent a lawman turning up on their doorstep. Conversely, if they lived in fear of being murdered for their faith, there was at least a fifty-fifty chance that they'd shoot first and save the questions for another time.

And, on the other hand, suppose he *hadn't* found the Haglunds. If Mel Waymire had misled him for whatever reason, or if Slade had botched processing his directions, he could be approaching some entirely different family's preserve.

Most likely, they'd be law-abiding folk. But if they weren't—if they were making whiskey, say, for sale to reservation tribesmen—Slade might never hear the shot that killed him.

He was still two hundred yards out from the house when someone stepped onto the broad front porch. A man, Slade thought, but couldn't swear to it without a closer look. The figure held something that might have been a rifle or a shotgun. Then again, it could've been a broom, even a shovel.

No such luck.

When Slade had halved the distance, he could tell it was a firearm, caliber unknown. When he had closed the gap to fifty yards, with no word spoken from the porch, Slade called out to the silent man. Identified himself by name and as a marshal.

"Come ahead, then," said the rifleman.

Slade watched the farmhouse windows, braced to leap and roll if anything resembling a gun barrel slid into view. Of course, the smart thing would be shooting him from well back in the house, leaving the sniper cloaked in shadow.

Smart and deadly. Nothing Slade could guard against.

"What brings you out this way, Marshal?" the farmer asked.

"That would depend on who I'm talking to," Slade said.

"You don't know where you are?" The farmer almost seemed amused.

"I've traveled quite some way to find the Haglund family," said Slade.

"Then you're not lost. I'm Dannell Haglund."

"Are you acquainted with the Oman family, out by Alva?"

"They are friends. Yes, sir."

"Then I'm afraid," Slade said, "I bring bad news."

"Hold on a minute," Hallace said. "Who's that, riding in?"

Tanner faced toward where Pratt was pointing and picked out a horseman approaching from south by southwest. He guessed the rider wouldn't see them, up there in the trees, and leveled his spyglass.

"Who is it?" asked Allred.

The question inflamed Tanner. "How would I know that? You think I should recognize him?"

"I just meant—"

"Quiet!"

Tracking the rider, he ran through the options. A neighbor. A farmhand. A drifter. What else?

Not a salesman. They traveled in wagons all jangly with products and painted with bold advertisements that promised the moon and the stars.

Not a doctor. The clothes were all wrong, and there was no bag of instruments strapped on the saddle behind him, to cure what ails you.

Not a preacher, for certain. There was no Mormon church hereabouts, and the gunbelt he wore didn't work for a man of the cloth.

At that point, Tanner hit a wall. The stranger didn't have a farmer's air about him, and he didn't look like anyone's hired hand. That just left *drifter*, but he wasn't scruffy, on the cusp of starving like most saddle gypsies Tanner had encountered.

What, then?

"Are we going in, or what?" Bliss asked him.

"Wait a bit. I want to see what's happening."

And as he spoke, the man he had identified as Dannell

Haglund stepped out of the house, holding a rifle ready at port arms.

"What's goin' on?" asked Allred. Like the others, he couldn't pick out any details from a distance without Tanner's spyglass.

"Seems they're not acquainted," Tanner told his men. "Be quiet, now, and wait."

It seemed too much to hope that the rider was an enemy of Haglund's, that he'd do Tanner's job while they sat in the tree shade and watched. More likely, he was a stranger passing through, and Haglund felt an isolated farmer's normal dread at the appearance of an armed and unfamiliar man.

They were talking now, and Tanner wished once again that he could read lips with his telescope. It stood to reason that they'd make the normal introductions first. And then, what?

Something that the rider had to say surprised Haglund. No, that was outright shock. The farmer took a little half step backward, not quite reeling from the news, but *feeling* it. No good news ever hit a man that way.

More words were passed between them, then the rider dismounted and stood by his roan with the reins in his left hand. Still keeping the right free and close to his pistol, in case there was a blowup.

Tanner knew there wouldn't be, when he focused on Haglund's face. His target wasn't weeping, but his cheeks had gone all blotchy, and it wasn't from the sun. Something distracted him—Tanner thought a question from the house; somebody waiting in there, asking if there was trouble—and he answered back. A moment later, women started to show themselves.

Tanner counted four, and saw their children peeping from the doorway, hanging back to keep from getting scolded in a stranger's presence. Haglund told the women something, scowling as he spoke, and they started crying, all at once.

"What's this?" Bliss asked. "They getting ready for a square dance?"

"Hush!"

"Amren, you give the word, I'll drop both men before the ladies know what hit 'em."

"Bliss, don't make me tell you time and time again to close your mouth. You'll fire when I say, and I won't be hurried."

"Amren—"

Tanner rounded on him, ferocious anger flaring, telescope forgotten as his right hand settled on his pistol.

"What?"

"Nothing. Forget it."

"Keep. Your. Mouths. Shut."

Saying it to all of them, before he turned back toward the farmhouse, peering through his glass.

"All dead?"

"Eleven found," Slade said. "One man, three women, seven children, if that's everyone."

"That's all of them," Haglund replied. "What happened, Marshal?"

"It was murder. Way it looks, three gunmen, maybe more, shot Mr. Oman in the yard, then burned the house with all the rest inside."

"Dear God!"

Slade read the farmer's shock and grief as genuine. If he could force that color rising in his cheeks above the beard, he should be starring in the theater, not plowing fields.

"This likely won't help much," Slade said, "but those inside the house were shot before the fire got to them. I'm still working on the how and why of it."

"It could have been the mothers," Haglund told him. "They'd have done it for their children, if it spared them needless suffering."

"I see."

"There's no need staying mounted, Marshal, if you'd care to stretch your legs."

"I would, thanks."

"Dannell?" called a woman's voice, from somewhere in the house. "Are you all right?"

"It's fine," the farmer said. "Our visitor's a lawman."

"Oh?"

There was a worried sound to that, matching the strained expression of the first woman who cleared the threshold. She wore her dark hair pinned up in some kind of swirl. A blue dress showed her belly swollen with a child-to-be.

"Marshal, my wife, Braylyn. Braylyn, meet Marshal Slade from Enid."

"That's a long way off," she said. "What brings you out our way, Marshal?"

Haglund answered the question for him. "Someone's killed the Omans. All of them."

A sob caught in her throat, and then her husband had his arms around her, whispering a lie that everything would be all right. The scene drew three more women from the house, the last in line nearly as pregnant as Braylyn. Behind them, children watched Slade from the shadowed doorway.

"I suppose you know about the Omans, then," said Haglund. "And about us."

"It's the reason why I'm here," Slade said.

"Marshal, it's one thing for the government to discount any vows we took in Utah, but there've been no marriage ceremonies here. We haven't broken any laws."

"That's none of my concern," Slade said. "I'm here about the murders."

"What?" three of the women asked him, all at once.

"Would it be possible to talk about this in some shade?"

"Of course," Dannell Haglund replied. "You'll want some water for your animal. Maybe some feed?"

"If you don't mind."

"No, no. I'll show you to the barn."

The women trailed their husband in a group, the youngest-looking of them pausing to instruct the children that they shouldn't leave the house.

"I mean it, now!" she told them, sternly, and a couple of the peering faces vanished from the doorway.

In the barn, Slade got his gelding settled with a water bucket and some hay, leaving the saddle on for now. Dannell Haglund assisted him, while introducing three more wives. Slade nodded to Alema, Tennys, and Vonelle, guessing at ages, clueless as to any kind of pecking order in the household.

Haglund spared Slade telling them about the Oman killings, bringing all of them to fresh tears with his brief description of the slaughter. Having finished that, he asked, "Now, Marshal, what is it you want from us?"

"I don't have any solid suspects," Slade replied. "Right now, I don't know if I should arrest you or start planning how to help you stay alive."

"Arrest us?" Vonelle Haglund was the other pregnant lady, which put ample color in her cheeks without another sudden shock. "You said you didn't care about—"

"He means for murder," Dannell interrupted her.

"Murder! But that's . . . that's . . ."

"Crazy," Tennys Haglund said. "The Omans were our friends."

"Our *only* friends," Alema added.

"Ladies, everyone who knew the victims is a suspect. That's how an investigation works. So far, there's hardly anyone in Alva who'll admit to speaking with the Omans, much less spending any kind of time with them."

"That's true enough, I'd guess," Dannell allowed. "Nice Christian town, that is, with everybody lining up to judge their neighbors."

"Bethuel could have taken better care," Braylyn suggested.

"Are you saying it's *his* fault they all got murdered?" Dannell challenged her.

"Of course not! But you saw the way he challenged them, taking his whole brood into town. *You* warned him to be careful."

"Still—"

Slade nipped their squabble in the bud. "Someone from Alva may have done it," he remarked, "but those I've spoken to were more concerned about keeping the whole thing quiet. Holding up the town's good name. It makes no sense they'd kill eleven people, knowing all the negative attention it would bring about."

"Well, Marshal, I can promise you *we* didn't kill them," Dannell told him, "but the only witnesses we have are one another. That won't count for much in one of your courts, I suppose."

"No one's on trial," Slade said. And thought, *Not yet.* "If you can think of someone else who might've done it, now's the time to say so."

Dannell Haglund and his wives exchanged dark, worried glances. Finally, Braylyn nudged Dannell with her elbow, saying, "Go on. Tell him!"

Another silent moment prompted Slade to prod him. "Tell me what?"

"About the Danites," Tennys said.

"Tennys!"

"You want to *hide* it, when they've killed the Omans? All those children!"

"We don't know that," Dannell answered.

"Who else would have done it?" Braylyn asked him, speaking softly.

Slade addressed the farmer. "Mr. Haglund, if you're holding information that can help me solve these murders, you're obliged to share it. Otherwise, I take you back in as a material witness. Let you try negotiating with Judge Dennison."

Vonelle reached out to clutch her husband's other arm. "For heaven's sake, Dannell!"

Surrounded by women, he cracked. "You don't know about Danites, I take it?" he asked Slade.

"The word sounds familiar. I can't pin it down," Slade admitted.

"They were organized in 1838," Haglund explained, "to guard the Prophet from his enemies, up in Missouri."

"Joseph Smith?"

"That's right. Their name comes from the book of Daniel, I believe. As things got worse, some of them went on the offensive, paid the unbelievers back in kind. They came to be known as the whistling and whittling brigades. After the move to Illinois, they served as the police in Nauvoo, but they couldn't save the Prophet or his brother at the end. Later, during the war for Deseret, President Young called Danites his Avenging Angels."

"Or *Destroying* Angels," Braylyn added.

"And they're still around today?" asked Slade.

"Officially," said Haglund, "you'll be hard-pressed to find any leader of the church who's willing to admit it."

"And unofficially?"

"You've heard of Porter Rockwell? He was one of yours, a U.S. marshal, out in Utah Territory. Dead these sixteen years, or so. But in his time, it's said he killed at least a hundred men on orders of the church."

"People who threatened Mormons?"

"Some, I'm sure. But saints, as well. Whoever might offend the powers that be. Are you familiar with the code of blood atonement, Marshal?"

"Not that I recall."

"We have a lot to talk about," said Haglund. "I suggest you make your horse more comfortable, then we go back to the house."

Tanner watched the Haglunds and their visitor retrace their steps between the barn and farmhouse, where a clutch of children watched them from the open doorway. They had put the stranger's horse away, but he was carrying a Winchester. Bright metal on his vest glinted in the sunlight.

"They're going in the house!" Bliss protested, breaking silence.

"I see that," Tanner told him. He stood watching while the six adults entered the farmhouse, women leading.

Dannell Haglund was the last in line and shut the door.

"And now they're gone," said Bliss.

"Gone where?" DeLaun asked. "Trapped, would be more like it."

"But I could've dropped the men," Bliss said. "You know it. Now, we have to—"

"Wait," said Tanner, interrupting him. "We have to wait and see what's happening."

"They're goin' in to supper, that's what's happening," said Zedek Welch. "And I could use some, too."

"You're packing jerky, like the rest of us," Tanner reminded him. "Eat some."

"Are we camping here, or what?" asked Hallace Pratt.

"Waiting and watching," Tanner said. "We'll sleep in shifts. No fire."

"Sleep, did you say?" Bliss sounded confused. "We're not just killing time till dark, so we can finish it?"

"There's no rush," Tanner said.

"No rush? How 'bout no reason we should put it off?"

"The reason is, I say so." Tanner turned to face him. "Now, is that a problem for you?"

Bliss delayed his answer for a crucial second, then relented and answered, "No."

"No, *what*?"

"No, *sir*, I've got no problem with it."

Tanner let that sink in with the rest, then told them all, "One thing you may have missed is that their company's not just some drifter. He's a lawman."

"Lawman? How—"

"I saw his badge," Tanner answered DeLaun's unfinished question.

"What's it look like?" Zedek asked him.

"Like a badge."

"I mean, what *kind* of badge. Is he a townie cop? A sheriff? What?"

"I couldn't *read* it," Tanner said, as if explaining complex matters to an addlepated child. "It's round, made out of metal, shiny. Good enough?"

"A federal badge is round," Zedek observed. "I've seen some. Course, them ain't the only ones."

"Who *cares* what kind of badge he wears, or why he's here?" asked Bliss. "He's in our way. Won't be our first lawman."

That was true. Tanner himself had slain the sheriff's deputy outside of Flagstaff, Arizona, six months back. The man had barged into their camp and come at them with questions, getting pushy when he didn't like the answers. Tanner shot him first, the others joining in to make a ceremony of it, then they'd worked together on the grave and ridden off by night to put the place behind them.

"I want to think about it some, before we stumble into anything," he said.

"More thinking." That from Bliss.

"Why don't you try it, sometime?" Tanner asked him. "While you're at it, give your mouth a nice, long rest."

Slade didn't like discussing murder with so many children in the room, but Dannell and the wives insisted on it. "This is what we live with," Dannell said. "It's all the younger ones have known since they were born."

Slade reckoned that the children ranged from fifteen years or so, down to the youngest, being four or five. He got their names and hoped that he could keep them straight.

Wandle June, the oldest, had her mother's eyes and rich

dark hair, together with the makings of a woman's figure. Slade had caught her staring at him, down the table, but he wrote it off to curiosity.

Posey Aldene, the next in line, was less inquisitive. Slade guessed that she was twelve or so, roughly the same age as the oldest boy, called Draycen Lee.

The second-eldest Haglund son, at nine or ten, was Heber Jamon, stuck with names Slade didn't recognize. Again, there was a close pairing of ages with his sister, Shaylin Zee. And last in line, so far, there was Moroni Cabel Haglund, still too young for school, if there'd been one around.

Six kids, and two more on the way. It seemed to Slade that Dannell kept his women busy in the bedrooms. Five of them inside the rambling house, to be exact, which worked out as one for each wife and two for the kids, split by sex. Slade pictured Dannell making his rounds, night by night, then shrugged it off.

They had more pressing business to discuss.

"You think the Danites may come here, next, Marshal?" Braylyn asked, as she was serving up a roast with carrots and potatoes on the side.

"I won't say Danites, ma'am," he answered, "since I never heard of them before today. But based on what's already happened with the Omans, I'd say there's a good chance *someone* you don't want to meet will pay a call."

Dannell Haglund swallowed a bite of beef, then said, "Marshal, it's been a long, long time since we left Utah. Left some of our family behind and all who once had claimed to be our friends. We have no contact with them, going on twelve years. How would they find us?"

"How'd they find the Omans?" Slade responded. "How does any tracker find his game? I found your place by talking to a neighbor who, I'm bound to say, is none to fond of you."

"That Melvin Waymire," Tennys said. "A filthy-minded little creature."

"Likely so," Slade granted. "But he's still a walking, talking signpost pointing your way, if somebody comes along who means you harm. And if the other folk around your neighborhood are anything like those in Alva . . . well, I doubt that he's alone."

"I wouldn't bet against you there," Dannell agreed. "So, what do you suggest we do, Marshal?"

"First thing, we need to keep the women and the children safe," Slade said.

"Look closely, and you'll see we live in something like a fortress, here. I've learned along the way, from folks who've fought Apaches and Comanches, rustlers, every kind of outlaw trash you can imagine."

"The Omans likely felt the same way," answered Slade. "But even forts can burn."

"I ask again. What's your suggestion?"

"Come with me to Enid. I can put you in protective custody until we get this sorted out and find the men responsible for what was done at Alva."

"And how long will that take?" asked Dannell.

"Well—"

"I have crops and animals to tend, Marshal," the farmer said. "I can't just up and leave them. Leave the home we've built together, for whoever happens by and feels like moving in."

"This wouldn't be for long," Slade said. "A few days, if we're lucky."

"I milk Maybelle twice a day," Posey informed him. "*And* I feed the chickens."

"Will you think about it, anyway?" asked Slade.

"I'll sleep on it," Dannell agreed. "That's only fair. But, Marshal Slade?"

"Yes, sir?"

"Don't get your hopes up."

6

Slade had volunteered to sleep out in the barn, but Dannell Haglund's wives would hear of no such thing. He finally relented, brought his bedroll in, and placed it near the hearth, when they were ready to retire. Wandle brought Slade a pillow, before going off to bed herself.

Turning away, she said, "Thank you. For caring what becomes of us."

"You're welcome, ma'am."

"Don't 'ma'am,' me, if you please! I'm not *that* old," she said, and left Slade smiling as she flounced away.

In deference to the ladies and the risk of an emergency, Slade slept fully dressed, except for his hat, vest, and boots. He did not literally sleep with one eye open but remained on near alert. He was awake before dawn and had his bedroll set aside, out of the way.

The Haglunds matched him as a pack of early risers, farming folk who didn't like to waste a moment's daylight.

Slade was forced to marvel sometimes at the way his life had turned around since Jim was killed. Instead of staying up till dawn with cards, whiskey, and the occasional obliging woman, he was commonly asleep by midnight and rose, if not with the rooster, at least with the hens.

The Haglund breakfast bustle started shortly before six o'clock, the older children joining in. Wandle gave Slade another fetching smile to start his day and said, "I hope you slept well, Marshal."

"Ma'am," he said, to make her blush, "I can't remember when I've had a better sleep."

"I was afraid the floor might be too hard."

"I've had worse in hotels that charged me dearly," Slade replied.

"You travel often, I suppose. Rescuing people."

"Not so many rescues, I'm afraid," Slade said. "But I've been known to cover ground."

"Your wife must miss you very much." Another blush.

"She might, if I was married," Slade replied.

"A single man, at your age?" Wandle caught herself and quickly added, "I don't mean you're *old*, of course. I—"

"But I am," Slade said. "Compared to you, at least. Ancient, in fact."

Turning, he saw Braylyn fighting a smile before she said, "Wandle, Posey, we need some eggs, and Maybelle needs attention."

"Yes, ma'am," both girls said, in off-beat unison, and both got busy lighting candles for their journey to the barn.

"Please don't let Wandle bother you, Marshal," Braylyn advised. "She's of an age."

"Mother!" A voice of outrage from the sidelines, undercut by Posey's giggle.

"It's no bother," he assured her.

"That's because you aren't required to live with it," Tennys chimed in.

"So, now you're ganging up on me," Wandle protested.

"Not at all, dear," said her mother. "It was just a simple observation that, of late, you've turning into—"

"A pathetic laughingstock?"

"Wandle!"

"Not strong enough? What, then?"

"A clown," Draycen suggested.

"You stay out of this!" his sister cautioned, almost fuming.

"If you had one of those red noses—"

Wandle shook a dainty fist at Draycen. "Keep it up. I'm telling you."

"Enough!" said Braylyn. "Kindly bear in mind that we have company for breakfast. And a man of prominence at that."

"Will someone else be joining us?" asked Slade.

"Marshal, I have no doubt that your exploits are known throughout the territory."

"Not to many that you'd care to meet, ma'am."

"Still, I'm sure you must be well admired," she said. And then, "Wandle! Posey! Have you both gone back to sleep?"

"No, ma'am!"

They hurried out, almost colliding with their father on his way back from the privy.

"Marshal, once again, I'm sorry," Braylyn said.

"Children bring their own light to the world."

Slade wasn't sure where that had come from and was reasonably sure that nothing similar had ever passed his lips before. And stranger still, he seemed to mean it.

"Marshal," Dannell said, distracting Slade, "I've thought about the talk we had last night. I thank you for your warning and concern, but we can't—"

Screams cut off the rest of Dannell's thought. They came from outer darkness, in the general direction of the barn. Slade grabbed his rolled-up pistol belt and bolted for the door.

•   •   •

"They found it," said Bliss Kimball, smiling in the pale light from a quarter-moon well on its way to setting.

"You think?" DeLaun replied, earning a glare from Bliss.

"We'll see what this does for them," Tanner said. "If all of you can hush."

He had sent two men down to prepare the surprise, choosing Allred and Welch because they complained less than others. Bliss may act impulsively, forgetting orders, and Pratt was not stealthy enough for the job.

It had been well past midnight when they set out on foot, the house before them dark and silent. Tanner and the rest had covered them by moonlight, knowing that the Haglunds and their guest might be awake, lying in ambush. There was nothing Tanner and his men could do about it, waiting for the muzzle flashes that would spell death for his scouts.

Tanner had watched them cross the half mile of open ground that separated him from the farmhouse, walking crouched over at first, nearly crawling by the time they reached the barn. He'd seen them disappear inside, some hesitation as the barn's door scraped across packed earth, then had to wait forever with his cheek against the rifle's stock, ready to fire if anything went wrong.

They had been half an hour in the barn, perhaps a little longer, finishing their task. Tanner had started to imagine someone catching them, killing them silently or holding them at gunpoint, but he'd known that couldn't be. If they'd been caught, there would have been a general alarm to rouse the family, preparing them to defend against attackers.

Finally, when Tanner felt as if his nerves had reached their breaking point, he'd seen his infiltrators slip out of the barn and start their slow journey back to the tree-topped ridge. Still undiscovered by the Haglunds, they had reached it and collapsed, spilling their whispered stories until Tanner hushed them both and resumed his watching.

In retrospect, he wished that he'd had them set the barn alight. It would have been spectacular, a stunning wake up for their targets, and would also have provided better light for sniping than the quarter-moon afforded. Still, he told himself, the plan he had crafted should be good enough.

When they had seen his gift, Tanner believed, they would respond in one of three ways. First, they might retreat and barricade themselves inside the house, in which case they would be trapped. Second, if panic gripped them, they might flee the property, which would make them easy targets in the open. Finally, the lawman might ride off in search of reinforcements, granting Tanner time to do the bloody work he'd already begun.

Three choices, any one of which would lead his targets to the same end.

Endless waiting followed, until lights showed in the cabin once again. Tanner couldn't see well enough by moonlight to consult his pocket watch, but he supposed it was nearly six o'clock. His stomach growled for breakfast, and he soothed it with a strip of jerky from his pocket.

"Anytime now," someone whispered in the dark, behind him. Bliss? Zedek? He didn't care.

He scanned the farmhouse windows with his spyglass. The shutters were closed against the hostile night outside but bleeding light around the edges. Proof that Dannell Haglund and his concubines were making ready for another day.

Their last.

Tanner was curious about the lawman. His appearance, in conjunction with their own arrival, mocked coincidence. But how could the authorities predict the Haglunds were in danger? He considered that the marshal, sheriff—whatever he was—might have come to confront Dannell about his wives, but that made no sense. It was obvious the Haglunds had been living here for several years, at least. To think the law would only notice them on the same day that Tanner and his men turned up was laughable.

The Omans.

Somehow, someone had connected them to Dannell Haglund's brood. Which meant the lawman was not hunting bigamists. He was hunting Tanner's crew.

The front door of the farmhouse opened. Two girls exited in a spill of light, cut off as one of them closed the door behind them. Pinprick candle flames led them across the yard and toward the barn. Seeing their youth, Tanner almost regretted the message he had sent them.

Almost.

Tanner waited, watched them reach the barn and enter. It would just take another moment for their weak lights to illuminate the scene. When they found it . . .

There.

The screams wafted to Tanner on a gentle breeze, music to his ears.

Slade hit the yard running, his Peacemaker drawn, with Dannell a long stride behind him. Haglund had detoured to snatch down a shotgun from pegs on the wall but was gaining on Slade with a terrified father's grim speed.

They were halfway to the barn when Wandle burst through the door, still clutching her candle in one hand, dragging her sister along with the other. Both girls were sobbing, Posey almost hysterically, struggling as if to escape from her sister's tight grip. Dannell gathered them into his arms, shotgun useless in one hand, his first instinct being to comfort his girls.

Which left Slade to protect them from any threat lurking in darkness ahead.

He pressed on toward the barn, hearing Wandle and Posey repeating, "It's Maybelle! Maybelle!" Something wrong with their milk cow? What could cause such a reaction?

Slade paused at the half-open door, noting faint light inside. A scuffing of footsteps behind him brought the Colt around, cocked, but he eased off the trigger at the sight of

Dannell. The farmer carried Wandle's candle in his left hand, shotgun still as good as useless dangling from his right.

"You cover me," Slade said. "And watch that buckshot."

"Go!" Dannell replied.

Slade went, scuttling through the doorway in a crouch, his pistol up and ready. He picked out the source of light at once. Posey had dropped her candle, and its flame had caught an errant patch of straw. There seemed no risk of any conflagration spreading, so he let it burn for light.

"Dear God!"

Dannell's voice, close behind Slade, almost made him jump. The ghastly scene in front of them rendered him speechless for a moment.

Maybelle the cow lay on her side, hooves toward them, at the mouth of what Slade took to be her stall. Someone had slashed her throat then drawn the blade along her underside, as if prepared to dress a deer. There seemed to be no system to it, after that, with entrails dragged and flung about in all directions. Milk spilled from the mutilated udder, mingling on the floor with blood. The barn smelled like a slaughterhouse.

Slade glanced at Haglund, saw he wasn't really looking at the cow's remains, and let his own eyes rise beyond the carnage. On the nearest wall, in foot-tall crimson letters, somebody had painted BLOOD ATONEMENT. Slade could see the "paint" already clotting, turning rusty brown.

"What's that supposed to mean?" Slade asked.

"I'll tell you all about it in the house," Haglund replied. "I need to see my family."

With that, the farmer left, running across the open yard. Slade half expected muzzle flashes from the darkness, but they didn't come. He stamped the small fire dead, then eased out of the barn, not trusting the shadows behind him. A gunman concealed in the barn would have fired by then, clearly. But still . . .

He felt a little better in the house, lamps burning, door

and shutters barred. Dannell was busy soothing wives and children, telling them that everything would be all right, caressing cheeks and kissing foreheads.

Thinking of the Omans, roasted in their home, Slade felt a pressing need to hurry things along. He drew Dannell aside, the others watching them, and said, "The message. What's it mean?"

"Blood atonement is a doctrine of our faith," Dannell replied. "According to the second Prophet—"

"Brigham Young?" Slade interrupted him.

"Correct. After the death of Joseph Smith, he called for vengeance against anyone who tries to harm the faith. That was allied with blood atonement, which requires spilling of blood in expiation of specific sins. A murder, for example."

"Plain old hanging isn't good enough?" Slade asked.

"It punishes the crime but does not wash the sin away. Endowment rituals also include a vengeance oath. When we receive the secrets of the temple, we agree that if we share them with the profane world, we shall submit to have our throats cut, bodies torn asunder, disemboweled—"

"Just like your cow?"

"That is the message. Yes."

Dropping his voice to something like a whisper, Slade inquired, "You teach your children that?"

"It's one reason we left. That and the pressure to recant our marriage vows."

"And now they've found you. Danites."

"It would seem so."

"Are you any closer to deciding on protective custody?" Slade asked.

"How can we leave now, Marshal? If they've been inside our barn, it means they're sitting in the dark right now, watching the house."

"They haven't started shooting yet," Slade said. "My guess would be they're waiting to see which way you'll jump."

"You can't imagine that they'll let us go."

"What's the alternative? Stay penned inside the house until your food runs out?"

"We have enough to last awhile," Haglund replied.

"And water? If you've got a pump indoors, I haven't seen it."

"Let's hear your plan," the farmer said.

It was more of a gamble, in fact. Dealing with criminals had taught Slade the futility of trying to read minds—particularly those of people whom he'd never met—and while he realized that any move to strike off from the farm might bring them under fire, it was a certainty that hiding in the house would get them killed.

Starved out or burned out, it was all the same.

If there was fighting to be done, Slade would prefer a battleground that granted some freedom of movement, a chance to outmaneuver his foes. He would have preferred waging war without women and kids underfoot, but the choice wasn't his. Dannell Haglund had made it, sometime in the past, when he bolted from Utah and left brooding grudges to fester.

Slade wasn't clear on why a church would risk embarrassment and prosecution fielding vigilante teams to hunt down members who had left the fold. Perhaps he didn't understand because he lacked a zealot's frame of mind, wherein the world and everything that it contained might hinge upon a single verse from scripture. Then again, perhaps religion and the church had less to do with it than simple human failings: anger, spite, a feral craving for revenge.

Things had been done in God's name that would not be found between a Bible's covers, even if you held it upside down and read between the lines. Some people used religion the same way that others used patriotism and charity, as a means to their own scheming ends.

Step one of getting out alive was packing up the bare ne-
cessities of travel. Weapons first, then food and water for the
trail. They had a two-day ride ahead of them, to Enid, if they
weren't ambushed along the way or forced to change their
route. Two camps in open country, where their enemies could
come at them from any compass point, at any time they chose.

Long odds. But staying holed up in the house, dying of
thirst, they had no hope at all.

Slade knew it would depend in large part on the unseen
enemy. If the Danites, or whoever they were, decided not to
let the Haglunds leave their spread alive, there'd be a battle
right away that would decide the issue. Some of Dannell's
brood were bound to fall. Conversely, if the hunters let
them go, Slade and his charges would be running a gaunt-
let, subject to sniping, or worse, all the way from the farmhouse to Enid.

It was a bad hand, either way, but Slade couldn't fold in
this game. He could only call or raise.

Four women and six children meant they'd have to take
the wagon—which, in turn, meant slower progress than they
could have made on horseback. On the sunny side, the wagon
would provide at least some meager cover during any confrontation with their enemies and when they camped at night.

Assuming that they lived to see the sun go down.

Just now, it was rising, suffusing the landscape with gray
light, then pink, brightening by degrees. Good news and bad
news, there, in equal measure. Daylight could reveal their
enemies, with any luck, but it would also give those enemies a clear shot at the Haglunds—and at Slade—while making muzzle flashes more or less invisible.

Look for the smoke, instead, Slade thought, knowing that
if the first shot took him down, there'd be no time to look
for anything.

Wandle was at his elbow, carrying a bundle of things she
planned to take away. "You will protect us, won't you?" she
asked Slade.

"I'll do my best," he promised. Smiling as he said it, to conceal his thought that nothing he might do would keep this woman-child and all the rest of them alive.

Eleven lives were in his hands—thirteen, if he counted the children yet unborn—and Slade feared he would prove unequal to the task.

"You need to hurry up," he told them all. "I want to get the wagon hitched and moving now, before full light."

"We're ready," Braylyn answered back. "Whatever's left behind is nothing that we haven't given up before."

"All right," Slade said. "Ladies and children, stay inside the house until we call, then run as if your lives depend on it."

Because, he thought, *they do.*

"Are we just gonna sit and watch 'em leave, now?" Bliss demanded.

"They haven't left," Tanner replied.

"You think they're hitching up the horses just to watch 'em stand there?"

"What I think," Tanner informed him, "is that you're forgetting who's in charge. If I have to remind you once more, it will be the last damned time."

They had not heard him swear before. It made Bliss hesitate, considering an answer, then step back without speaking.

In fact, Tanner could see they meant to leave the farm. Flight was among the various responses he considered, prior to sending Welch and Allred off to leave the message. What he hadn't worked out, yet, was whether he should let the Haglunds run a bit or take them now.

Bliss had the only weapon capable of dropping man-sized targets at their present range. He was good, but his Sharps was a single-shot weapon. At top speed, its falling-block action allowed for no more than eight to ten shots per minute. It was impossible for him to drop a dozen people in the time required for them to reach the house and button up.

And even Bliss was known to miss his mark, from time to time.

Then came another siege, perhaps with two armed men inside the house. So far, he'd seen two long guns, plus the lawman's pistol, and it wouldn't surprise Tanner to find more guns within the farmhouse. He was convinced that he could find some way to starve or smoke the Haglunds out, but at what cost?

The lawman was a problem. Not because Tanner opposed killing him. Rather because his presence indicated that *someone knew.* He had not happened by the Haglund spread through some unlucky accident. No. He'd been *sent.* And that meant other lawmen, somewhere within easy riding distance, might be thinking about ways to frustrate Tanner's mission.

If he let them run—not far, just far enough—Tanner would have the Haglunds and their escort to himself. Each hour on the road presented another opportunity for him to cut them off, annihilate them all before they reached their goal, whatever that might be.

Which towns were nearest?

Alva, if they headed west, but it seemed unlikely. Why would Dannell Haglund lead his wives and children toward the place where his last friends on Earth were buried? Sentiment? Not likely.

Tanner had a map of Oklahoma Territory in his saddlebag, along with others. He did not consult it now. There was no need. He'd memorized the parts that now concerned him. Enid was a two-day ride to the southeast. They had a court there, if he was not mistaken, and more lawmen. In between the Haglund homestead and that town, there was a flyspeck on the map.

What was it called, again?

He had it. Blaze.

It was an odd name for a town, but that appeared to be the rule in some parts of the country Tanner had traversed, pursuing heretics. Sometimes he wondered if the people of a given place sat down on purpose, to select the worst name for a town that any drunken lout could think of.

Blaze.

Perhaps they'd had a fire. Or would, soon.

He heard a whispered mutter behind him, hissed at the others to be silent, and resumed watching the lawman and Dannell. They had four horses hitched up to the heavy wagon, with a fifth tied to the tailgate in reserve. There was nothing stowed inside the wagon yet, but Tanner reckoned there was ample room for ten slim bodies, if they cozied up a bit.

The wagon was a handicap. So were the pregnant women, who would not take jostling well. Tanner began to picture how his problem would resolve itself.

The open prairie was his friend.

"We wait," he told the others, deaf to their complaints. "Until I give the word."

Slade kept expecting gunfire, without knowing where it might come from. He'd double-checked the barn and thought the distant line of trees was too far off for rifles or marksmen to attempt a shot. Still, after the surprise that had been waiting for them in the barn, could they expect to ride out unopposed?

They finished hitching up the horses, one step closer to departure, and he saw no riders on the open plains surrounding them. The spread had blind spots, granted. From the dooryard, anyone approaching from due south or west was screened from view by Haglund's house and barn, but spotters in the house were watching from its windows, ready to cry out at the first glimpse of strangers.

So far, so good. But Slade was burdened with the thought of children dying from a choice he'd made. He pictured women screaming, falling bloodied to the ground, and wondered how he'd live with it.

Slade didn't let the morbid thought take root. Whatever happened in the next few minutes, or the next two days, he knew the Haglunds—the adults among them, anyway—had chosen their own path. They'd known about the Danites, blood atonement, and the rest of it before they left Utah and started on the long trek that had brought them to their present circumstance.

As for the children, as in any family, they were the hostages to grown-up whims and choices, forced to march one way during their early years, until they aged enough and found the gumption to break ranks. Draycen was close to grown-up, only a year or so younger than Slade when he had taken off to find a new life, and Wandle wasn't far behind her brother.

Would they get the chance to make their own choices? Their own mistakes?

Slade might not have the final say on that, but he would do his best to keep the lot of them alive as long as possible.

"Ready," Dannell announced.

"Stay under cover while I fetch my horse," Slade told him.

It was strange that last night's prowlers hadn't touched his roan. Slade couldn't figure it, unless they lacked imagination or were acting under strict, specific orders. Either way, he'd caught a break.

He had the gelding saddled, waiting for him on his last trip to the barn. They had already tossed a few things in the wagon—ax and shovel, with a toolbox for repairs—and as he mounted, Slade could think of nothing more to add except the passengers.

The living targets.

They had discussed the plan, such as it was. Dannell

would back the wagon closer to the house, and Slade would place himself between it and the distant trees, the only sniper's refuge he could pick out from the yard, unlikely as it seemed. When Dannell called his brood, they would come rushing from the house and pile into the wagon, children first, staying as low as possible to frustrate any watching riflemen.

Then, all they had to do was clear the property and spend the better part of two days crossing open country, without getting ambushed anywhere along the way.

Simple as drawing three cards to complete a royal flush.

He'd filled one, once. Out in Nevada, that had been. A little nothing town they called Las Vegas. The one time in his life he'd seen those five cards staring up at him, and something in Slade's face had spooked the other players, causing all of them to fold. The pot he'd won was less than twenty dollars, and one of the hard-bitten miners had still accused him of cheating.

"Okay, let's do it," Slade told Haglund, as he cleared the barn. Chickens scattered before his roan, already cackling complaints at being left behind.

Haglund was handy with the wagon, backing it around on his first try, placing the tailgate within ten feet of the porch. He called out to his family, and in another moment they were spilling into pale daylight, each with a bundle clutched beneath one arm, vaulting or scrambling to a semblance of cover in the wagon's bed.

The women trailed their children, Braylyn and Vonelle helping Tennys and Alema climb into the wagon, awkward with the weight of growing life inside them. Slade rode back and forth along the wagon's length, watching the skyline, hoping he might glimpse a gunman in advance, before a killing shot was fired.

And do what?

Try to drop him from a distance? Spur his mount to take the bullet that was meant for someone else?

"All ready!" Draycen called out from the wagon as it lurched into motion, leaving the farmhouse behind. Slade kept pace through the yard, past the barn, and beyond.

It was a good day for a ride, he thought.

And hoped it wouldn't be his last.

1

Tanner led his men down from the ridge, toward the farmhouse. He felt exposed, crossing the open grassland, passing cultivated fields as they drew closer. Even knowing that the spread was now deserted, Tanner felt as if he was being watched.

He pivoted in his saddle, making sure his men were on alert as he'd instructed, not just staring at his back. They were fanning out now, circling wide around the house and outbuildings as ordered, none showing the least interest in Tanner.

Why the feeling, then?

He wondered, for a heartbeat, whether God was watching him, judging his choices and performance of the task assigned to him. A twinge of apprehension followed from that thought, sparked by a fear that he was being arrogant, or even blasphemous.

On one hand, Tanner had been taught from infancy that God sees everyone and everything. His eye is on the falling sparrow. At the same time, though, it had been drilled into his head and heart that God reserved his closest scrutiny for those who matter most. The Prophet and his handpicked aides were the elect.

Tanner entered the dooryard, shrugging off his vague sense of anxiety, willing himself to focus. While the Haglunds and their lawman had departed, there was still an outside chance they might have left surprises of their own behind, to welcome trespassers. A trap gun in the house, perhaps? Aimed at the door, to send the first intruder off to his reward?

It seemed unlikely. Haglund would want every firearm he possessed for their lonely ride to nowhere, but complacency could kill. Aside from guns, he had seen traps rigged up with axes, sharpened stakes—and once, a bucket filled with kerosene above a door, with sandpaper and matches on the jamb.

"Bliss!" he called out. "Check the house."

For just a second, Tanner was reminded of King David in the Bible, sending Joab off to war. Except that Bliss had no Bathsheba to be coveted, and there was virtually no chance he'd be killed by entering the Haglund home.

A captain parcels out assignments to his soldiers. It's the way of war. Tanner could always ask forgiveness of his savior later, if his idle fantasy came true and Bliss was shot or fried.

The marksman didn't give a second thought to danger as he climbed down from his saddle, tied his chestnut's reins to a porch post, and clomped to the threshold. There was no hesitation as Bliss shoved the door open, passing inside.

Tanner frowned and released his breath. He told himself that he was not disappointed.

Silent moments passed, then Bliss returned, shaking his head. "They left most everything behind," he said. "O' course we knew that, having watched 'em leave."

Tanner ignored that. He told him, "Light it up."

Bliss cracked a smile. "House only? Or the lot?"

"All of it," Tanner said. And turning to his other men, two of them just emerging from the barn—DeLaun and Zedek, going back to view their handiwork—repeated it. "Burn it all!"

They went to work, Allred and Welch retreating, fumbling matches from their pockets. Bliss went back inside the house, and Tanner heard him smashing glass. Maybe a lamp or two, for fuel. A moment later, he saw pale flames through the open doorway, washed out by the sunshine in the yard, but no less dangerous for that.

Bliss did not leave immediately. Why linger inside, once he had set the fire? Again, Tanner allowed himself a flight of fantasy. Perhaps a rotten floorboard, snapping under Kimball's weight. His leg trapped, panic overwhelming calm and common sense. He screams, but flames surround him. Tanner could not reach him, even if he cared to try.

The daydream dissipated as Bliss emerged from the house, a rag doll dangling from one hand. "Someone forgot her toy," he said.

"You plan to take it with you?" Hallace asked him, not quite sneering.

"No, I reckon not," Bliss said and casually flung the doll back toward the spreading fire. He untied his gelding and led it well back from the house, as smoke bled from the windows and doorway.

Smoke poured from the barn as Allred and Welch cleared its door for the last time. Around their feet, chickens ran wild, every which way. Soon, gray tendrils were escaping from the loft, as well.

"What now?" Bliss asked him.

"Now," Tanner replied, "we hunt."

"Oh, no! Please, Lord!"

Slade turned at the sound of Vonelle Haglund's voice

and found her facing northwestward, along their back trail. He saw the smoke at once and knew what it must mean.

"Is that our house?" asked Posey, not quite crying yet.

Dannell reined in the horses, turning on the driver's seat to watch the smoke rise for a moment. Those riding behind him in the wagon's bed were torn between eyeing the smudged horizon and the visage of their patriarch.

"It doesn't matter," Dannell said at last, over the muffled sounds of weeping. "We're alive and well. That's all that counts."

"The good news," Slade observed, "is that they lost time hanging back, to get that done. The bad news—"

"Is that they can travel faster than our wagon," Dannell finished for him. "And there's nothing else to stall them."

"That's about the size of it."

"We'd best be moving on, then," Haglund said.

"I can double back and try to head them off," Slade told him. "But it wouldn't be that hard for them to slip around me, riding off a mile or so to either side."

"Marshal, I'd rather have you with us," Dannell answered, "if it's all the same to you."

"Yes, stay!" Wandle chimed in. "Don't leave us out here all alone!"

That started several of the younger children clamoring, their mothers soothing them as best they could.

"I was about to say that we should stick together," Slade replied.

For all the good that it would do.

He still had no idea how many gunmen were pursuing them, whether it was the three-man minimum he'd worked out for the Oman raid, or several times that number. Even three could flank them on both sides, ride on ahead and catch them in a cross fire at the first convenient place with any cover.

And without it . . . what?

Suppose the trackers had to show themselves. They

could hang back at the edge of rifle range and try their luck.
Say a hundred yards for the standard .44-40 Winchester
cartridge, and several times that if they packed something
larger.

Slade wasted no time second-guessing marksmen he had
never met. He didn't know if they could hit the broad side
of a barn at anything past twenty feet, or if they favored
torching houses with the occupants inside, waiting to pot
them as they tried to scramble clear. The numbers also made
a difference. Six snipers had a better chance of scoring lucky
hits than three would, all else being equal.

Slade supposed the countryside would work against them,
as they moved closer to Enid. Open grassland helped them
now, but in a few more hours there'd be rolling hills to hide
their enemies, some scattered woods along the way, and
who knew what else that would work against his vulnerable
party. Wagon travel was a handicap, but riding double would
be problematic, since the Haglunds' five had no tack or
saddles. Pregnant women made it hopeless.

There was another town ahead of them, before they got
to Enid, but Slade couldn't recollect its name. Something to
do with fire, he thought, which struck him as ironic, in their
present circumstance. He wasn't on the railroad line and
had no telegraph connection. No hope there for bringing
reinforcements out to meet them, but a town full of witnesses should keep the hunters at bay.

At least until Slade's party cleared the other side, continuing along their way.

Or would they even get that far?

Their present speed told Slade they wouldn't reach the
first town—*Blaze*, he thought it was—before nightfall. Rather
than plow ahead and miss it in the dark, or risk an accident
that might leave them afoot, he would prefer to camp and
mount a guard. No fire to make them better targets. Let the
hungry children sleep inside the wagon, or beneath it, with
their mothers warming them.

Slade didn't favor playing cat and mouse, particularly when he had to be the rodent. Other men had stalked him in the past with killing on their minds, but he had not been saddled with a mob of innocents whose safety was his first concern. It didn't suit him, but he had to play the cards that he'd been dealt.

And hope it didn't prove to be a dead man's hand.

"Where will we live now?" Posey asked. "There's nothing to go back for."

"Someplace," Wandle answered vaguely, wishing she could offer reassurance. "Don't be scared. He'll save us."

"Papa?"

"Marshal Slade."

Heber leaned over, whispering, "Is he your *hero*, Wandle? Is it *love*?"

"Shut up!"

"He can't do magic. No one can."

"He got us out of *there*," Wandle replied, and nodded toward the skyline and its pall of smoke. "Are you forgetting that?"

"We could have fought them off, inside the house," Heber replied. "Like at the Alamo."

"The men inside the Alamo got killed," Wandle reminded Heber. "Anyway, you heard what happened to the Omans. *They* stayed in their house."

"We should have more guns," Shaylin chimed in.

"Too late for wishing," Wandle answered. "What we have is what we've got."

"You're a genius," Heber taunted.

Wandle pinched him, made him squeal, and earned a glare from Tennys, sitting nearest to them. She was pale and worried-looking, one hand resting on the round swell of her stomach.

Wandle was suddenly afraid she'd never see her new

brothers or sisters, maybe one of each to keep the balance. Would a baby killed before its birth still go to Heaven? Wandle longed to ask but didn't dare.

"I hope they didn't kill the chickens," Posey said.

"Why would they?" Heber asked.

"For meanness, same as Maybelle."

He had no answer for that, chewing his lower lip.

"The chickens will be fine," Wandle told Posey.

"Better off than us," said Heber. Wandle saw tears welling in his eyes, about to spill down freckled cheeks.

"You'd better not," she warned him.

"What?"

"Set off the others, crying."

"I'm not crying!" he insisted, outraged.

"See you don't." She hoped the anger would sustain him for a little while, at least.

"You're not the boss of me!"

Better.

She left him to his brooding, staring at the distant smoke, imagining her things incinerated, transformed into tiny particles that traveled on the breeze. It was a kind of miracle and made her heartsick.

Marshal Slade was constantly in motion. Not just moving forward, like the rest of them, but riding on the left side of the wagon for a while, then circling to its right, next falling back to trail them for a bit, before he caught up. Wandle reckoned that he'd travel two or three times farther than the rest of them, before they reached wherever they were going.

Somewhere, she decided.

Maybe *nowhere*, if the strangers overtook them. If her father and the marshal couldn't fight them off.

She'd never really pictured dying. Oh, the odd thought that was unavoidable when there were chickens to be killed for supper or her father chopped a rattler's head off with his hoe. And talk of Heaven made it almost sound desirable, sometimes. She'd asked, once, years ago, why Christians didn't kill themselves and hurry off to Paradise and had been scolded with a warning that it was a sin against the Lord and mocked his sacrifice on Calvary.

There was so much that she might never have the chance to learn or understand.

The marshal rode by on her left and smiled at Wandle as he passed. It seemed to strike a spark inside her, warm hope spreading from her stomach in a way that almost made her squirm.

He'd noticed her; she'd made it unavoidable. But it was often hard to tell what grown-ups really thought. They fibbed sometimes or put a brave face on to keep from scaring children.

I am not *a child,* she thought. Wandle was changing, had been since last autumn, and had come to see herself as, if not quite a woman, at least as a woman-in-waiting.

Waiting for what? A man?

She looked at Marshal Slade again and felt the same warm flush of feeling, even though he wasn't smiling at her, wasn't even facing the wagon.

Wandle had no idea how old he was, but she'd seen girls close to her own age marry older men. In Utah, it had been routine, unquestioned. They were sealed before the Lord, within his Temple, and went forth to multiply.

He'll save us, Wandle told herself, almost a silent prayer. *He'll save* me.

Tanner took his time trailing the Haglunds, ever mindful of the discontent that simmered in a couple of his men. It might be that he needed to thin the pack, and if it came to that, he would not hesitate. Tanner had dealt with mutinous subordinates before and had no questions asked.

He pictured two young men. Their names escaped him, but he saw their faces with a kind of crystal clarity. The first had disgraced himself, trying to force himself upon one of the errant wives they had been sent to execute. Perhaps believing Jesus and the Prophet wouldn't mind a little extra degradation heaped on top of death. Tanner had caught him in the act and blown his rotten brains out, then had turned his pistol on the sobbing woman just as easily.

Thy will be done.

The other had been more like Bliss, an upstart know-it-all who'd started out content to follow orders, then decided over time that he should be in charge. Tanner had warned him twice, with witnesses, and on the third time shot him from his saddle without thinking twice about it. He'd stripped him of his guns and anything that might identify him and had left him for the scavengers.

Word got around on things like that, but no one higher up the ladder had complained or sought to punish Tanner for his style of leadership. The very fact that he was on the trail again, leading one of the Prophet's most extensive campaigns yet against the godless heretics, was proof that he'd found favor in the eyes of the elite.

He was in no rush to overtake the Haglunds and their escort now, because the open country worked against him in broad daylight. Following their wagon tracks was easy; any fool with one good eye could do it. There was no reason for haste, which generally bred mistakes.

And in the trade of hunting men, mistakes are often fatal.

Times like this, Tanner reflected on what he had accomplished in his life. Sometimes he risked comparing his record to Porter Rockwell's, knowing he fell short but still striving to achieve what might be unattainable. Raw numbers did not tilt the scale, so much as the intent and faith behind them. Did it mean more to exterminate a hundred minor heretics, or to avenge the death of Joseph Smith by punishing a handful of his murderers?

Tanner had no control over the tasks he was assigned,

but he controlled his men and would eliminate whichever ones among them failed to render full obedience to his commands. If that left him to carry on alone, so be it. Tanner's duty was to God and to his church, which in his mind were indivisible.

He heard Bliss muttering behind him, not quite whispering. It was as good a time as any to be done with it.

"Bliss!"

"Yes, sir?"

"I want you to ride ahead and scout their party for me. Eyeball them, but do not—I repeat it, *do not*—under any circumstances let yourself be seen. You understand me?"

"Yes, sir!" He visibly brightened by the thought and was more respectful in a heartbeat.

Kimball had his chestnut trotting when Tanner called after him, "Wait! I'll hold the Sharps while you do that."

Bliss gaped at him, pretending that his own ears had deceived him, then said, "What?"

"The rifle. Give it here. You won't be needing it."

"But, what if—"

"What if *what*?" Tanner inquired, sweet reason smiling. "I've instructed you to spot them without being seen. That means you're in no danger and you'll have no need to shoot across a thousand yards. Any close-range trouble you run into, snakes and such, you have your six-shooter."

Bliss hesitated, then said, "The Sharps is *mine*."

"Of course, it is. I'll keep it safe and sound for you."

They'd reached the point of no return, of do or die. If Bliss refused him, Tanner would have no choice. His hand rested lightly on the curved butt of his Colt, ready for anything.

Bliss scanned the other faces. Tanner didn't bother, knowing none of them would shoot him in the back. Whatever happened next was just between the two of them, and Tanner had the edge. He was prepared to kill, while Bliss clearly was not.

"Okay, then. Sure," Bliss said, at last. He nudged the chestnut forward, drawing his Sharps from its saddle boot.

It could still be a trick. Tanner knew that Bliss carried the rifle unloaded, but its long heavy barrel could fracture a skull if swung with the requisite force. At the first hint of a double cross, he was prepared to drill Bliss on the spot.

But there was no trick. The heavy rifle changed hands. Kimball turned slowly and rode off, defeated. Tanner propped the long rifle across his saddle horn, urging his pinto to a slow and steady walk.

They had, he thought, all the time in the world.

Two pregnant women and a load of children dictated that the wagon had to stop from time to time. Their first break for necessity came three hours into the trip—a bit longer, in fact, than Slade had expected.

The first complaints caught them in flat, open country, with nothing for cover. No one wanted to crouch beside the wagon while the others seated in it stared away toward the horizon and pretended they were deaf. By mutual consent, they spent another twenty minutes on the trail, then stopped where boulders jutted up from the earth to six or seven feet in height.

Slade rode around behind the rock pile, checking it for snakes and snipers, then reported it was clear. He sat and watched the flat land for a trace of horsemen, while the girls and women made their journey fist, followed by Dannell's sons.

In other circumstances, Slade supposed there would have been some joking, childish teasing, maybe even horseplay, but the rest stop was a somber interruption of their journey. He imagined each one of the Haglunds thinking of their home, in ashes now, and wondering if they'd be taken by surprise or shot down from a distance while they crouched to do their business.

It was hard enough on soldiers in the field, much less on women and their children, but Slade couldn't change the facts of frontier life. Farmers who triumphed over drought and storms, insects and withering diseases still fell prey to other men, and no one was exempt.

Again, Slade thought of all the various decisions that had brought Dannell Haglund, his wives and children, to their present state. It had begun with choosing their religion—or, perhaps it had been chosen for them, by their parents. Then, despite the church reversing its position on polygamy, they'd chosen to preserve the old discarded ways and risk an ostracism that could lead to violence. At last, they'd fled, determined to survive and multiply with no one but themselves for company.

Slade wondered how they'd planned to make a go of it, alone and isolated in a hostile world. Did they intend to keep their children out of school? Teach them at home? And where would the Haglund children look for partners when they came of age?

So many questions that he didn't dare ask.

Slade concentrated on the landscape, watching for his faceless enemies. It angered him that some men felt they had the right to murder others for a difference of opinion over subjects that might well be nothing more than fairy tales.

A part of Slade's mind hoped he'd have a chance to meet them soon. The rest dreaded the confrontation, with so many innocents caught in the line of fire.

There was still no sign of their pursuers when the Haglunds finished and piled back into the wagon. The men who hunted them had missed another opportunity, and Slade could only wonder why.

Were they afraid to fight in daylight? And, if so, why were they satisfied to gut a cow last night, instead of lighting up the farmhouse? Flames and panic would have given them the perfect opportunity to finish it, with little risk.

Cowards or cunning strategists?

Slade doubted that his presence with the Haglunds would have put the killers off. If these hunters were true fanatics, they should have no qualms about adding a lawman to their death list—if they even knew he *was* a lawman. And there'd be no glory for them, either here on Earth or in the Great Beyond, if they allowed their victims to escape.

Whether in gambling or real life, Slade hated being placed on the defensive. He preferred attacking to retreating, overcoming obstacles by open confrontation or by stealth, whichever worked the best. Retreating, dodging, playing bodyguard was not his style, but at the moment there were no alternatives.

Slade couldn't chase an enemy who was invisible.

He couldn't fight the prairie wind.

But he could try like hell to keep eleven people breathing until they were safe in Enid, under guard. He could do that, or give his life in the attempt.

Dusk overtook them, as Slade knew it would, well short of Blaze. They'd reached a hilly stretch of country, wooded here and there, as if a giant had passed through and plucked most of the trees, while leaving clumps and copses in a pattern that defied all logic. There was cover to be had, for both the Haglunds and their enemies.

Slade took a chance and rode ahead, seeking a campsite that would minimize their risk. He'd covered half a mile and felt his nerves drawn bowstring tight, and was set on turning back to join the others when he found a spot that suited him.

Four weeping willows formed a kind of semicircle, with the open side facing southeastward, in the general direction they were traveling. The big trees offered shelter from the elements and prying eyes. Better, a spring cut through the grassy clearing, which would let them keep the horses close and under guard.

He rode back to the wagon, everyone aboard it watching him as he drew near. Dannell, driving all day without relief, showed weariness around his eyes and in the grim set of his jaw.

"How does it look?" he asked, dry-mouthed.

"I found a place," Slade said. "There's cover, grass, and water."

"Fair enough."

Slade made another pass behind the wagon, watching out for shadows on their trail, then led Dannell to his selected campsite. He dismounted then and led his roan to drink, but kept a sharp eye on the landscape they'd vacated.

Still nothing.

Wandle found him, carrying her bundle and a rolled-up blanket while her mother and the rest were making camp. "It's good that no one's found us, isn't it?" she asked.

"It's good so far," Slade granted.

"But you're still worried."

"I get paid to worry," he replied.

"Because they might sneak up on us tonight?"

"It's crossed my mind," he said. No point in lying when she'd see right through it.

"You can stop them," she said confidently. "You and Papa."

"We'll do our best," Slade told her, putting on a smile he hoped would be encouraging.

"I know you wouldn't let them hurt me. Hurt *us.*"

"Not if I can help it," Slade assured her.

"Well, I'd better help the others."

"Right," he said and, looking past her smile, Slade saw a couple of the younger kids collecting wood.

He interrupted them, telling the group, "There'll be no fire tonight."

"No fire?"

"What about supper?"

"We'll get cold!"

Slade overrode their voices. "We've been lucky that they haven't found us yet," he said. "They shouldn't have a problem following the wagon tracks, but we don't want to give them any extra help. No beacons in the dark to guide them, right?"

No one replied to that, so he pressed on. "As far as supper goes—and breakfast, too—you packed food that would keep, already cooked. It won't be hot, but it'll fill you up. As far as warmth goes, overnight you should be all right if you bundle up together."

"What if they *do* find us?" Tennys asked.

"We'll keep watch through the night. Between Dannell and I, we ought to have it covered."

"I'll help," said Draycen. "I'm a better shot than Papa."

"And so modest, too," Dannell answered. But when he smiled, it was with pride.

Slade cut it off before the younger boys rose to the challenge, saying, "Three on watch should get us through till morning, if we take three-hour shifts. The main thing to remember is to rouse the camp if someone's coming. Don't try taking on the whole pack by yourself."

Braylyn approached Slade while the other wives were passing out smoked meat and biscuits to the children. He saw worry in her face, no great surprise, as she addressed him.

"Marshal, do you think they'll come for us tonight?"

"I wish I knew, ma'am," Slade replied. "They missed one chance, last night. I don't know if they're spooked or working through a plan. Not knowing them, it's hard for me to peer inside their heads."

"If these are Danites, they won't stop at anything," she said.

"Which doesn't mean they can't *be* stopped."

"But if they reach the children—"

"We'll do everything within our power to prevent that happening," Slade said.

And hoped that it would be enough.

8

"They're settled for the night," Bliss told the others, when he finally got back to camp. He didn't mention riding past the landmark oak tree twice, afraid that they would think he was stupid.

"How far out from here?" asked Tanner.

Bliss had trouble calculating distance, worsened by the extra passes he had made, trying to find his own camp in the dark and no fire at either end to light his way.

"Few miles, I guess," he said and punctuated it with a quick one-shoulder shrug.

"A few miles," Tanner echoed. "Would that be closer to two, or ten?"

Bliss bit the bullet and said, "It's hard for me to figure in the dark."

"Well, did you count the steps your horse took, coming back?" asked Tanner.

"What?"

"Because from that, it's no trouble to work the distance out."

"I didn't think of that."

"All right. So they're *somewhere* ahead of us." Tanner was fairly sneering at him now. "How do they look?"

"Same as they looked leaving the house," Bliss said. "But tired."

"What were they cooking?"

"Nothing. There was no fire when I left."

"Refresh my memory. How long ago was that?"

The darkness of their cold camp hid his angry blush. "I didn't check my watch," Bliss said. He hated the others—Hallace, Zedek, and DeLaun—for standing silent, letting Tanner torture him without a word of protest. Nothing said on his behalf.

"Aside from being tired, how were they?" Tanner asked him. "Any problems that you noticed, with the young ones? Or the pregnant women?"

"Nothing I could see," said Bliss. "I wasn't close enough to overhear 'em, mind you. Had to leave my horse and crawl a ways to watch their camp without them seeing me."

"Your suit could use a brushing. I see that."

Bliss longed to curse him, maybe swing at him, but didn't dare. Instead, he said, "From where I was, they looked like anybody else who's lost most everything and hasn't got used to it yet."

"Well, that's a start," Tanner allowed.

"We going after them tonight?" asked Zedek, finally remembering that he too could speak.

"Too risky, without solid battlefield intelligence," Tanner replied. "We ride off without knowing whether we'll be going two miles or fifteen—"

"It ain't *fifteen*," Bliss told them, no one looking at him.

"—and with no precise direction," Tanner pressed on. "Not even a description of their camp to help us find it."

Damn it! Bliss thought.

"Weeping willows!" he blurted out. "A circle of 'em, like. It kind of faces north. Looked like there was a stream, too."

"None of which we stand a chance of finding in the dark, with no fixed line of travel."

"They've been following the road all day," said Bliss. "They haven't left it."

"Good. That ought to help us in the morning, catching up," said Tanner.

"You don't want to take them while they're sleeping?" Zedek asked.

"Not this time," Tanner said. "We've missed our best chance for tonight."

"There's no doubt I can find 'em," Bliss told anyone who would listen.

"Time for sleep," Tanner replied. "We're riding at first light."

"I'll have my Sharps back, then," said Bliss.

"It's on the oak."

He found it hanging from the stub-end of an old limb, by its sling. Retrieving it, he was glad to feel the weapon's solid, reassuring weight. Bliss wished that he had the nerve to draw a bead on Tanner and be done with it, but he'd seen Tanner kill and feared him.

Anyhow, the rest might turn on him. Most likely they *would*. And what about their mission, if the leader fell? What would he tell the Prophet about Tanner, back in Salt Lake City, if he ever got that far?

Not yet, Bliss told himself. *But if he keeps on riding me . . .*

Tomorrow was a new day. They could overtake the Haglunds, deal with them, and see the last of Oklahoma. Bliss couldn't remember if their next targets lived in Missouri or in Arkansas. More long days on the trail lay ahead of them.

Heavenly Father, give me strength.

"What have we got to eat?" he asked nobody in particular.

"Whatever's in your pockets or your saddlebag," Tanner replied, already stretched out on the ground, black hat over his eyes.

Hardtack again. It made his teeth ache, thinking of it. Better just to let his stomach growl and hope it wouldn't keep him awake.

Bliss wondered whether the crusaders had it this rough, fighting for Jerusalem in olden times. One thing he knew: they could have used a few Sharps rifles when they faced the infidels.

Maybe tomorrow, Bliss consoled himself, tending his horse. *Maybe we'll get it right.*

Slade was up before daybreak, after a nearly sleepless night. He'd taken the first watch, then stayed awake for Draycen's, dozing fitfully at last when Dannell took the last shift. Slade was tired, trying to hide it, and he knew most of the Haglunds had passed restless nights, only a couple of the youngest snoring in their mothers' arms.

Slade had watched to see which wife Dannell would huddle with for warmth, just curious, and he had been surprised to see the farmer spread his solitary blanket near the wagon's tailgate, lying down with just his Winchester for company. Slade wondered if Dannell was trying to avoid any semblance of favoritism, or if he feared that killers creeping into camp might fire upon him first.

Draycen had walked his beat around the camp with his father's shotgun, giving up the rifle after Slade persuaded him that moving targets in the dark were easier to hit with buckshot. They'd been lucky, getting through the night without an incident, but pale daylight only increased Slade's sense of dread.

Some soldiers he had known preferred to stage their raids at dawn, catch people dozing in their beds or still not quite awake, maybe preoccupied with breakfast or a call of nature. Sunrise also made it easier to pick out targets from a distance, when their guard was down.

Slade could only do so much in preparation for a fusillade of gunfire from an unknown point of origin. Instead of letting worry paralyze him, he got busy saddling his roan, stowing his bedroll, helping out the kids as best he could—all with a roving eye alert to any movement that betrayed a stranger's presence within rifle shot of their campsite. He saw Dannell doing the same, toting his Winchester and trying to be casual about it as he made his morning rounds, dispensing hugs and kisses.

Family.

Sometimes it saved your life. Sometimes it got you killed.

Without cooking, there was no need for a sit-down breakfast. They were packed in record time and on the trail before the Haglund women started handing biscuits to the children, passing a canvas bag they'd refilled with spring water last night. Slade wished for coffee, eggs, and bacon, settling for a corn dodger and tepid sips of water from his own canteen.

With any luck, if no one overtook them on the road, they should be rolling into Blaze around midday. A straight ride on from there to Enid meant arriving several hours after sundown, with the risks that traveling by night entailed. Slade was inclined to spend their second night in town, with help nearby—or witnesses, at least—but Blaze was strange to him. He'd have to size it up and get a feel for its inhabitants before he made that call.

Meanwhile, they had another half day to survive while traveling through unfamiliar country, mostly in the open, with a gang of unseen killers on their tail. Or running parallel. Or waiting somewhere up ahead.

It was a risk, Slade knew. Instead of taking them in camp, the hunters might have ridden on through darkness, found a place to lay their ambush, maybe catch Slade and the Haglunds in a killing cross fire. He might recognize the setup from a distance when he saw it—and then, what?

Go around it? Take the wagon off-road, hoping that the stalkers wouldn't notice? It seemed laughable, when Slade considered it, but would there be another choice?

Ride on ahead, he thought, *and see what's waiting.*

And another voice inside his head answered, *How far? What happens to the others while you're gone?*

No good.

They were together now, whatever happened, until they reached Enid or the hunters cut them down. Slade had a job in front of him, and he was doing it. He'd see it through.

Down to the bitter end.

One thing he knew, beyond the shadow of a doubt.

Before that job was done, someone was bound to die.

Slade hadn't been impressed with Alva at first sight, but it was a metropolis compared to Blaze. Alva was small, as towns went in the territory. Blaze looked like a camp prepared by squatters with some skill at carpentry.

The town's main street—its *only* street, if you could call it that—was roughly one block long. Some might have said there was no street, since all of Blaze's five commercial buildings stood in line and faced the same direction, windows turned southeastward as if staring off toward Enid with vague longing.

Blaze was not on any railroad line and therefore needed no hotel. Its structures, tracking west to east as Slade approached them in the early afternoon, included a small church, a lawyer's office, a general store, a blacksmith's shop, and a little saloon. A motley clutch of dwellings ranged behind the five main buildings, as if using them as cover, while their flanks and rear were wholly unprotected.

"Doesn't look like what you'd call a lively town," Dannell observed from his perch on the wagon driver's seat.

"They can't roll up the sidewalk," Slade acknowledged, "since they don't have one."

He pictured residents of Blaze roaming their short, one-sided street, praying for something—anything—to happen and relieve the drab monotony of life in such a place. Now Slade had come, bringing a nine days' wonder to their doorsteps, trailing danger in his dust. He hoped it wouldn't lead to trouble. Most of all, he hoped the killers following his tracks would think Blaze large enough to put them off a raid that night.

The children and their mothers needed proper sleep, and while there'd be no roof over their heads again tonight, the skies were clear, and they could have a fire, hot food, whatever was available for sale in Blaze. Slade didn't guess religious folk were much for drinking, though he'd known some parsons in his time who weren't afraid to pull a cork. When they had found a place to camp and settled in, Slade thought he might make time to have a whiskey for the road.

Or maybe two.

A tall, thin man emerged from the church as they passed it, regarding Slade and the Haglunds with skeptical eyes. He had a preacher's look about him, face drawn from a losing battle with the baser side of man, his narrow shoulders slumped beneath the weight of burdens shared. The frown looked permanent, more of a healed wound on his face than an expression.

Another lone observer watched them from the lawyer's office. He was shorter than the preacher by a good four inches, carrying an extra thirty pounds or so. His suit, presumably selected to inspire a certain confidence in clients, once upon a time, was dated now and straining at the seams. The round-faced lawyer didn't scowl, but neither did he smile.

Slade couldn't blame him.

Frontier towns were much like farms where risk from passing strangers was concerned. Of course, they welcomed visitors with money in their pockets, but you always had to wonder if the next one through the doorway had come to loot and kill, instead of buying what was on the shelves or racked behind the bar. It wouldn't take a large gang to destroy a town this size. Slade reckoned one or two determined outlaws could accomplish it, if no one shot them first.

Now, here he came, wearing a badge and escorting a family like nothing anyone in Blaze had likely ever seen. The townsfolk wouldn't know a witness from a prisoner until they checked for shackles. In the meantime, trusting strangers was a luxury that most inhabitants of the frontier could ill afford.

"How's this look for a place to camp?" Slade asked Dannell, when they were roughly in the middle of the small one-sided town. He'd stopped directly opposite the silent blacksmith's shop, still short of the saloon and fifty feet or less from the general store.

"Suits me, if we're not trespassing," Dannell replied.

"I'll ask around," Slade said. "If nothing else, the lawyer ought to know."

"I see a pump," Braylyn remarked and pointed out a kind of trough arrangement Slade had missed, resembling those he'd seen in certain desert towns.

"I'll ask about that, too," Slade said.

Dismounting, he tied his roan to the wagon's left-rear wheel, leaving enough slack in its reins for the gelding to graze. He angled toward the lawyer's office, glad to stretch his legs, aware of other eyes upon him and ignoring them.

"Marshal," the lawyer said, when he was close enough to speak without shouting. "We don't see much of lawmen here in Blaze. Hank Brannigan, attorney, but I don't suppose you need legal advice."

Chuckling at his own joke, the lawyer stuck his hand out. Slade pumped it twice and let go.

"Jack Slade," he said. "We're on our way to Enid, but

we can't make it tonight. Is there a problem with us camping where the wagon stands?"

"There shouldn't be," Brannigan answered, after thoughtful contemplation. "No one's claimed that side of Main Street, yet."

"And water from the pump?"

"We don't charge travelers for that," said Brannigan. Then winked, adding, "At least, not yet."

From where they stood, the lawyer had a clear view of the Haglunds, stepping from the wagon two by two, with helping hands. "That's quite a group you've got there, Marshal."

"Burned out of their place by hooligans," Slade said. "A day and something north of here."

"What kind of hooligans?" asked Brannigan.

"It's hard to say."

"They won't be headed this way, will they?"

Slade replied, all honesty, "There's been no sign of them since we set out."

"Still, it's a troubling thought. Perhaps we should—"

"Perdition! Damnation!"

Slade turned toward the sound of a harsh, dried-up voice and saw the preacher coming at him from next door. Despite his agitation, he was smart enough to stop beyond Slade's reach.

"Is there a problem, Parson?" Slade inquired.

"Indeed there is. You've brought corruption to our midst!"

"Meaning?"

"We are not blind here!"

Slade craned his neck, peering back toward the church. "Who's this 'we,' if you don't mind my asking?"

"The people of Blaze."

"And you speak for them, do you?" Slade asked. "Would you be the mayor, by some chance?"

"I'm the shepherd. These folk are my flock."

"Well, the people you're calling corrupt have just lost all they own to a gang of outlaws. They're under my protection, headed for the federal court in Enid. You'd be ill-advised to make their situation any worse."

The stew smelled good. No, make that *great*. Wandle was startled, after everything, to realize that she had eaten no hot food since supper the night before last. Finding May-belle the next morning had canceled breakfast, and they had been running since then, hiding out in the night from strangers who wanted them dead.

She understood why it was happening. Papa had warned all the children at various times to beware of strangers coming to their farm or asking questions if they were in town. She could remember bits and pieces of the flight from Utah for herself—mostly the wagon, dust and heat, together with some Indians they'd see along the way—and had the rest filled in by Papa when he taught the younger ones about their faith and breaking with the church that had gone wrong.

It made a kind of twisted sense that people from that church would try to silence Papa, to prevent him spreading stories that they wanted to keep quiet. Wandle also understood that strangers to the faith were prejudiced against grown-ups who lived the principle of plural marriage. And against their children, too.

It wasn't right, but she could live with it. She had her family.

So far, at least.

The man and wife who ran the general store in Blaze had gawped at Wandle and her mothers as if they all had two heads, when they were buying beef and vegetables for the stew. It didn't take a mind reader to know they disap-proved, but they were quick enough to pocket Papa's money.

When they'd left the store, a skinny man wearing a black suit and string tie was standing off to one side, glaring dag-

gers at Braylyn and Tennys. They ignored him, but when
Wandle spent a moment too long looking at him, the man
raised a Bible clutched in both hands, holding it out in front
of him as if it were some kind of shield.

Protecting him from what?

Her eyes found Marshal Slade—*Jack*, as she called him
when she practiced conversations in her mind—tending his
horse. He'd come back looking stormy from his first encounter with the townspeople, advising Papa and the mothers to be careful. He'd told them to stick close to the wagon
when they'd finished shopping and avoid unnecessary contact with the locals.

Wandle didn't mind. She'd never seen these folks before
and likely never would again after they pulled out in the
morning. For tonight, though, having them nearby meant hot
food and a chance to sleep in something more like peace.

And there was always Jack, keeping her safe and sound.
Just knowing he was near at hand made Wandle feel all
warm inside.

"So, that's Blaze?" Hallace asked.

"It doesn't look like much," said Zedek.

"We could likely ride in there and turn the whole place
upside down," DeLaun remarked.

Tanner made note that Bliss was keeping quiet, wasn't
pushing it. "How many people do you reckon live in there?"
he asked the group at large.

"Maybe a hunnert, hunnert fifty," Zedek said.

"You want to fight a hundred people for the Haglunds?"

Tanner saw the three of them glancing at Bliss, expecting him to make some comment, Hallace frowning when he
didn't.

"More than half of them are likely kids and women,"
Zedek said at last.

"You're right. Let's say two-thirds, for the sake of argument. If there's a hundred people in the town, that still leaves thirty-three. We'd be outnumbered more than six to one, not counting Haglund and his lawman."

"Why would any of 'em risk their skins for Haglund?" asked DeLaun.

"Most of them likely wouldn't," Tanner granted. "But some won't care to see the wives and children harmed. Others will fight to save their town."

"Who cares about their town?" Hallace sounded honestly confused. "We don't want anything from them."

Tanner turned from his spyglass and peered at Hallace for a moment. "How are they supposed to know that, when we ride in shooting?"

"Oh."

Bliss spoke at last. "You mean to let 'em have another night, then?"

"They've already claimed it, camping out in town," Tanner replied.

"What's next down the line?" Zedek asked.

Tanner recalled his map, saying, "A town called Enid. Likely better size than this one."

"If they get there . . ." DeLaun left it hanging, reluctant to finish.

"They won't," Tanner told them. "We'll rest here a bit, then ride on. Circle wide of this burg and find someplace ahead where they won't be expecting a party. Bliss can use his Sharps, then, and we'll finish up whatever's left."

He yawned, trail weary, leaving them to hash the details out amongst themselves. Tanner sat with his back against one of the poplar trees that screened them from even a sharp-eyed observer in town, still a half mile distant.

Tanner wished he had something that would help him stay awake. The Prophet's Word of Wisdom forbade tea and coffee, along with alcohol and tobacco. Tanner was accustomed to life without stimulants, but the older he got, the harder it seemed to keep going on too little sleep.

I'll rest up after this, he thought but knew that when they were finished with the Haglunds they'd be running again, trying to get out of Oklahoma Territory with their skins intact. Maybe, when they'd crossed over into Arkansas, they could afford to steal a day or two and catch up on their rest.

How many of them would be left by then?

The Haglunds and their lawman wouldn't go down without a fight. Tanner was convinced of that. He was having second thoughts about restraining Bliss, back at the farm, but it was too late to second-guess himself. There was no profit in regret, only in lessons learned from past mistakes.

And when this mission was completed? If he lived to see its end, then what?

First thing, he must return to Salt Lake City and report. If more work was already waiting for him there, then Tanner would have to decide if he could do it. If he *wanted* to do it. Did he still have God's own calling for the task of meting out his blood atonement? Had he done and seen too much?

Not yet.

At least, until this mission was behind him.

Tanner still had heretics to punish, dissidents to silence, for the sake of others. He would never meet most of the Saints who were depending on his strength and fortitude. The generations yet unborn, who may read something of him in a book someday or possibly forget him altogether.

In the end, it made no difference.

As long as God remembered Tanner, there was nothing else of any consequence.

Slade ate a second helping of the stew and washed it down with water, since the Haglunds brewed no coffee. Vonelle had informed him that hot drinks were banned by Joseph Smith, back in the old Missouri days, after a revelation from the Lord. He didn't ask why God would be opposed to coffee, which He had supposedly created in the first place.

Slade was not concerned with challenging or testing anybody's faith. He simply wanted to deliver them alive, in Enid, to Judge Dennison.

What happened after that would be a matter for the law.

Slade was about to ask Dannell and Draycen if they favored last night's lookout schedule when a muttering of voices from the farther end of Blaze distracted him. Tracking the sound, Slade saw a clutch of townsmen standing with their minister outside the boxy little church. Most of the noise was coming from the parson, he supposed, and while Slade couldn't catch the words, he had a fair idea that they spelled trouble.

Talk was one thing, but a mob in motion was a hungry animal.

Slade watched the preacher wave his Bible, pointing with his free hand toward the Haglunds' camp. Some heads were turning, but they needed more encouragement. Slade saw a couple in the last rank sipping theirs from whiskey flasks.

God-fearing drunks. The last thing he needed.

Dannell came to join him, saw the preacher's grumbling audience, and said, "They smell like trouble."

Picking up his rifle, Slade advised, "Best to have your weapons ready, just in case."

Dannell retreated to the wagon but was back a moment later with his Winchester. Beside him, Draycen held the double-barreled shotgun.

"If they come," Slade told them, "let me do the talking. If there's shooting to be done, I'll start it."

"Yes, sir," Draycen said.

"I hear you," said his father.

And the mob *was* coming, several members bearing lanterns, with their chaplain in the lead. Slade reckoned it was sixty yards between their campsite and the church. He let the townsmen cover half of that before he called out to them, "Stop right there, before you cut a slice of trouble you can't swallow."

The preacher answered back, "That badge you wear stands for the law of man, Marshal. This book"—he said brandishing his upraised Bible—"represents the holy law of God. It tells us sin must be uprooted and cast out!"

"You aren't uprooting anything tonight," Slade said. "Unless you figure God has made you bulletproof."

"You dare make sport of the Almighty? May He damn your soul to Hell!"

"He just might, Preacher," Slade replied. "But as one sinner to another, I'll make you a promise. Any man who takes another step in the direction of this family will go to his reward before I do."

Some of the angry men looked paler now by lamplight. Several were whispering behind the parson's back, but if he picked up their misgivings, he wasn't letting on. Thrusting his Bible out in front of him, the preacher took another forward step.

"You can't stop all of us, Marshal!"

"You may be right," Slade said. "But come what may, you'll be the first man down. As for the rest, any still standing when the smoke clears can expect to face Judge Dennison in Enid. Try explaining this night's work when you're on trial. And if you harm these folks behind me, you can make your last excuses on the scaffold."

"Reverend," one of the others said, "we ought to reconsider this."

Another raised his voice. "It's just one night. They're moving on tomorrow."

The preacher half turned, snarling at his pack. "So, how much degradation is acceptable? Where do we draw the line? I draw it here!"

He faced Slade once again, raising his Bible overhead as if it were a torch, and took another long stride forward.

Slade's shot stunned the crowd, raised gasps behind him from the Haglund women. When his bullet struck the upraised Bible, plucked it from the parson's fingers, spilling pages on the mob like snowflakes, most of them began retreating. Scared to turn their backs on Slade, they edged away from him, cringing.

"Go home, the lot of you," he ordered. "We'll be gone at daybreak. If I see you on the street again, I won't be aiming high."

They scattered, then, leaving their minister to grovel in the dust, retrieving scattered pages from his book. Slade left him to it, with a last word of advice.

"You find the part about not judging others," he suggested, "take a minute and refresh your memory."

9

They passed a long but quiet night in Blaze, with no one on the street. Even the small saloon stayed dark and silent, its proprietor apparently preferring one night's loss of business to whatever might occur if he got people liquored up. Or maybe, Slade reflected, those who liked a drink or two were scared to show their faces after his encounter with the mob.

Either way, it suited him just fine.

Slade took the first watch, interrupted once when Braylyn and her daughter had to use the privy they'd found tucked away in back of the saloon. He walked them over to it but made sure to keep his distance, standing back where he could see the outhouse and the Haglund camp at the same time. Returning from their errand, Wandle looked embarrassed, but she still gave Slade one of her bashful-teasing smiles.

That's trouble, said a small voice in his head.

But not for long.

By early afternoon tomorrow, they would be in Enid, Slade would have reported to Judge Dennison, and Dannell Haglund's brood was in the judge's hands from there. Slade doubted that there would be any charges filed against them for their lifestyle. A bigamy indictment needed marriage licenses as evidence, and sex outside of marriage wasn't punishable under federal law. The reservation tribes enforced a stricter code, including laws against adultery, but that had no effect on whites unless they married Indians and went to live with them.

As for the Danites—if they *were* Danites—Slade knew he might be sent to run them down. Nooses were waiting for them, for the Oman killings, and if that case failed, there'd be an arson charge for burning out the Haglund homestead. Slade wasn't convinced the killers he had yet to see would stick around once Dannell Haglund and his family were in protective custody, but he supposed that anything was possible.

It hadn't been that long ago that crazed fanatics had come gunning for Judge Dennison, inside his own courthouse. The madness that occasionally flowed from politics and from religion prompted men to throw away their lives for hopeless causes, taking others with them as they fell.

Come morning, they rose early to a silent town where window curtains parted to reveal curious eyes, but no one ventured out onto the dusty street. Slade stayed alert, prepared to open fire if any of those windows opened, sprouting gun barrels, but Blaze remained in hibernation, its inhabitants concealed.

They got the wagon packed, then Slade stood watch over a long privy parade, while Dannell and Draycen harnessed their team. One of the horses that had pulled their wagon yesterday switched out, giving the extra animal a turn. Daylight was still a pink haze in the east as they rolled out of town.

Slade had considered riding down to rouse the preacher, tell him there were no hard feelings, but he didn't like to lie.

The wagon's pace and the requirements of its passengers would finally determine their arrival time in Enid. Slade was hoping they'd be safe in town by one or two o'clock, with any luck. He would have liked to stop and visit Faith, but didn't want to leave the Haglunds dangling like bait for any longer than was absolutely necessary.

Meanwhile, he had killers on his mind.

It seemed impossible to Slade that they had shaken off the men who'd burned the Haglunds' home. Unless the hunters chose to let them go, and fired the homestead as a parting shot, he knew the wagon's tracks would tell them where the family had gone. It puzzled him that they had not been jumped already, prior to reaching Blaze, but since Slade didn't know his adversaries, he could not presume to see things through their eyes.

This morning was their last chance, short of slipping into Enid for a raid that could be suicidal. And the pressing question on his mind, now, dealt with where and when the enemy would strike.

Slade hadn't seen them on the trail, so far, but they'd had thirteen hours to catch up, while he and his companions camped in Blaze. Slade took for granted that they had been glimpsed, at least, if only from a distance. But then what?

Would the hunters wait to follow them away from town? Perhaps ride parallel on either side and swoop in for the kill when they were safely clear of Blaze? Or had they used the night, riding ahead to lay an ambush somewhere up ahead?

It galled Slade, knowing that he'd simply have to wait and see what happened next. It went against his grain and made him worry that he wouldn't save the Haglunds after all.

But he would damn sure try. And God help anyone who tried to stop them now.

• • •

"What's keeping them?" asked Hallace.

"How should I know?" Zedek answered back.

Tanner cut through the hot air. "Give them time," he said. "Figure they had to get up, do their business, have some breakfast, pack the wagon. If the folks in town give them a send-off, that'll take some time."

"I did some thinking," said DeLaun.

"Uh-oh." The jibe from Bliss.

"I'm serious!"

"So, spit it out," said Hallace.

"What if they don't come this way?" DeLaun inquired. "We could be waiting here all day, for nothing."

Tanner fielded the question. "They've been heading down toward Enid since they left the farm. There's no place else a U.S. marshal would escort them."

"Okay, sure. I see that. But suppose they don't come *this* way? Who's to say the lawman doesn't know a shortcut? They could pass a mile on either side of us, and we'd be none the wiser."

It was a troubling thought, but Tanner trusted in probability. "You see those wagon ruts in front of us, DeLaun?" he asks.

"Sure do."

"That's what we call a road," he said, and heard the others start their snickering. "It's not much of a road, I grant you. Nothing fancy. That's a fact. But it's the *main* road linking Blaze to Enid. Now, unless you know for sure the lawman has another way to go, and you can point us to it . . ."

"Nope," DeLaun admitted, defeated.

"Well, then, let's give them some time, shall we? We're fifteen miles from town. Take 'em five hours in that wagon, even if the women and the young ones don't need any breaks."

Tanner wished they could have laid the ambush closer in, toward Blaze, and not halfway to Enid, but the landscape dictated his selection of a vantage point. They waited for Haglund and his brood in cover granted by a jagged line of upthrust granite slabs, half screened by hackberry and sawtooth oaks, set back some twenty paces from the wagon road. He wished they were closer, and there were no other trees or boulders on the field to help their targets duck and hide, but Tanner could not change the countryside to suit himself.

Their plan was relatively simple. Bliss would drop the lawman with his Sharps, then try for Dannell Haglund, while the others opened up with everything they had and made a sieve out of the wagon. Anyone still moving when the smoke cleared could be finished off with pistols, at close range.

He thought about the horses, wondering if they are branded—and, if not, whether it was too risky to appropriate any survivors of the ambush for their ride to Arkansas. Spare mounts would be a boon, but there was a good chance that the wagon and its lifeless cargo would be found within a day or two. And extra horses were the kind of thing that might provoke a lawman to confront them, somewhere down the road.

Tanner decided it would be better to release the animals, if they weren't killed in the initial fusillade. He'd shot horses before—one of his own, most recently—but didn't like to do it. Joseph Smith had taught that animals have souls, calling them "angels in their sphere." Tanner accepted it, as with any other teaching of his faith, and did his best to live the principle.

Humans are something else entirely.

To his knowledge, there had never been an animal that sold its soul to Satan or betrayed its kind for personal reward, while humans did it every day. Some took it as a point of pride, in fact. The heretics he hunted had betrayed their people and their Lord.

It was his job to seek them out and punish them.

He was thankful for the shade this morning, as the sun

began to bake the soil around him, browning grass that clearly needed a taste of rain. The sky was cloudless, offering no respite from what promised to be another scorching day.

But it was hotter where the Haglunds would be going.

Hot as fire and brimstone in the pits of Hell.

Wandle Haglund was tired of riding in the wagon. Even though she sat atop a folded blanket, the wooden slats of the wagon bed still numbed her backside and made her shins ache if she sat too long with her legs tucked beneath her. The side boards were worse, rough enough to snag clothing or prick her with splinters, while leaving her shoulder blades bruised.

The good news was that wagon travel granted her a constant, unobstructed view of Marshal Slade.

Wandle tried to be subtle about it, casually turning her head when he passed in another direction, as if she were scanning the landscape for features of interest. And it *was* more interesting since they'd left the dreadful town of Blaze behind them. There were more hills, more trees, and craggy rocks that looked as if they'd fallen from the sky.

But mostly, Wandle studied Jack.

She hadn't dared to speak his first name yet, of course. Young ladies couldn't be that forward with an older man, unless familiarity had been invited. Wandle didn't think that Jack would mind, but there was still the matter of her father and her mothers. Not to mention siblings who were absolutely wearing on her nerves.

"He isn't going anywhere," said Posey, as she caught Wandle watching the marshal ride by.

"I'm sure I don't know what you mean," Wandle replied, stiffly.

"You'll scare him," Posey whispered, "if he sees you staring at him like you want to eat him up."

Wandle imagined that her burning cheeks must be bright

crimson. Lowering her head, half turning it toward Posey, she hissed, "I do not! And besides, he isn't scared of anything."

"Papa says everyone gets scared."

"That's *normal* folk," Wandle replied. "Lawmen are different. The good ones, anyway. They live with danger all the time. Bandits robbing their towns or gunfighters trying to shoot them."

"It must be lonely," Posey ventured.

"Why?"

"Just think. Who'd want to live with someone when he keeps on getting shot at all the time? He'll never find a wife."

"Don't be so sure."

"And when he's off like this, away from home," Posey continued. "Wouldn't that be awful? Gone for days or weeks, and Mrs. Marshal never knowing whether he's alive or lying dead?"

It *would* be awful, Wandle realized, but Jack could obviously deal with anything that came his way.

"You saw the way he got rid of that mob, last night," she said. "Their preacher was a crazy man."

"I didn't watch," Posey admitted, lowering her eyes. "I hid under the wagon with my eyes closed. When I heard the shot, I almost had an accident."

"You should have seen it, Posey. One shot through the crazy preacher's Bible. He was wonderful!"

"Does that mean that he'll go to Hell?" asked Posey.

"What? Why would you say a thing like that?"

"Shooting the Bible has to be a sin. It's dis . . . disre . . ."

"Disrespectful?"

"Yes, that! Papa says the Holy Bible and the Book of Mormon are the words of God."

"He's right. But Marshal Jack was standing up for us, against the bad men. He was doing God's work, don't you— What's so funny?"

"You said, 'Marshal *Jack.*'" Posey replied, giggling.

"I did not!"

"Did, too!"

"Well . . . suppose I did? So, what? That *is* his name."

"You like him!"

Face on fire, Wandle said, "We all like him. He's saving our lives."

"You *really* like him!"

"Keep your voice down!"

"Wandle and the marshal, sitting in a tree—"

Wandle pinched Posey hard enough to leave a bruise, clapping a hand over her mouth at the same time. She leaned in close and said, "I swear, if you say one more word, I'll tickle you until you cry and wet yourself."

Reluctantly, her sister nodded, signaling surrender. Wandle took her hand away and checked to see if anyone was eavesdropping.

"It's no one's business who I like," she whispered, sounding fierce to her own ears.

"Papa won't like it," Posey said. "Our mothers will be angry."

"You just mind your business," Wandle cautioned. "I'll take care of mine."

Jack chose that moment to ride past them, raising two fingers to his hat brim in a gallant gesture as he smiled. Wandle could feel her heart leap, thumping hard against her ribs.

"There's someone coming!" Hallace said, sudden excitement in his voice.

Tanner was close to dozing, but the words revived him instantly. He rose to a crouch, clutching his spyglass as he duckwalked down the line of waiting riflemen to reach the point where Hallace knelt, peering off northwestward.

"There," said Hallace, pointing.

Just a speck, but drawing nearer by the minute. Tanner pulled his spyglass out to full length, hoisted it to his eye, and found his target after searching for a moment. Tiny figures, still a mile or more away, sprang into sharp relief.

He spotted Dannell Haglund, still in the driver's seat behind four horses. And behind him, heads bobbing in the wagon's bed, some of them barely visible. Tanner made no attempt to count them, knowing some were too short to be visible. Haglund would not have left any behind in Blaze.

The lawman held more interest for him, at the moment. Circling left and right around the wagon, back and forth, he kept a cautious eye out for the first suggestion of a trap or anyone pursuing them. He clearly didn't think that one man riding rings on horseback could protect a wagonload of targets from determined rifle fire, but he did it to soothe the Haglunds—and to give himself a better view of the landscape on every side.

A cautious man. No doubt a fair hand with a gun.

"It's them, all right," he told the others as he heard them shifting anxiously. "All in the wagon, like before, except the marshal. They're alert, so keep your heads well down and out of sight until the shooting starts."

He turned to Bliss at last, saying, "That's you. First shot, as soon as they're in place."

Bliss smiled. "I'm ready. Anyplace within a thousand yards," he says.

"That's too far for the rest of us, with only Winchesters and Henrys," Tanner says. "It's no good hitting one or two of them and letting the others get away."

"Why can't we ride them down?" asked Bliss.

"We've laid an ambush for a reason. That's to catch them by surprise and take them all at once. No stragglers and no running fight across the plains."

"I'm not afraid of fighting," Bliss replied, some of the old resistance creeping back into his voice.

"Nobody said you were," Tanner replied, his left hand

slipping toward his sheathed knife. "There is such a thing as fighting smart. That's what we aim to do." The blade unsheathed an inch. "Is that all right with you?"

"I'm with you. Absolutely," Bliss agreed.

"Good. Then, what I need for you to do is drop the wagon's driver when they're close enough for us to do the rest."

"The driver? Haglund?" Bliss appeared confused. "But what about the lawman?"

"Taking out the driver stops the wagon. Then, the lawman comes to us. And when he does," Tanner instructed them, "Bliss and I will put him down. You others, concentrate your firing on the wagon. Make sure no one wriggles out and finds a place to hide."

He knew this was the tough part, when the gun work turned to women and their children. Every handpicked member of his team was briefed on that, before they left Salt Lake to start their mission. Every man agreed that he could do what must be done.

But still, it was hard. The killing took its toll.

Tanner returned to his original position, pleased to see the others hunching down as ordered, slipping off their high-crowned hats that only made a bigger target when the shooting started. He trusted them to obey his orders—even Bliss, since he was included in the marshal's execution.

Though, in fact, Tanner intended to do that job himself.

It took time to reload the Sharps. Not much, but time enough for Haglund's escort to see him drop. Time for Slade to spur his horse toward the source of the shots, with the good of the children in mind.

And Tanner would be waiting for him, staring down the barrel of his Henry rifle, ready for the killing shot.

A grim sense of anticipation made him smile.

Slade didn't like the countryside they were traversing. He preferred the open plains, where he could see the hunters coming and be ready for them. Hills and trees and boulders made his job more difficult, if not impossible.

How many miles to Enid? Ten? Fifteen? Call it five hours of steady travel at their present pace, with no more stops for overloaded bladders. But he knew they faced a greater danger now than at any other time since they had fled the Haglunds' farm.

If someone meant to stop them, it would have to be sometime before they got to Enid's outskirts. Any gunplay within sight or earshot of the town would bring out any marshals not engaged on distant business and perhaps civilian possemen, as well. The hunters wouldn't risk it, if they'd been afraid to try their luck in Blaze.

Again, Slade entertained the wishful thought that Dannell Haglund's enemies had given up the chase, that they'd be satisfied with leveling his home and ruining his years of labor on the spread. Slade *hoped* it might be true, but he did not believe it for a minute.

Say four hours and a fraction, then, before they had the town in sight and he could let himself relax. Until then—

Something flickered at the corner of his left eye, made him turn as Dannell's hat flew backward, off his head. There was a breeze of sorts, but nothing strong enough to bare the farmer's shaggy scalp.

Another heartbeat passed before Slade heard the shot, somewhere between a crack and distant thunder, rolling toward them from their front.

"Get down!" he shouted, as he bent and drew his rifle from its scabbard. "Get the wagon over to those trees!"

Haglund was there ahead of him, already hauling on the reins, flogging his team into a gallop toward a line of bald cypress and ash, off to their left. Slade paced the wagon, guessing it was suicide to stay in one position now, and watched for rifle smoke around the rocks and trees ahead.

His forward motion saved him when the next puff came, rising from a stand of trees with boulders at their base.

Slade heard the heavy bullet pass somewhere behind him, followed by the echo of a second rifle shot. It sounded like a Sharps, coming and going.

Gun enough to knock him down, and then some, if the shooter scored a hit.

Slade galloped toward the trees and reached them as a third shot struck one of the bald cypress trunks, spraying slivers of moist living wood. The slow rate of fire confirmed a Sharps buffalo gun in Slade's mind.

One shooter? Or were others waiting for the distance gun to do its work before they chimed in with repeaters? If so, they'd missed their chance, but how long could Slade trust them to wait before they rushed the Haglunds?

When Slade reached the wagon, Dannell Haglund had already jumped down from the driver's seat, holding his Winchester in one hand, shotgun in the other. Draycen was scrambling over the tailgate, rushing to take the twelve gauge from his father. Braylyn was standing in the wagon, holding a long-barreled Colt in both hands, its muzzle pointing down for safety's sake.

Slade dismounted, tied his gelding's reins off to a wagon wheel, and drew his rifle from its saddle boot. Children were stirring in the wagon's bed, frightened, seeking release of frazzled nerves in motion.

"Best to stay right there, for now," Slade cautioned them, before addressing the family members with weapons. "That scattergun won't reach from here," he told Draycen, then turned to Braylyn. "Neither will that Colt. The Winchesters should reach, but burning too much ammunition without targets is a bad idea."

"It's Danites, isn't it?" asked Tennys, close to tears and maybe to hysteria.

"I don't know who it is," Slade answered honestly, "or how many there are. One's shooting now, but there could well be others lying back. That's what we need to know, first thing."

"And how will you find out?" Dannell asked him.

"By going over there," Slade said.

"Alone?" The question barely squeaked out of Wandle June.

"I make a smaller target than your family," Slade said. "And most of you aren't armed."

She seemed about to burst with anger, worry, something, but Slade didn't have the time to soothe the Haglunds individually.

"What I mean to do," he said, "is work my way along this side of the road, under cover, and try to surprise them. It may work, may not. If it does, be ready to go when I come back to join you. Top speed, all the way in to Enid or bust."

"And if it doesn't work?" Dannell asked.

"They'll be coming for you, one way or another," Slade replied. "Keep watch. Don't let your guard down for a second. When they come, don't fire until you're guaranteed of making hits. Aim true and shoot to kill."

With that, Slade doffed his hat and hung it on his saddle horn, then struck off following the tree line southward toward its end, where scattered boulders and tall grass would be his only cover.

At his back, Slade could've sworn he heard a voice call out, "Be careful, Marshal Jack!"

Careful he was, proceeding in a crouch until the bald cypress and ash ran out, then crawling on his belly through the grass, hoping he didn't veer off-course now that he couldn't see the road or any other landmarks.

Hope was all Slade had, until he reached a point where he could cause some damage to their enemy. Hope that the sniper or his still-unknown companions wouldn't see the grass moving, to mark Slade's crawling progress. Hope that he would not surprise a rattlesnake along the way and either sustain a lethal bite or have to give himself away by killing it.

No snakes, in fact, and nothing to suggest that Slade had been spotted as he wriggled through the grass, judging the distance he had covered by his own fatigue and the raw discomfort of his knees and elbows. Slade got help when the Sharps shooter squeezed off a round, its report much closer now.

He crawled another twenty yards or so, to reach a heap of stones on his side of the road. It stood some fifteen feet tall, crags and hollows gray-green with lichen that smeared and stained Slade's fingers as he climbed, going for height.

He found a niche of sorts, supported by a narrow ledge that granted purchase for his boots, and risked a look across the road. More boulders, jutting up through hackberry and oak, set back some distance from the wagon track. He knew it for the sniper's roost, but couldn't say exactly where the long shooter had fired from.

He waited. Five, six minutes passed, before Slade saw a stirring in the shadow of a rock off to his right. He watched a head pop up, then drop from sight again. More waiting, then it was a head and shoulders rising, with the Sharps attached, angling downrange toward where the Haglunds were concealed.

Slade didn't wait to look for any other spotters. Lining up his shot before the sniper had a chance to fire again, he thumbed back the Winchester's hammer and squeezed its trigger, willing the slug to fly true.

Slade saw his shot strike home, a puff of crimson mist before the sniper tumbled backward, out of sight. Some kind of muscular convulsion in the dead man's trigger finger fired the Sharps once more, skyward, as it was slipping from his view.

And then, all hell broke loose.

Heads started popping up along the rocky crest in front of Slade, across the wagon road and eighty feet or so away from him. Slade pumped his rifle's lever action, rapid-firing three rounds, right to left along the line, without counting the startled faces. They dropped out of sight while his slugs were still flying, and Slade heard a voice shouting garbled instructions he couldn't translate.

Time to move.

Slade broke from cover, charging toward the heap of stony slabs that hid his targets. Knowing it was crazy, maybe suicidal, he kept going, heartened when Dannell Haglund's Winchester chimed in to cover him, long-range bullets chipping granite, whining off across the countryside in ricochets.

Slade kept expecting gunfire, knew someone was bound to rise in front of him and slam a round into his face or chest, but nothing happened. He had nearly reached the rock pile when he heard the sound of horses hooves retreating, leaped onto the rocks, and scrambled up left-handed, ready with the rifle in his right hand.

Too late.

As he reached the pinnacle, Slade saw four black-clad riders racing out of range, trailing a horse with an empty saddle. He fired after them regardless, knowing it was wasted, and could only grimace as a couple of them ducked their heads in reflex action.

Down below and to his right, the sniper he had shot lay sprawled beside his Sharps, no longer fit for battle. Slade turned back in the direction of the stand where Dannell Haglund's family waited, free hand raised and waving them across.

At his first glimpse of movement in the trees, Slade started his descent to check the corpse and claim its weapons for his side.

10

The man was absolutely dead. He was still quivering when Slade topped the rock pile, firing at his four companions in retreat, but that had passed. Slade's .44-40 round had drilled a tidy hole behind the man's right ear, but it had done a messy job emerging from the other side.

Thirteen grams of lead, traveling at close to 1,200 feet per second, creates a shockwave on impact that not only kills but also distorts and deforms. Even so, there was enough face left for Slade to peg the corpse's age as somewhere in the mid-twenties. Old enough to make a choice that had ended him.

And was it all because of faith in God?

Slade heard the Haglunds coming, called up to them from the killing ground, "No need for women or the kids to see this."

Still, they came, with Braylyn and Tennys holding the two youngest children, keeping their faces turned into soft bosoms. The rest, Slade supposed, had a need to confirm that their stalkers were mortal and could be defeated.

Dannell Haglund crouched and peered into the dead shooter's misshapen face. He looked the body up and down, then rose and took a backward step, almost colliding with his eldest son. Draycen's expression had been caught somewhere between excitement and revulsion.

"You don't know him, I suppose?" Slade asked.

"I've never seen him, but he's bound to be a Danite."

"You can tell that . . . how?"

"Aside from shooting at us," Dannell answered, "see the clothes he's wearing. Did you see the others? Were they all dressed just alike?"

"I couldn't vouch for any details," Slade replied, "but all of them were wearing black."

"It's like their badge or uniform," Dannell explained. "You find a gunman dressed in black and hunting Saints, you won't lose any money betting he's a Danite."

"There were five in all," Slade said. "They're running now, but we'd be foolish to suppose they won't come back and try again. We need to get a move on, while we have some time to cover ground."

"We're ready now," Dannell assured him. Turning to his brood, he said, "I need you all back in the wagon, right this minute."

Slade was unfastening the dead man's bandoleer of rifle cartridges, rolling the body to facilitate removal of the ammunition and the pistol belt, when Haglund said, behind him, "Thank you for my family. I make it three times that you've saved us, Marshal."

"It's my job," Slade said, hoisting the double belts and stooping for the heavy Sharps. "But truth be told, I've never had much tolerance for people telling others what to think or how they should behave."

"Sounds funny for a lawman, I admit," Haglund replied.

"Oh, I believe in order," Slade confirmed. "No killing, raping, stealing, this and that. But when it comes to faith and politics, I can't help thinking people should be left alone. Or, maybe I just don't like bullies."

"Either way, you have my thanks and everlasting gratitude. If I or mine can ever help you out in any way . . ."

"Just keep that wagon moving at a decent pace," Slade said. "If anyone comes back at us, at least we've got more guns to welcome them."

"I've never fired a Sharps," said Haglund, as they neared the wagon.

"Nothing hard about it but the recoil," Slade advised and took him through the basic steps of using the rifle's falling-block action. Pull down and forward on the trigger guard to open the action. Remove and replace the spent cartridge, then close up the breech. Peer through the open ladder sight, adjusting it for range if there was time. Ease back on the first of the double-set triggers, then gently squeeze the second to send the 475-grain projectile howling downrange.

"It'll kick like a mule," Slade reminded Dannell. "But by the time it bruises you, the slug's long gone."

"I'll remember that," said Haglund, as he stowed the Sharps and ammunition bandoleer beneath the driver's seat. Before mounting the seat, he asked Slade, "Will they let us get to Enid?"

"There's a decent chance they'll try to stop us," Slade admitted. "But I just might have a backup plan."

"What's that?" asked Haglund.

"When I've got it all worked out," Slade said, "you'll be the first to know."

Amren Tanner told himself the failure wasn't his fault, that he couldn't see the lawman sneaking up on them, and he hadn't sparked the panic, even after Bliss had half his head blown off. But none of it relieved his sense of shame. He was their leader—or supposed to be—and any fault for failing ultimately rested on him.

He still wasn't sure what had gone wrong, aside from the lawman flanking them. It had been shocking, certainly, to see the rifle slug drill Bliss, and hear the next few chipping granite overhead, but they still had him four to one and could have run him down on guts alone, if all else failed.

Tanner believed it was DeLaun who squealed, although he couldn't prove it. The unearthly sound of panic might have been an animal, gnawing its own leg in a trap, the way it twanged his nerves like fingernails on slate. It *was* De-Laun who bolted first, Tanner had seen that with his own eyes, but instead of calling Allred back, or even shooting him to stiffen up the rest, Tanner had found himself bolting, as well.

His weathered cheeks burned with the shame of it. His jaw ached from grinding his molars in fury. Inside, Tanner raged at all of them—but at his damned self, worst of all.

They'd ridden well beyond the lawman's line of sight, beyond the range of Bliss's Sharps, abandoned in their flight, when Tanner hauled back on his pinto's reins and hollered at the rest to stop. He was surprised and gratified when they obeyed, instead of simply racing on without him.

He knew better than to challenge them for running, since he shared their guilt. Seeing DeLaun, the left side of his face painted with Bliss's blood and brains, Tanner could hardly blame him for the squeal, the bolting.

Still . . .

"We have to go back," he informed them, waiting for a protest, hearing none. "We can't leave it like this and claim we did our best. What will the Prophet say? Or our Heavenly Father?"

"They're gone by now, Amren," said Hallace. "On their way. You know they are."

"And *we* know where they're going," Tanner answered.

"They may get off the road," Zedek suggested. "I would, if it was me."

"It makes no difference," said Tanner. "Enid isn't moving. We can ride ahead and wait for them, outside of town. Spot them a couple miles beyond the city limits, anyway, and finish it before the lawman has a chance to rally anyone against us."

"What about Bliss?" asked DeLaun, while wiping his face with a formerly white handkerchief.

"He's gone," Tanner replied. "Like Weldon. Like Nordell. It happens when you're in a war. You all were cautioned at the outset. No one was misled."

"I worry more about the Sharps," said Hallace, always practical. "They've got range on us, now."

"It only matters if they see us coming," Tanner said. "We've got a few tricks left, I'll bet."

No one responded. They sat astride their animals, staring at him and at each other, as if beaten and demoralized.

At last, he said, "I'll understand if any of you wants to go back home. You weren't compelled to join this mission, and you won't be forced to stay against your will. Riding back, avoid the places where we've done our business, if you can. Whoever goes, just tell the Prophet that I'm finishing the work."

They chewed on that a while, then Zedek said, "Reckon I'll stick."

A nod from Hallace. "Yeah."

DeLaun considered pocketing his bloody handkerchief, then gave it to the prairie wind. Watching it sail away like hope escaping, he made it unanimous. "I'm in."

"We'll need to push it," Tanner told them. "Haglund and the marshal won't be dawdling any longer. We can best them, but we'll have to ride straight through. I make it ten miles, plus the five we lost running away."

"We'd best be getting started, then," DeLaun replied.

And so they did, riding for all they're worth—whatever

that may be. Four horsemen racing toward their own apocalypse.

He knew that back in olden times, the Bible's final book, describing how the world would end, had once been called Apocalypse, instead of Revelation. Both originally meant the same thing, a revealing of the answers to all mysteries. A tying up of all loose ends.

Tanner was ready for his revelation.

He could almost smell the brimstone now and hear the sinners screaming as they burned in hellfire hot enough to purge his own humiliation and relieve him of his shame.

Slade's backup plan was hastily conceived, around the time he saw the four surviving Danites fleeing westward, and it left him with several misgivings. There were risks involved, no doubt about it, and while he was paid to put his own life on the line, he hated placing others in harm's way.

The Haglunds were already there, of course, but Slade's idea made matters worse, because it posed a threat to Faith.

The thought had come to him, watching the would-be killers ride away, that they would likely circle back and try again before he got the Haglunds safely into Enid. While he didn't know the gunmen and couldn't honestly predict what they'd do next, they struck him as fanatics who would not give up a mission once they'd set their teeth in it.

Slade's plan was simple, as the best ones always seemed to be. They had to pass Faith's place en route to Enid, as it was, and Slade would ask her if she'd let the Haglunds wait there for him, while he rode on into town and got some reinforcements from Judge Dennison. With extra marshals, they should make the last three miles without a problem.

All of which depended on a set of circumstances Slade could not control.

First, he would not consider using Faith's spread as a hideout for the Haglunds if he knew the Danites were watching his fugitive party. The landscape was mostly wide-open from there on to Enid, and Slade would be on high alert for a sign of their stalkers. One glimpse, one threat of leading them to Faith, and he would scrub his plan and ride on to Enid with the Haglunds by himself.

And there was always the one-in-a-million chance Faith might refuse his request. He doubted it, knowing the lady and seeing her boundless compassion firsthand as he had, but who knew? They'd never really talked about religion, much less Mormons or polygamy. Faith might have strong opinions on the subject that had never surfaced, since they seemed irrelevant.

Six miles, and Slade had seen nothing to suggest that they were being watched or shadowed. There were ways to do it, he supposed, using a spyglass or binoculars, and he made a mental note to purchase one next time he had a chance. For now, though, it appeared that they were safe.

It felt like home, crossing the boundary onto Faith Connover's land. Slade was accustomed to that feeling now, but still, it never failed to touch him. One of Faith's outriders spotted them when they were halfway to the house and left them with a wave on recognizing Slade.

More welcome eyes to watch their back.

Faith wasn't waiting for him on the porch this time, but she appeared as Slade was starting to dismount. The Haglunds kept their places in the wagon, Dannell watchful from the driver's seat and Draycen with the twelve gauge close behind him, all the others skittish, somewhere short of scared.

"Hello, Jack." Greeting him without the customary kiss. "You brought me company, I see."

Slade felt embarrassed, now that he'd come down to it. "This may have been a bad idea," he said. "Turns out the family that got killed out by Alva was the start of something. Or the middle of it; I'm not sure. Long story short, they were a bunch of Mormons, like these folks. Hard men are hunting them, some craziness to do with their religion."

"Oh," Faith said. "I see."

"They jumped us, eight or nine miles back, but we got out from under it. As far as I can tell, they haven't trailed us here, but I expect they know we're on the way to Enid. I was wondering—"

"Of course, Jack. I'd be pleased to make them comfortable while you fetch some marshals back from town."

"You *do* read minds," he told her, smiling.

"I've had practice reading yours," she said.

Dropping his voice another notch, Slade said, "I bet you don't know what I'm thinking now."

"I bet I do," Faith said. "But it would scandalize the church folk." Giving Slade's hand just the shortest, lightest squeeze, she asked him, "Will you make the introductions, or shall I?"

"You have a lovely home, Miz Connover," Vonelle Haglund remarked.

"Lovely," the younger Tennys echoed.

"Well, it's been a long time growing into what you see," Faith said, "but I am pleased with the result."

"Ma'am, I just want to thank you one more time for helping us this way." Dannell, the husband four times over, held his hat in both hands, fairly kneading it.

"You're more than welcome," Faith assured him. "It's a pleasure to have children on the place."

"You don't have any of your own, then?" asked the eldest Haglund daughter. "None with Marshal Slade?"

"Wandle June!" two of the mothers snapped in unison. The older of them, Braylyn, swiftly added, "You apologize this very second!"

"Sorry, ma'am."

"There's nothing wrong with curiosity," Faith said, feeling the warm blush on her cheeks.

"That may be true," Braylyn replied, still glaring at her daughter. "But this is not the time or place."

"I *said* I'm sorry, Mama."

Faith caught something in the girl's eye as she turned away and focused on the stone fireplace with feigned interest. It struck her that the child—young woman, really—was infatuated with Jack Slade.

Why not? Faith thought, half smiling. *So am I.*

Or was there more to it than that?

She thought so, had herself nearly convinced of it, but if Jack couldn't speak the words—

"I pray we haven't placed you or your home in any danger," Braylyn Haglund said.

"We should be fine," Faith said. "I'm sure the marshal wouldn't place your family at risk. Besides, it's just an hour's ride to town from here. He should be back with other deputies in no time."

"Still, it's very gracious of you to accept us," said Alema Haglund, speaking up for the first time. "There's many who would not."

"I don't hold with religious prejudice, or any other kind," Faith said. Hoping to change the subject, she inquired, "When is your baby due?"

"October," said Alema.

"And yours?" Faith asked Tennys.

"Two more months. September, ma'am."

"Please, call me Faith. The ma'aming always makes me feel like I have one foot in the grave."

Too late, Faith caught herself on that, but Braylyn started laughing, followed by the other wives, a couple of the younger children joining in because it was contagious. Dannell Haglund looked embarrassed, as if women were a species he would never understand, despite the evidence of his experience at tending them.

"I don't know where I left my manners," Faith said, when

the laughter had begun to wane. "You must be hungry. There's some cold beef, bread I baked this morning, and no shortage of potatoes. I could—"

"Ma'am . . ." Dannell stopped short, then tried again. "Miz Connover, we didn't come to eat you out of house and home."

"It's nothing, really. Just a snack to tide you over, while we wait."

"Just a snack, Papa," one of the younger boys said. Faith believed it was Heber.

"We shouldn't," Dannell said, but Faith felt him weakening.

"What if I told you that I'd be insulted by any refusal?" she said.

"Oh, no insult intended," he answered. "It's just . . . well . . ."

"Perhaps not the beef," Braylyn said. "It has to do with our religion."

"The Word of Wisdom," little Moroni contributed.

"No beef then. I'm convinced there must be beans," Faith said.

"If it's no bother," Braylyn said. "Please let us help you in the kitchen."

"I'd appreciate it."

As the women rose in unison, Faith was discomfited by her mistake. She'd never met a Mormon, to her knowledge, and had only known two Jews—Aaron Shapolsky and his wife, who ran a yard-goods shop in Enid. There were several dozen Catholics in town, and Faith knew that some of the Protestants regarded them with vague suspicion, which seemed *very* odd, since both claimed Jesus as their master.

Faith decided she would take her cues from Braylyn and the other wives, trying her best not to embarrass them or make a spectacle of her own ignorance. It could be educational.

But looking at the children, she was moved to worry. If Jack couldn't keep them safe in Enid, how many would live to see their newest siblings greet the world?

Slade was nervous on the ride to Enid, wondering if he had made a serious mistake. It felt wrong, for a start, letting the Haglunds stray out of his sight before he'd placed them under guard by deputies. His worrying became worse still when Slade thought of bringing danger to Faith's doorstep through his own miscalculations.

Still, as he was covering the last three miles to town, he saw no trace of any hunters on his track. No silhouette of riders on the skyline, nothing to suggest that he was being shadowed.

And it still felt wrong, somehow.

Slade almost doubled back, then cursed himself for being stupid. The best thing that he could do was get to town, file his report, and lead a team of deputies back out to Faith's place. With the extra men and guns, Slade guessed the Danites would be forced to reconsider their assignment. Either give it up entirely, or begin to think of ways to reach the Haglunds inside Enid.

And he would be waiting for them when they tried.

Slade told himself that Faith was safe without him. She had four hands on the place, all men she trusted, armed and capable of dealing with intruders under normal circumstances. Beyond that, the Haglunds were prepared to fight, and Faith herself was no slouch with a Winchester, although Slade knew she'd never had to drop the hammer on a man.

First time for everything, he thought. And desperately hoped it wasn't true.

Three miles had never felt so long to Slade before, but mindful of the distance he'd already covered since sunrise, Slade held his roan to a trot, instead of a gallop. There was plenty of daylight remaining, ample time to speak with the judge, retrace his path to Faith's with help, and bring the Haglunds into safety in broad daylight.

Time enough to keep them all alive.

Unless . . .

The trouble with fanatics, as he'd learned from others who had tried to kill Judge Dennison, was that they weren't afraid to die. Slade had been startled when the four remaining Danites had fled their ambush site instead of standing fast and dueling with him, but he'd finally decided it was likely a strategic move. Retreat to fight another day—or later on the same day, if the opportunity arose.

Still nothing on the far horizon. Nothing when he veered off track to check three lonely trees that stood north of the wagon road. A lizard scuttled out of sight at Slade's approach, and that was all.

Could it be that easy, after all?

Slade didn't think so. He was drawing to an inside straight and wasn't thrilled with how the cards had run, so far.

He let his thoughts stray far enough off track to wonder how Faith was getting along with the Haglunds. She had cheerfully welcomed them into her home, but he reckoned the tribe could be overwhelming for someone who rarely had more than one guest at a time. Faith had been gracious, concerning their strange situation and lifestyle, but what would she *really* be thinking?

Slade knew he'd find out in due time and hoped that it wouldn't rebound to his sorrow. One man with four wives, and two of them pregnant, was bound to be startling. Faith knew he was escorting them, not joining in the strangeness, but mere contact with a group so different from "normal" could unhinge some folks—as Slade had seen in Alva and while talking to the Haglunds' hostile neighbor.

None of them were Faith, of course. If she had been like them, Slade would have wondered what his brother had ever seen in her, instead of falling into . . . what?

Why can't I say the word? Slade asked himself.

He had no answer for himself.

Reflection on his own shortcomings could be left for later, when he didn't have eleven strangers counting on him for another day of life. Make that thirteen, if he counted the unborn, and Slade was glad he'd never picked up any superstition that would make him count the number as unlucky.

For the Haglunds still might need some luck, before this day was done. And Slade suspected they were running short.

"He's by himself," said Tanner, holding out the spyglass as an offering to anyone who'd take it.

Zedek was the nearest, first to grasp the telescope and raise it to his eye. He tracked the distant rider for the best part of a minute, then passed it on.

"He left 'em somewhere," Zedek muttered, not quite making it a question.

"Must have," Hallace said, now peering through the glass.

"You're right, he must have," Tanner said. "Because we damn sure didn't stop them on the road."

None of the others could remember ever hearing Tanner swear. The "damn" he uttered was as shocking to them as if he had dropped his pants on Temple Square at home. None of them knew how to respond.

DeLaun tried first. "He's going in alone to ask for help. More marshals, or a posse."

"I imagine you're exactly right," said Tanner.

Hallace growled, "We need to find out *where* he left them."

"And be done with 'em before he brings an army back," Zedek suggested.

"All true enough," Tanner replied. "But first, let's just allow him to ride out of sight."

Their cover wasn't much to speak of, just a swale gouged in the landscape, some three-quarters of a mile south of the wagon road. It was deep enough to hide their grazing horses, with the spare that Bliss would never need again, and let them lie in grass damp from a recent cloudburst, hatless heads and shoulders raised to scan the countryside.

Not much but good enough. The lawman hadn't seen them. He continued riding past. When Tanner took the spyglass back and turned it eastward, he couldn't see as far as Enid, where the marshal'd going.

That was encouraging. It meant a ride ahead of him, and even farther back, to wherever he'd stashed the Haglunds. Tanner needed to solve that mystery, and soon, before they finally ran out of time.

"How should we do it, then?" DeLaun inquired.

"Only one way *to* do it," Tanner said. "Ride back along the way he came, looking for places where a family can hide."

"There can't be many," Hallace offered. "Specially not with the wagon and horses."

"No, I expect not."

Tanner folded his spyglass, stowed it in a pocket, and descended the grassy slope to reach his pinto. He could hear the others following before he had his left foot in the stirrup.

He calculated that they were roughly twelve miles from the point where Bliss was killed, their ambush frustrated by one determined man. The shame of it still gnawed at Tanner, giving him a sour-stomach feeling that reminds him of the one and only time he sampled coffee, feeling like a rebel as he swilled it down.

God always had the last laugh, but he wouldn't be laughing if they let the Haglunds get away somehow. The Prophet wouldn't be laughing, either, if they straggled back to Salt Lake with their mission incomplete.

Tanner swallowed the bitter gall that came from having failed the first time and determined not to make a habit of it. Twelve miles wasn't much—four hours, maybe, plus their time for searching any likely hideouts found along the way—and nothing on God's Earth would stop him from completing what he'd started with the Haglunds earlier that day.

Before they started, he told the other men, "I owe you an apology for running out on Bliss. For letting *you* run out, the way we did. It wasn't right. I've asked Heavenly Father to forgive my weakness. If we don't succeed next time, no one goes home alive."

His three companions seemed as startled by the word "apology" as by his swearing, moments earlier. DeLaun looked like he'd seen a ghost, perhaps his own. Hallace and Zedek seemed uncomfortable, making little noises in their throats and looking anywhere except at Tanner's face.

He let them off the hook, adding, "That's all I have to say. Let's go and do it right this time."

II

Slade entered Enid as he had so many times before, alone. Main Street was busy, as on any weekday afternoon. A marshal passing without prisoners in tow or draped across a saddle wasn't cause for any special comment. Here and there, a hand or hat was raised in greeting as Slade passed, but otherwise, he might have been invisible.

He couldn't blame the townsfolk. Few of them would know why he'd been sent to Alva in the first place, and none could know he'd brought the Haglunds back, fleeing from gunmen bent on wiping out the family name. Slade couldn't blame his neighbors for proceeding with the business of their lives, and yet he *did* resent the fact that they were free to look the other way, remain oblivious to strangers in distress.

He reached the courthouse, stopped in front of it, and tied his roan up to the nearest hitching rail. A bailiff smoking on the sidewalk nodded to him as Slade passed.

Inside, Slade climbed the staircase where he'd killed one of the men who'd shot Judge Dennison during the bloody courthouse raid. He couldn't see the stains, now, but he knew the spot, regardless. If they never had that kind of trouble in the court again, it would be too damned soon.

It doesn't have to be your *trouble,* said a small voice in his head, but Slade was too busy to listen.

When he reached the judge's chambers, there was no sign of the clerk. Off on some errand, filing orders or whatever. Slade moved past the clerk's small desk, approached the judge's private office, knocked, and waited for the summons.

"Enter!"

Judge Dennison was rarely taken by surprise, but now he frowned at seeing Slade before him. "Jack?" he asked, as if confirming it, but didn't wait for a reply. "I would've thought you'd send a wire if you'd resolved the case."

"Well, that's the problem, Judge. It's not resolved."

"Care to explain?"

In simple terms, Slade sketched what he had learned in Alva from the townspeople, and how the constable had sent him off to find the Haglunds.

"Mormons, eh?" Judge Dennison remarked. "I'd heard there might be some scattered around the territory. Not our problem, if they live within the law. Most of their children aren't legitimate, the way things stand, but that's a matter of inheritance, not crime and punishment."

"No, sir. But someone's out to punish them."

Slade forged ahead, from his arrival at the Haglund spread to the next morning and their flight to Blaze, then on from there to Enid, winding up with Dannell and his brood hiding at Faith Connover's house.

"And you've seen nothing of these Danites since the ambush?" Dennison inquired.

"No, sir."

"Which doesn't mean that *they* have not seen *you*."

"It's preying on my mind."

"You made a hard choice. I won't say it was the wrong one. But," the Judge reluctantly went on, "we have a problem."

"Sir?"

"While you've been gone, some other things came up," said Dennison. "The Riley gang's come back from Texas, running wild and raising Hell along the Washita. I've sent Tom Ward and Dooley Schmidt to round them up, or run them back across the border, anyway."

"That still leaves Pat and Don," said Slade.

"Unfortunately, Marshal Horn is presently in Woodward, looking into several rapes that have occurred over the past two months. An ugly business."

"What about—"

"And Marshal Kallinger is running down a rumor on Dan Clifton. We'd supposed he might have left the territory, after he was wounded in the Ingalls shooting, but it seems he's back, as well. Most likely trying to pick up with Doolin and that bunch. The so-called Oklahombres."

"So, there's no one."

"On the contrary. There's you, Jack," Dennison replied.

"I should have brought them straight in."

"You were forced to make a judgment call. I'm not inclined to second-guess it. Now, however . . ."

"Best to bring them here, as soon as possible."

"I'd say so. Yes."

"Well, then," he told the judge, "I'm on my way."

Tanner was tired—of riding, hunting, killing, take your pick—but there was no rest for the weary. He had also heard it said another way, claiming there was no rest for the *wicked*, but he couldn't place himself in that class. He was absolutely wicked, if examined in the light of man-made laws, but Tanner answered to a higher judge. His bloody work had been ordained and sanctified.

If only he could finish it.

It galled him to consider that he was just a little over halfway through his list of heretics, that so much work remained undone.

It had occurred to him before that he might not survive this mission. Bliss Kimball's death had helped remind him of the others and his own mortality. Tanner was getting old for service in guerrilla wars and was well beyond the life expectancy for gunfighters. Even if no one shot him this time, or the next, he was aware of little aches and pains, of critical reactions slowing down.

In Tanner's line of work, it only took one slip, one heartbeat of delay, to end a soldier's life.

When he was younger, he'd believed God would protect him. How could his Heavenly Father permit a loyal servant to fail? That train of thought derailed itself on the headstones of martyrs, from Prophet Smith back through the ages. Men of God—some women, too—were sometimes called upon to sacrifice themselves.

Tanner did not pretend to know the will of God. Experience had taught him to be satisfied with orders from the Prophet and the elder Saints. He did not question them, or seek the rhyme and reason for their issuance. He was a humble tool.

Sometimes a blade, employed to excise evil from the sanctified Body of Christ.

Sometimes a bludgeon, wielded against those who have been reckoned past all hope.

A voice cut through his reverie. He realized that the others had been talking for some time now, unnoticed.

"How long you reckon that he'll be in town?" DeLaun inquired.

"A couple hours, anyway," said Zedek. "Maybe more, if he can't raise a posse."

"It's already been an hour," Hallace said.

"Yeah, but he hadn't *got* to town, remember," Zedek answered.

"Where do you think Bliss is, right now?" Another question from DeLaun.

"In Heaven," Hallace said. "Where else?"

"But which one?"

The old conundrum. Joseph Smith had preached a five-tiered afterlife. Declaring that all souls will find a measure of redemption, he explained that Heaven has three tiers, ranked from the lowest to the highest as Telestial, Terrestrial, and Celestial. Before attaining any of those levels, souls were either sent to Paradise for sorting, or to Perdition— also called Spirit-Prison Hell—where the dead still had the option to repent. A person's long-dead relatives could be assisted in their journey from Perdition by the prayers of those still living who were dedicated to their soul's salvation.

Tanner had no idea where Kimball's soul has gone, or those of Weldon Killebrew and Nordell Lambourne. He was content to know that those he has dispatched to Spirit-Prison Hell would have another chance to save themselves, although they'd spurned that opportunity in life.

By killing them, he saved them from themselves.

It was a priceless gift he offered them, if only they could understand.

Something made Tanner pause, rein in, and wait. "Hear that?" he asked.

"I smell it," Zedek said.

"What is it?" asked DeLaun.

"Cattle," Tanner replied. And smiled.

It seemed a long way back to Faith Connover's ranch. Slade made that journey twice a week, on average, either to visit or to tell Faith that Judge Dennison was sending him away somewhere, in search of badmen. Usually there was time to linger over conversation, food, or private moments.

Not today.

He had to get the Haglunds packed once more and take them back to Enid by himself, without the escort he'd been counting on to ward off any more attacks. Four guns, with Draycen on the twelve gauge, Braylyn on the extra Colt. Or call it five, if any of the other wives could use the extra pistol he'd retrieved after the ambush.

Numbers weren't the main thing, though. Slade couldn't speak for Dannell Haglund, but he knew damn well that Draycen and the wives had never shot a man. There was a world of difference between just knowing how to shoot— the raw mechanics of it, from the loading of a weapon through the aiming, knowing when and how to breathe— and shooting when your life was on the line.

The trick-shot artists Slade had seen were good at drilling cards and tumbling coins, but most of them had never faced an armed man bent on killing them. They didn't have the edge required to be a man hunter. Most would hesitate at the critical moment and die.

The men who hunted Slade—who he'd be hunting, once he had the Haglunds safely under wraps—apparently fell somewhere in between the mass of ordinary people who had never seriously harmed another soul and those who stayed alive because their aim was fast and true. They were assassins, in a word, accustomed to picking off targets who were either defenseless or outnumbered, taken by surprise. Hired killers, even though Slade guessed their payment was a sermon promising them heavenly rewards.

The good news was that they hadn't shot Slade from his saddle, so far. The *bad* news was that Slade now had to wonder why.

He'd been convinced that the Danites would try for the Haglunds once more, before they reached Enid. So far, there'd been nothing, and that was what worried Slade most.

If the stalkers had seen him within rifle range, then he ought to be dead. They should have stopped him short of Enid, guessing that he would find help and sanctuary for their targets waiting there. No ambush meant the Danites either hadn't managed to catch up with Slade, or—

"Damn it!"

If they *had* seen Slade, without the Haglunds, it could mean they'd let him pass because he wasn't their primary target. They were still on track, seeking the targets they'd been sent to kill in the first place. Still searching.

And if they'd seen Slade on his own, they must know that he'd left the Haglunds someplace where he could retrieve them. Someplace between the ambush site and the point where the Danites had seen Slade alone.

If they'd seen him.

A jolt of something close to panic made him flinch. Slade couldn't swear that there was any truth behind the scene his mind was sketching, knew that his imagination might be playing tricks on him, but he could not afford to take that chance.

If the Danites had seen him riding solo, they'd be scouring the countryside for any hideaway Slade might have picked. And if they stuck to the road, it would lead them to Faith.

Slade kicked his roan into a gallop, praying to forgotten gods that he would not arrive too late.

"You like the marshal. I can tell," said Wandle June.

Faith nodded, smiling as she said, "Of course, I do. He's a good man."

"I guess he rescues people all the time." The girl seemed almost wistful as she helped Faith clear the table from their meal.

He rescued me, Faith thought, but simply said, "His job is more about locating people who've harmed others, making sure they don't hurt anybody else. Unfortunately, by the time he's called, the damage has been done."

"The men we're running from already killed our friends," said Wandle.

"I'm sorry for your loss," Faith told her. "It's small consolation when the guilty come to punishment, but it may help you put the pain behind you."

"If we're still alive."

The answer startled Faith, coming from one so young. "Of course you'll be alive," she said, feeling a twinge of guilt for such presumption, even as she spoke.

"I'm not so much afraid as sad," said Wandle. Glancing toward the parlor, where her father and his wives sat, talking quietly among themselves, she added, "Papa's done his best to make us ready for this day."

"How so?"

"He told us that the Danites could be coming for us, anytime. They never rest, he says. I've prayed for them to pass us by since I was old enough to understand. I guess God wasn't listening."

"He listens, Wandle," Faith replied. "Sometimes we just don't understand his plans."

"Why would he want my family to suffer? Or the Omans? Why'd he let them die that way?"

"I can't explain it," Faith said, honestly. "Maybe these Danites are supposed to be here, so the law can stop them."

"Marshal Jack, you mean."

"And other deputies. Judge Dennison. The law."

"There must be law in other places, where it could have stopped them sooner," Wandle said.

Faith heard her mother's voice in memory, saying, *There's nothing to be gained by arguing religion. All you'll do is lose your friends.* She longed to change the subject but was strapped for things to say.

At last, shifting by small degrees, she asked, "Who are these Danites, anyway?"

"Avenging Angels of the Prophet," Wandle June replied, as if discussing any common occupation. "They hunt people who have left the church or threaten it somehow."

"How can a child threaten a church?"

"By growing up, I guess. By having children of her own and telling them the Prophet doesn't really speak for God on Earth."

"It seems to me," Faith said, "that if he *was* God's chosen voice, he wouldn't worry about things like that."

"That's what my Papa says. His fury proves him false."

Faith didn't have to ask why no one jailed the so-called Prophet for the crimes committed by his "angels." She'd known other men who got away with murder, thanks to wealth or their alliance with selected men of power. One such man had killed her fiancé, Jim Slade, back in the days before she'd met Jim's twin and learned that feeling didn't vanish altogether just because a heart was broken.

"I think that maybe Marshal Jack is our avenging angel," Wandle said. "I reckon he was sent to help us."

By Judge Dennison, Faith almost said, but caught herself in time. Instead, she told Wandle, "He's only human, I'm afraid."

"What happens if they find us here, before he comes back with the other marshals?" Wandle asked.

Frowning at that, Faith said, "I have some other men here. They're out working on the property. They won't let anyone get through."

But Faith felt new fear kindle in her stomach, thinking, *Will they?* Her employees might be rugged men, but they weren't killers. Not like the Avenging Angels.

Not like Jack.

She didn't really think of Slade that way, but realized and accepted that he was a hunter of men. And sometimes his prey refused to be taken alive.

Faith missed him now, wished he was there, protecting her by escorting the Haglunds from her home, out of her life. That sparked a pang of guilt, in turn, making her feel ashamed.

And still, she thought, *Please hurry, Jack. Hurry!*

"There's people coming," Hallace said.

Tanner saw the riders, tiny men and horses growing larger by the second. It upset him that he hadn't spotted the strangers first, but kept his anger at himself concealed. They were still more than a hundred yards away, to the northeast, as Tanner freed the hammer of his Colt from its retaining thong.

"Keep riding, nice and easy," he instructed the others. "When they reach us, let me do the talking. And I do mean *all* the talking."

DeLaun said, "They might ask us questions."

"And I'll answer for you," Tanner told him. "Anyone not clear on that? I want your mouths stitched shut, and don't make any moves before I do."

"Suppose they—"

"Hush, DeLaun!"

The riders halved the distance separating them from Tanner's men while he was giving instructions. The one on Tanner's left was taller and thinner than the other, his long face shaded by a flat-brimmed hat. His sidekick had a stubbled jaw—not like he was trying to grow whiskers, but as if the act of shaving bored him.

Both wore pistols and had long guns snug in saddle boots. The tall one also had a knife sheathed on his belt, but Tanner didn't plan on letting him get close enough to use it.

"Can we help you gentlemen with something?" asked the taller one.

"We're doing fine," Tanner replied.

"I'll have to disagree with that. You're trespassing on private property."

He feigned amazement. "Someone owns all this?"

"That's right."

"But not you boys."

"We work here," said the shorter one.

"And part of that is keeping strangers off the place?"

"You're right again," the tall one said.

"You have a watchful eye," said Tanner.

"When it's called for," said the taller cowboy.

"Then, you've likely seen some friends of ours. They would've passed through here this morning, bound for Enid."

Tanner saw the stubbled rider cut a sidelong glance toward his friend, but the taller one missed it. He was all business, watching the strangers. Watching their hands.

"We haven't seen your friends," the tall one said. "No other trespassers come through, today."

A little tic there, at the corner of his mouth, told Tanner that the cowboy was lying. Stubble-jaw looked nervous, too. A child caught with his grubby little fingers in the cookie jar.

"Maybe your boss saw something you all missed," said Tanner. "We'll just ride along and ask him."

"No."

"You're saying we can't even *ask*?"

"I'm saying you can turn around and leave the way you came. Stick to the public road."

"You're not what I'd call neighborly."

"We know the neighbors," Stubble-jaw replied. "And you ain't none of 'em."

"I'm sorry you boys feel that way," said Tanner.

And he drew while he was still speaking. He shot the taller cowboy in the chest from ten or twelve feet back, then turned his pistol on the shorter target, catching him still in the first flush of surprise.

The second shot was hurried, with the cowboy groping for his pistol. Tanner saw the bullet strike—a lung shot, painful but survivable—and now the cowboy was hauling on his grullo's reins, turning, as if to flee.

A third shot echoed over flat land, but it wasn't Tanner's. As the shorter cowboy tumbled from his saddle, Tanner turned to see DeLaun with gun in hand, stone-faced and pale.

The taller cowboy, first to fall, was still alive. His dapple gray had bolted, bound for home without him, but the stricken man was not convinced that it was his time to die.

Tanner holstered his Colt, dismounted, and drew his own belt knife. They'd made too much noise already, as it is.

"Them horses will be home before you know it," Hallace said.

"I only need a minute," Tanner told him, stooping lower with the knife.

The last mile in to Faith's house was the worst. Slade kept expecting gunfire, every time he passed a boulder or a stand of trees, then felt a letdown when it didn't come. It kept his nerves tight strung and twanging, like piano wire.

None of Faith's hands rode out to greet him, either, but Slade knew they were spread thin and guessed that they ignored him half the time, even if they were watching from a distance. If they knew the boss's private business, they were also smart enough to know that interfering wouldn't win them any points—and might just get them fired.

If Slade had been a stranger, though . . .

Then what? he asked himself. Four hands weren't nearly enough to patrol Faith's ranch against intruders while doing their own full-time jobs. He knew the men would challenge any trespassers they met, but slipping past them likely wouldn't be the hardest thing professional assassins ever did.

Slade urged his roan to a near gallop for the last half mile, feeling a great swell of relief at the first sight of Faith's house, smoke rising from the kitchen stovepipe, rather than the doors and windows. He had pictured tragedy and found them cooking supper.

Gratefully, he slowed the roan, entered Faith's dooryard at a walking pace. A moment later, Faith was standing on the porch before him, Dannell Haglund coming through the open door behind her.

Slade was angry at himself over the sudden, stupid pang of jealousy he felt. The last thing on the Mormon's mind right now was looking for another wife. And Faith would not have bought the package under any circumstances. Still, Slade supposed it must be normal for a man to feel somewhat inadequate beside another who could satisfy four women at a time.

Wiping that image from his mind as he dismounted, Slade heard Faith ask, "Are the others coming soon?"

"Nobody's coming," Slade replied. "The other deputies are all out on assignment. I'm what's left."

"What do we do now?" Haglund asked.

"Pack up," Slade said, "and head for town while it's still daylight."

"But the Danites—"

"May have lost our trail," Slade said, not sold on that idea by any means. "The only thing we know, for sure, is that they didn't jump me on the way to town or coming back."

"Because they want my family, not you," Haglund replied.

"Let's say you're right. I won't argue the point," Slade said. "What's the alternative? The judge's other deputies aren't coming back for days. Some of them may be gone for *weeks*. The longer you sit still out here, beyond the reach of any help, the more likely you are to find yourself surrounded."

Haglund was still mulling over that thought when Faith said, "Jack! Look there!"

He followed her slim upraised arm to the west, where a riderless horse was approaching. Slade noted the saddle, with rifle in place, and rode over to meet it. The dapple gray's rump bore Faith's brand.

"One of yours," he announced, as he reached for the reins, led it back toward the porch.

"It's Smoky," Faith said. "Handy's favorite."

Slade knew Faith's foreman, Handy Cartwright, well enough to greet in passing. He was competent and then some, but the rider wasn't born who'd never fallen from a horse at some time.

But if Handy'd fallen off . . .

Slade saw the blood, then, smeared across one side of Handy's saddle and streaking the horse's right shoulder. The animal's skin was unmarred, otherwise, with no trace of a wound.

Handy's blood, then.

"Oh, God!"

Slade thought Faith had seen it, but glanced up to find her staring past him. Turning with his right hand on his Colt, he saw a second horse—this one a grullo—coming back without its rider.

"Quick!" he told them. "Back inside the house!"

Finding the other lookouts wasn't difficult. The pistol shots attracted them, one after the other. First came a lanky cowboy mounted on a snowflake Appaloosa, cautiously approaching with his Winchester in hand.

Tanner already had his Henry rifle drawn and took his first shot at a range of eighty yards. He winged the rider, nearly made him drop the Winchester, but nearly wasn't good enough. Hallace and Zedek fired before Tanner could pump the Henry's lever-action, one or both of them on target, and the rider plummeted from his saddle to the unforgiving ground.

The next and last cowboy to face them was an olive-skinned vaquero who'd have been more at home in Texas, maybe somewhere even farther south. He saw them, recognized trouble on the hoof, and was reversing his direction when a round from Tanner's Henry drilled him from behind, between his shoulder blades. Against all odds, the dead or dying rider didn't fall. They watched him gallop off toward home, slumped over his perlino's neck, arm's dangling free.

And twenty minutes later, they were staring at a farmhouse, barn, corral, outbuildings—all the trappings of a large, successful spread. Tanner couldn't see the Haglunds' team or wagon from his present vantage point, but instinct told him that his prey was close at hand.

And fate confirmed it, when he saw the lawman moving from the barn, back toward the house.

"I've got him," Hallace said, already squinting over rifle sights.

"No," Tanner told him, reaching out to push the weapon's muzzle down.

"He's *right there*!" Hallace argued.

"And he isn't going anywhere," Tanner replied. "None of them are."

"More waiting?" Zedek asked. "Seems like we've done enough of that, already."

"We're committed here," Tanner assured him. "But there's still a smart way and a stupid way of doing things. Stupid is rushing in before we're ready, getting all shot up before we even have the targets spotted."

"*He's* a target!" Hallace answered. "He's the one killed Bliss, in case you don't remember."

"And we'll settle up for that in good time," Tanner said. You bear in mind why we were sent. Remember the priorities."

"We've lost him, anyway," DeLaun observed. They look in time to see the front door of the farmhouse close behind the lawman.

"No one's lost," Tanner replied. "No one gets out of here unless we let them, and that won't be happening."

"That marshal's been to town and back," said Zedek. "Who's to say there won't be others coming out to join him?"

"Do you think they'd send him back alone, to wait?" asked Tanner.

"How should I know?"

"Use your noggin," Tanner said. "And watch the sky."

It was nearly dusk, losing daylight by the minute. Shadows growing long around the house and other buildings set before them.

"If they had help coming," Tanner told the others, "it would be here. All we need, now, is a little patience and the night."

12

"I'm scared," said Posey Haglund, sniffling on the verge of tears.

Wandle slipped an arm around her younger sister's shoulders and pulled her closer on the rancher lady's sofa. "There's no cause to be," she lied.

"The Danites found us," Posey answered, stubbornly refusing to be comforted.

"They haven't yet. But if they do," said Wandle, "that's *their* problem. Marshal Jack and Pa will make them sorry that they ever bothered us."

"When can we go home, Wandle?"

"I don't know. Be quiet now. Try not to worry."

That was poor advice, but what else could she say? The Danites frightened anyone who knew a thing about them, and the thought of them lurking outside, watching and waiting as the sun went down, gave Wandle chills.

The bad news, first. She knew that they were trapped and going nowhere, for tonight, at least. The grown-ups tried to keep it quiet, but she also knew that four of Faith Connover's men were missing now. Two horses had returned without their riders, and the other pair of men who worked the place were running late. Wandle did not expect to see them. Not alive, at any rate.

The only good news: Marshal Jack had made it back from town alive and well, past any Danites lurking on the road. Of course, he'd come alone and had arrived too late to get them out before sunset.

Nobody's perfect, Wandle thought.

So, there they sat, behind latched shutters, with the lamps turned down and barely burning. Marshal Jack said it was better for night vision, something Wandle understood from peering out of lighted rooms into the dark. She guessed that Jack was also hoping for the little ones to fall asleep and pass a peaceful night.

Until the killing started, anyway.

Wandle felt tears spring to her eyes and wiped them surreptitiously, hoping that no one else would notice. Posey nudged her with an elbow, whispering, "It's okay if you're scared. I won't feel so alone."

"You're *not* alone," Wandle replied. "We're all scared, in our own way. All but Marshal Jack."

"Don't he get scared?"

"It's *doesn't*, and I don't believe he ever feels a lick of fear. How could he go out chasing bad men all around the country, if he's frightened?"

"Papa worries," Posey said. "I hear him talking to our mommies."

"Well, of course he does. He has to think about all kinds of things. Us children, and the ones to come. Our mothers. Work around the farm."

"Not anymore."

"We'll find another place," said Wandle, as she dabbed another tear. "Papa will build it better than before, and we'll all help. You wait and see."

"Not if the Danites get us," said Posey.

"And I told you, Marshal Jack and Papa won't allow that. You should trust me. Have I ever lied to you?"

A quick headshake. "I trust you, Wandle."

But I'm lying now.

A surge of shame made Wandle's stomach clench, threatened to bring her supper up, but fourteen years had taught her that some lies were mandatory in polite society, no matter what the Bible said about bearing false witness. No one on Earth would have any friends if they always spoke the unvarnished truth. A simple question like "How are you?" would unleash a torrent of complaints that drove people away like skunk fumes.

Lying to her little sister at the moment was an act of mercy, Wandle thought. The plain truth might drive Posey to hysterics, and what good was that for anyone?

If they were bound to die here, at the rancher lady's house, at least Wandle could do her best to help her younger siblings face death bravely. She would need a weapon if the Danites came inside, or if her family was forced into the night. Something to fight with, that would wound her enemies.

A gun would be the best thing. Marshal Jack and Papa had their rifles. Draycen had the shotgun. Mother Braylyn carried Papa's six-gun. The sister-wives had quietly discussed who ought to have the pistol Jack had taken from the dead Danite, deciding Mother Tennys was the best shot of the three.

That left the big gun, what they called a Sharps, propped up beside the front door. Wandle knew she couldn't take it without being seen and thought she likely couldn't aim it, anyway.

What, then?

The rancher lady's kitchen offered an array of bright, sharp knives. Wandle had seen them earlier, and knew exactly where to find them. All she needed was a moment unobserved.

"Where are you going?" Posey asked, as Wandle stirred.

"To get a drink of water from the kitchen. I'll be right back."

"When we get our new house," Posey said, "I hope we have a pump inside."

"Tell Papa, and I bet he'll get you one."

"I'm getting sleepy, Wandle."

"Good. I hope you have sweet dreams."

"Sorry about your men," Slade said.

"It's not your fault," Faith answered, barely whispering, trying to let the Haglunds rest if that was even possible.

"Who's is it, then?" asked Slade. "I brought this trouble to your doorstep; now you're caught up in the middle of it. That was foolish, and it's wrong of you to let me off the hook."

"I do believe that's my decision," she replied.

"You're too forgiving."

"Count your blessings, mister."

Slade was forced to smile at that. "I have been," he informed her. "Now, I've put them all at risk and can't see any way to make it right."

"I guess we'll have to wait and see what happens, Jack."

"By that time—"

"Ssshhh." She pressed a finger to his lips. "It's not like you to worry."

"Sure it is," he said. "I worry all the time."

"I've never seen it."

"That's because . . ." He stalled, ran out of words.

"Because of what?" Faith prodded him.

"Because when you're around," Slade said, "I feel like everything will be okay."

"I'm right here, Jack."

"Proving that I was wrong," he said. "I stepped in something, and I've tracked it home to you, instead of dealing with it somewhere else."

"You did what you thought best for all these innocents," Faith said.

"Well, I thought wrong. And who's to say they're innocent?"

"They're children!"

"Not them," Slade replied. "I mean their so-called parents. Putting that religious mumbo-jumbo first, before their kids, and knowing all the time that this could happen."

"Would you say the same if they were Catholics or Baptists?"

"Faith, if they were Catholics or Baptists, they'd be safe at home right now. We wouldn't know the lot of them existed. And your men would be alive."

"We'll be all right."

When Slade made no reply to that, she asked him, "What about Judge Dennison? He was expecting you to fetch them back this afternoon. He must be worrying, right now."

"That doesn't help us. If he had a man to spare, they'd be here. We'd have taken these folks out of here on time."

"And if the Danites were already here," Faith said, "they would have found me all alone."

"Jesus! You see the mess I've made?"

"So, now the judge knows something must have stopped you coming back. What will he do?"

"What *can* he do? Ride out here in a buggy with his cane?"

"Can't he deputize some men from town?"

"He has the power," Slade replied, "but that takes volunteers. He can't snatch people off the street and shove them in the line of fire."

"You must have friends in Enid," Faith said. "I do."

"I have friends who say hello in passing, or make time to play a hand of poker. Anyone who might risk dying for me wears a badge, and they're all otherwise engaged."

That silenced Faith for half a minute, then she said, "All right. We'll have to deal with it ourselves."

"It means killing," he said.

"In self-defense."

Slade nodded. "I was thinking more of the mechanics than the morals. If you've never shot a man—"

"As you well know," Faith said.

"There's two things to remember," Slade pressed on. "First, speed's important, but it's better to be accurate than fast. Unless you're close enough to touch your target, take your time and aim."

"Not *too* long," Faith replied, half teasing him.

"Dead center, if you can," Slade said, not seeing any humor in their situation. "Squeeze the trigger then. Don't jerk it."

"Jack, I know all this."

"It's not the same with people as with cans and bottles."

"I've been hunting."

"Deer and rabbits don't shoot back."

Faith took his hand and squeezed it. "I won't let you down," she said. "I swear."

"I never thought you would," Slade answered, knowing where the blame lay, even if Faith wouldn't let him shoulder it alone.

Four gunmen, waiting somewhere in the dark outside, were prepared to kill for God. Slade swore a silent oath that even God could not protect them if they laid a hand on Faith.

"We gonna get this done or what?" asked Hallace Pratt.

"We're getting there," Tanner replied.

"They're all inside the house," said Zedek Welch. "Let's flush 'em out."

"Thirteen inside," Tanner reminded him. "And how many guns?"

"I wouldn't know."

"Then you're a fool to rush in blind."

Tanner felt Zedek fuming, didn't have to see his face to know his cheeks were mottled red. He kept them waiting for another moment, peering at the farmhouse from concealing darkness, then began to speak again.

"Two Winchesters we're sure of and a shotgun. Haglund had a pistol when he left the farm. The lawman has another. Figure they got Bliss's sidearm and the Sharps. We know the hired men carried guns. Who wants to bet there's no more in the house?"

"What does it matter if they've got a hundred guns?" asked Hallace. "Half of them are children."

"Children fighting for their lives, and two or three of them, at least, grown-up enough to shoot." Tanner let that sink in, before he said, "Fact is, we could be going into this outnumbered two to one."

"You want to quit? Is that it?" Zedek asked.

"Nobody's quitting anything," Tanner replied. "I mean to see it through *and* live to finish off our list. I can't do that by letting some kid drop me just because I'm in a hurry."

The others settled into restless silence, then. Tanner continued studying the house and outbuildings, imagining what tactic may work best to force his prey outside, or help his men gain access to the house.

He didn't like the fiery wagon ploy this time. There were two wagons on the property—the Haglunds' and another, no doubt the rancher's—but neither was positioned close to any kind of flammable supplies or to the farmhouse. Tanner's dwindling team would risk more than they stood to gain by any repetition of their tactic from the Oman spread.

Firing the barn or stable was an option, but it seemed the horses had been moved into an open paddock, clearly visible from several windows of the house. Tanner did not believe the lawman or his host would send the Haglunds out to save an empty building.

What else?

A hostage would be useful, but he didn't have one. Only

two things he could think of might incline someone to leave a building under siege: a shortage of water or a call of nature. Tanner saw a privy near the bunkhouse that the rancher's hired men wouldn't be needing anymore, but its remove from the main house suggested the landowner had built one of the newer septic systems. And if there was plumbing in the house, it meant the occupants had water, too.

Tanner could feel the night slipping away from him. And who could say what the new day would bring?

The marshal had had no luck recruiting possemen in town that day, but Tanner took for granted that his boss—a judge, most likely, or some kind of prosecutor—would be working on that problem through the night. Help might arrive at any time, but it was more likely after sunrise, when reinforcements could see what they were doing and who might be trying to kill them.

Dark work was best performed in darkness, anyway.

"I want you three to work your way around the house," he said, at last. "Surround it. Pick your fields of fire, and make sure that you won't be hitting one another when I start the party."

"We're just gonna try and shoot 'em through the walls?" asked Zedek.

"Do what you're told. Don't fire until you get my signal."

"Which is what, again?" asked Hallace.

"The start of Armageddon."

"And you're doing what, exactly?" asked DeLaun, the quiet one.

"I'm working on the details," Tanner told them. "Get a move on, now. Be ready when it happens."

They slunk away through darkness, single file, taking the long way to surround the house. Watching them go, Tanner wondered if he had sent them to their deaths. He still had no ideas for how to crack the house, no glimmer of a plan. Something would come to him, but would it be in time?

Hoping for inspiration, Tanner turned and scuttled through deep shadows, toward the barn.

Judge Isaac Dennison was worried, and his second glass of whiskey hadn't helped. He checked his pocket watch against the wall clock in his chambers, found their times identical as always, and admitted to himself that something had gone wrong.

Faith Connover's property line lay three miles north of Enid, a fair hour's ride if the horseman was taking his time and letting his animal walk at its own normal pace. Slade wouldn't have been idling when he left the courthouse, headed back to Faith's after his talk with Dennison.

Say twenty minutes at a trot, then. Maybe fifteen, at a steady gallop. Coming back, he'd have to slow down for the wagon filled with people—call it two or three miles per hour, unless they were whipping the team into a lather.

Unless they were met and stopped on the way.

He pictured Jack Slade dead, an exercise he practiced with his deputies across the board. They led a rugged life, dealing with killers and the dregs of so-called civilized society day in, day out. The life expectancy of U.S. marshals in the Oklahoma Territory wasn't anything to brag about. Nine killed within the past two years alone, and twice that many wounded in the line of duty. Dennison began anticipating each new marshal's death the day he donned a badge.

And he avoided making friends with any of the men who might be killed as a direct result of following his orders. As it had been during military service in the war, so it remained in the endless struggle to tame a frontier. Commanders who fraternized with their troops bred disrespect and opened themselves up to heartbreak.

Granted, Slade was special. He had tracked, identified, and punished the fanatics who had tried to murder Dennison himself not long ago. Before that, he'd unmasked a

family of killers who'd eluded justice for the best part of a
quarter century—and, in the process, he'd stopped what
could have been a new Indian war. The list went on, but
Dennison was in no mood to reminisce.

If Slade was lying dead somewhere along the road to
Faith Connover's spread, Judge Dennison would mourn him
briefly, then begin the process of identifying, capturing, and
executing his killers. Assuming that any survived.

Jack Slade had a way of settling such matters himself.
He wasn't a hair-trigger lawman, like some the judge had
known and driven out of service for abusing their authority.
Slade delivered most of his prisoners alive and fit for trial,
but when the chips were down and there was no alternative
to deadly force, he didn't hesitate.

The Mormon angle of Slade's latest case had taken Judge
Dennison by surprise. He'd been expecting something more
mundane: a range war in the making, or a squabble between neighbors that had ended in blood. Religion might
confuse the issue, but the law made no allowances for personal beliefs where murder was concerned.

The judge had watched a preacher hang three years ago.
No one in Enid had suspected that the parson lusted after
one of his parishioners, until the woman's husband turned
up dead, knifed in an alley on a Sunday night. There'd been
a witness to the stabbing, though—a stable hand returning
from an evening at the saloon, but still sober enough to
recognize the pastor of his church. The witness couldn't
stop himself from weeping when he testified, but Dennison
had shed no tears as he pronounced the sentence, or when
he had seen it carried out.

Some people claimed there was a higher law than any
codified by man. Judge Dennison was undecided on the
subject, but he knew one thing beyond all fear of contradic-
tion: only man-made laws restrained the worst impulses of
humanity within the Oklahoma Territory, and their proper
execution was his sole concern.

Tomorrow, at first light, he would begin to knock on doors—twist arms, if necessary—to collect a posse for the ride to Faith Connover's ranch. He feared what they might find but was prepared to deal with it.

As for tonight, Jack Slade was on his own.

"There's someone in the barn!" said Wandle June. "I see a light!"

Faith moved to join the girl, peering through slits cut in the shutters on a window facing eastward, toward the barn and stable. Sure enough, faint light was visible inside the barn, moving, as if someone had lit a lamp and turned its wick down low.

Slade was beside her seconds later. Faith could feel his warm breath on her neck as he bent down to take a look outside. She took the opportunity to touch his arm, then cautiously withdrew her hand.

"Could it be one of your men?" Braylyn asked.

"I doubt it," Faith replied. "We should have heard them riding in."

"And heard the others shooting at them," Dannell Haglund said.

Even with two men obviously dead, Faith had allowed herself to hope that Guy McElwain or Pat Fluett had survived to ride for help. Their horses hadn't come home yet, but that proved nothing. In a corner of her mind, she'd thought the news that they were trapped, cut off, might stir someone in Enid to coordinate a rescue effort. Now, at last, she let that notion die.

"It's just a barn," she said. "I don't care if they burn it. Jack, you have to promise me you won't do something foolish just to save an empty building."

"I never strive for foolish," he replied. "But we need to do *something*."

"Like what?"

"I'm still thinking."

"I could go out and talk to them," Dannell suggested.

"I don't think they're in a talking mood," Slade said.

"You may be right," said Haglund. "But you wouldn't be here, if it weren't for me. They followed me from Utah with a score to settle."

"Not just you," Jack said. "You need to mind your people."

"That's exactly what I'm doing," Haglund said.

"Then think about the Omans for a minute," Jack suggested. "No one at their place got out alive. These lunatics aren't hunting single men. They're killing families. You think they'll ride away and leave a dozen witnesses because you sacrifice yourself?"

"Give me another choice."

"Stay put awhile," Jack said. "We'll need you if they storm the house. Worse comes to worst, you can go out and let them shoot you later."

"If you have a plan—"

"I'm working on it," Jack assured him. Turning back to Faith, he said, "I need to be outside."

"Jack, no!"

"Don't worry," he said, smiling. "I don't have an ounce of martyr in me."

"Out there, it's four to one against you," Faith reminded him. "Together, we can beat them."

"Haglund's got a point, about just sitting in a cage and waiting for the ax to fall. They've done this kind of thing before. I can't afford to let them call the shots."

"They'll shoot you down before you clear the porch," she said, feeling a hard lump in her throat, eyes stinging with the first onset of tears.

"I won't be going out the front door," Jack replied.

"What? How—" She had it then, immediately feeling foolish. "Through the cellar?"

"It's our best shot."

"But—"

"Bearing in mind the way they like to play with fire," he interrupted her, "I'd fill some pots and pans with water, just in case. Help keep the others busy, too."

"I hate this!"

"I'm not loving it, myself," Jack said. Then he added in a whisper, "I prefer it when we don't have all this company."

That almost made her smile.

"You *will* be careful," Faith demanded.

"It's my middle name."

"Is not. But make-believe it is."

"I've got a fair imagination."

"I remember."

"I'll be going, then," he said. "Don't open up for anyone, no matter what they say."

Faith didn't understand at first, then realized that Jack was warning her he might be captured. Swallowing the fear that sparked inside her, she replied, "I won't."

"And if you have to run for any reason, go out shooting. Hear me? Aim to kill, and put the bastards down."

Tanner assumed his prey could see him from the house. He'd left the barn door halfway open, and the lantern cast a pale light, even with its wick turned down as far as possible. He hoped the lawman might be lured out to face him, but he wasn't counting on it.

He was trying to devise a plan.

The others had begun to doubt his leadership. He knew this and could hardly fault them for it, since their ambush of the Haglunds had turned into a shameful rout. He wondered if they would respect him more in memory than presently, if he had stayed behind and died fighting the marshal.

Useless speculation, now. He needed to reclaim their confidence and loyalty by thinking up a plan to drive the

Haglunds and their two protectors from the house or else destroy them in their hidey-hole.

But how?

The lamp he held could be his weapon. He could rush the house and fling it high onto the roof, shatter its reservoir of kerosene, and set the shingles blazing. He would probably be shot in the attempt, however, so he kept the notion in reserve. A last-ditch scheme.

Another possibility: begin to shoot the horses in the paddock. Not to kill them, but to *wound*, and let their squealing torment those inside the farmhouse. Tanner was not cruel by nature—or, at least, he didn't think so—but there was a chance the rancher might emerge to halt the slaughter.

One *slim* chance. An outside chance at best.

Not for the first time, Tanner wished that he'd kept one of the rancher's men alive. Make *him* squeal, and they'd have a better shot at drawing someone from the house. He'd played that game before—a girl, five years ago, in Arizona— and had been successful, if you didn't count the nightmares afterward.

The rancher's cattle came to mind, glimpsed only once and from a distance, passing by, but it was too late to round them up and turn a stampede toward the house. His three companions likely couldn't find the herd at night, much less control it, and the Haglunds might relocate in their absence. Lay an ambush of their own and turn the hunters into prey.

It was looking grim. Only the lamp available, if Tanner couldn't come up with something better in a hurry. He'd already lost another day, and now the night was slipping through his hands like smoke.

Which gave him an idea.

The Haglunds might be trapped, but they weren't starving. Tanner smelled their supper cooking, earlier, and he could still smell wood smoke rising from the chimney. If he could scale the roof, or have one of his soldiers do it, it should be a simple thing to cap the chimney, fill the house with smoke, and flush its occupants outside like honeybees from an endangered hive.

It was a simple law of nature: even die-hard smokers needed oxygen. And if they couldn't breathe *inside* the house, they'd have to take their chances *outside.*

Possible defenses? Once the smoke had started backing up, someone could always douse the fire, but that was likely to produce more smoke, in the short-term. Tanner couldn't be sure the plan would work, but if he managed to coordinate his men, lay down some fire to keep their shooters near the windows and away from the fireplace, he had a chance.

Better than charging at the house and being cut down on the run, he thought. How shameful it would be to come this far, accomplish so much for the Prophet, and be slain in such a stupid manner with the mission incomplete.

Tanner owed more than that to his faith and his Heavenly Father.

Searching now for a specific item, Tanner feared he might not find it, but at last the lamp's faint light revealed a ladder, propped up in the farthest corner of the barn. He hurried to it, tucked it awkwardly beneath his left arm, then remembered he must douse the lamp before he left the barn, to keep from being shot down in the doorway.

Even in the dark, he ran a risk, but with his plan now firmly fixed in mind, Tanner was ready for the challenge. He regretted sending the others on ahead of him, and had to find them now and sketch his plan, coordinate their roles, but even the relentless tingle of frustration motivated him now.

Poised on the threshold, half expecting to be killed before he clears it, Tanner drew a deep breath, gripped the ladder as a drowning man might clutch at flotsam from a sinking ship, and dove into the night.

13

Slade had to stop and tell the Haglunds what he had in mind, so none of them would think that he was sneaking out to save himself. The last thing that Faith needed in his absence was a panic in the ranks.

They all had questions that he couldn't answer: When would Slade return? How did he know the plan would work? What should they do if, God forbid, he didn't make it back? Slade tried to keep their hopes up, fended off Dannell's request to tag along and help, and caught Faith smiling at him with a raised eyebrow when Wandle rushed to hug him in the kitchen doorway.

Women. Never mind the age, they always took him by surprise.

A door beside the kitchen pantry opened to reveal a flight of stairs descending steeply into darkness. Slade paused long enough to light a lamp and double-check his Winchester, then started down into the pit. He'd only seen Faith's cellar once before, retrieving some preserves for a late breakfast, but he still recalled its earthy smell and claustrophobic feel.

Tornadoes were a fact of life in Oklahoma Territory, striking damn near anytime they felt like it, with no apparent season to confine them. Any rancher with a lick of sense had one or more storm cellars on his property, accessible at momentary warning. It could mean the difference between survival and rebuilding from the rubble or a screaming death.

Faith Connover had gone the normal hideaway one better. Guessing that a flattened house could block the kitchen exit from her storm cellar, she'd had a tunnel dug ten feet below the surface of the ground, trailing away some thirty feet to the southwest and coming out inside a tool shed set beside her chicken coop. If *that* blew down, pushing the boards aside would be a relatively simple job, compared to crawling out from underneath a shattered house.

They hadn't talked about it, but Slade would've bet his life she'd never thought about the tunnel as a means of slipping past a siege.

Another case of live and learn.

It was the *living* part that posed a challenge at the moment.

There was no door to the tunnel's mouth, downstairs, only a dark hole in the earth, shored up by wooden beams. Slade had to stoop a little as he entered it, holding the lamp in front of him with his left hand, Winchester in his right.

Shadows retreated from his lamplight, then closed again behind Slade as he moved along the tunnel. Three or four years after its construction, the passageway still had a moist and cloying earthy smell about it, giving Slade a foretaste of the grave. He knew it was secure, but still imagined sudden tremors bringing the roof down on top of him, stealing his last breath in stifling darkness.

How much farther?

Slade cursed himself for failing to count his own footsteps. Pausing, he turned back to face the way he'd come but couldn't see the tunnel's entrance, since he'd left no light behind him in the cellar. It was easy to imagine that the earthen tube ran on forever, leading him away from Faith and toward some fate that he could not imagine.

Slade shrugged that sense of doom away and started plodding forward once again. Each step brought him a little closer to the shed and his next problem. When he reached it, when he raised the wooden hatch that was a portion of the tool shed's floor, would he be staring into gun sights? Was a Danite waiting there to finish Slade, before he had a chance to move against the others?

No.

If he'd believed that, then the wisest thing would be to turn around, retrace his steps, and join Faith and her guests in defending the house. Die there, beside her, instead of ending his life in a grave someone else had dug for him.

There was no reason he could think of for the Danites to be lurking in Faith's tool shed. It might serve for cover, but the shed possessed no windows and wouldn't let them watch the house. Perhaps a sniper might conceal himself *behind* it, but he would be wasted crouching in the dark inside.

So, he would keep his promise, being careful when he raised the hatch, making as little noise as possible. If no one shot him right away, it should be clear for him to stand inside the shed, listen for any sounds of men close by, then creep outside to take the Danites by surprise.

One step at a time, Slade reminded himself, silently. He had to get out of the tunnel first, before he started looking for a fight.

Another step, and suddenly he saw a short ladder in front of him, planted in dirt, its top rung snug against a wooden trapdoor.

Thinking through the moves ahead of time, Slade stepped up to the ladder, placed his right foot on the bottom rung so that he couldn't lose it, then blew out his lamp and set it down so there would be no stray light to betray him. He reached up overhead, felt for the hatch, and raised it slowly, inch by inch, into a pitch-black void.

Dannell Haglund wished he could pace the floor, burn off some of the nervous energy that made his ears ring and his skin feel like a swarm of ants was crawling over him, but he was stationed at a window facing into darkness, looking for a target.

Anything at all would do, as long as he could vent his rage on one of those who'd turned his nearly perfect life into a kind of Hell on Earth.

The good news, he supposed, was that his worst fears had been realized. For years, he'd lived in dread of facing retribution from extremists in the church he'd left behind, had warned his wives and schooled his children to beware of strangers, trust no one, check constantly for shadows coming up behind them.

Now, the shadows had arrived and taken solid form. They'd left his family homeless and were still intent on killing any Haglund they could reach. It was the worst time of his life, by far surpassing the embarrassment of excommunication and exile.

But now, at last, he had a chance to *fight*.

Dannell was wracked with guilt over the choices he had made, the hardships he'd inflicted on his family, but they had built a life in Oklahoma Territory, had offended none but the self-righteous bigots who enjoyed taking offense at disparate beliefs. Now, that quiescent life had been destroyed, and Haglund meant to punish those responsible.

Unless they killed him first.

That was entirely possible, he realized. Jack Slade was trained at hunting men, but Dannell didn't share that skill. He'd never fired a shot in anger, but he trusted his paternal love and instinct to make up for any shortcomings in that regard. Whoever tried to harm his wives and children had to deal with Dannell Haglund first.

Which, he supposed, would be exactly what the Danites had in mind.

"Are you all right?" Faith Connover asked him in passing. She was making rounds, the rifle in her slim hands seeming badly out of place.

"I'm fine," Haglund replied. "And you?"

"A little nervous, I suppose."

"Only a little?"

"Well . . ."

"Did Marshal Slade get out all right?"

"He's out," Faith said. "I can't say whether he's all right."

"No shooting, though," he said, trying to reassure her.

"No."

"You have a good man there."

"I think so, too."

As she moved on, Dannell glimpsed Wandle, sitting with her younger siblings near the fireplace. Watching him—or was she watching Faith? Her rush to hug the lawman as he left had startled Haglund, but it wasn't something that required attention at the moment.

He could always deal with puppy love tomorrow, if tomorrow ever came. If they were still alive to see another sunrise.

Dannell knew it was wrong to wish hardship on others, much less pray for their demise, but he could not help sending up a silent prayer to Jesus, asking for the opportunity to smite his enemies, the strength to put them down and *keep* them down.

And if his prayer was answered? If they won this fight? Then what?

The Danites were like ghosts—or like the hydra, in old tales of Hercules. Cut off one head and two appeared to take its place, both venomous and deadly. Killing four Danites would not erase the threat that colored every waking moment of his life and haunted Haglund's dreams.

He could change names, of course. That wasn't difficult. But hiding three spare wives in a monogamous world would not be so easy.

Another problem for tomorrow, he decided, drawing his inspiration from Matthew 6:34: *Take therefore no thought for the morrow: for the morrow shall take thought for the things of itself. Sufficient unto the day is the evil thereof.*

And there would be more evil, soon.

Dannell could feel it in his bones.

"The roof, you say."

Tanner could hear the resistance in Zedek's voice. He nodded and said, "That's right."

"Cap off the chimney," Hallace said, "and smoke 'em out."

"Exactly."

"What's to stop them shooting anyone who tries it," Zedek asked, half whispering.

"Look at the house," Tanner replied.

"I'm looking at it!"

They were crouched together at the southwest corner of the bunkhouse, having slaughtered its inhabitants that afternoon. The farmhouse stood about two hundred feet southeastward, silent, mostly dark.

"At the corner, there," said Tanner, pointing, "just across from us, they have a blind spot. Once you've covered half the distance, more or less, no one can see you from the windows off to either side."

"Why me?" Zedek demanded.

"Why not?"

"Hallace is faster on his feet!"

"Says who?" Hallace replied, angry.

"I'll do it," said DeLaun.

They all stared at him for a moment. Tanner asked him, "Are you sure?"

"Why not?" DeLaun replied.

"Okay. We'll keep them busy."

"One thing," said DeLaun.

"What's that?"

"What should I use to block the chimney?"

Tanner saw the flaw in his design. "Wait here," he said and scuttled toward the bunkhouse door, which faced westward, away from the farmhouse. The door wasn't locked, but it was dark as a coal mine inside. He groped around, bruising his knees and one hip on assorted bits of furniture before he found a rumpled bed. Stripping a blanket from the mattress, he retreated to join the others, folding it along the way.

"Use this," he said, handing the folded blanket to DeLaun.

"You'll cover me?"

"I guarantee it. Give us time to spread out," Tanner said, "then make your move when we start shooting."

"Right."

"Good luck," said Hallace, reaching out to pat DeLaun's shoulder.

"You'll do all right," said Zedek, sounding sheepish.

"Come on, now!" snapped Tanner.

As they left DeLaun alone, Hallace whispered, "I never woulda thought he had it in him."

"We surprise each other every day," Tanner replied.

He dropped off Hallace first, beside a chicken coop located on the south side of the house. The birds inside were sleeping—for the moment, anyway.

"Remember," he told Hallace. "Not a movement or a sound until you hear me fire. Got it?"

"I hear you."

"If it takes five minutes or an hour, *wait for me*."

"I *said* I heard you!"

Tanner left him angry, hoping it would make him more alert. He moved on, trailing Zedek, till they reached a point facing the northwest corner of the farmhouse, where an oak provided fair cover.

"Did you hear what I told Hallace?" Tanner asked him.

"Sure I did."

"Same word to you. I want you quiet as the grave until I fire the first shot. Got it?"

"Yep."

Tanner left Zedek crouching in the shadows, skirted the house, and kept on circling toward the barn. He'd come full circle now and had a clear view of the front porch, ready when targets started emerging in a swirl of smoke.

But first, he had to cover for DeLaun. Give him a chance to plant and scale the ladder without being gunned down in the yard. If he fell, there'd be no second chance at executing Tanner's plan. Nothing for them to do but storm the house with three men both outnumbered and outgunned.

Cover fire was tricky. It should be enough, but not too much. Buy time for Allred to approach the house and start his climb, but don't leave any other member of the team with empty guns that need reloading at a crucial moment. Tanner's Henry rifle held sixteen rounds in its magazine, one in the chamber. He could spare six, maybe seven, with enough left over for the job he has in mind.

Adults first, concentrating on the ones with guns. When they were down and the rest were helpless, Tanner and his men can hunt the children at their leisure, finish them like chickens as they scattered aimlessly.

He cocked the Henry, sighted in on the nearest shuttered window, drew a breath and held it as his finger tightened on the trigger.

Faith ducked and spun to face the nearest window as a bullet drilled its shutters, followed half a heartbeat later by the echo of a gunshot from the yard. She reached the window in a crouching run, gripping her Winchester with force enough to blanch her knuckles. Rising when she reached the wall, trusting the heavy lumber there to stop a slug before it reached her, Faith rose slowly, leaning toward the window for a look outside.

"Watch out!" Dannell Haglund called after her, just as more bullets struck the house, coming from three sides now. Faith heard a gasp from one of Haglund's women, then the younger children started squealing in alarm.

"Stay calm!" Faith urged them, trying not to use an angry tone. She knew they must be frightened, but the racket from outside was bad enough without a wailing chorus from her living room.

"They're up to something," said Dannell, after he risked a peek outside. Faith followed his example, picked out muzzle flashes from the darkened yard, but saw no gunmen moving toward the house.

"Trying to draw our fire?" she asked.

"Could be. Or keep our heads down, while they move in closer."

"Jack said that only four of them are left."

"Three firing," Haglund said, "means one of them is free to move."

Faith did the calculation swiftly, understanding that diversions were intended to *divert* attention. If their enemies were firing from north, east, and the south, it had to mean—

"Look to the west!" she snapped, already moving as she spoke. Whatever was about to happen, whether it involved some penetration of the house or setting fire to it, she knew where the attack would come from.

Dannell passed her at a gallop and pressed his face against one window where no slugs had penetrated, staring into darkness. "Nothing here, that I can see," he said.

Faith left the living room, opened her bedroom door, and rushed inside, seeking its westward-facing window. She and

Jack had watched the sun go down from there on more than one occasion as they—

"Anything?" asked Haglund, from behind her.

"Not as far as I can tell," she answered.

But there *was* something. A scraping sound against the eaves, beyond her line of sight, and then . . .

"There's someone on the roof," Haglund declared, craning his neck to stare up at the bedroom ceiling.

Faith could hear the footsteps now. No doubt about it, there *was* someone walking on the roof above her head. Haglund reared back, aiming his rifle as he tracked the sound.

"No, wait!" she said. "I have an attic. You won't hit them, shooting from down here."

"How do I get up there?" asked Haglund, speaking through clenched teeth. Clearly, the wailing of his children grated on his nerves.

"This way."

Faith led him to the central hallway, pointing to a trapdoor in the ceiling. Haglund couldn't reach it, leaping from a standing start. He growled and sprinted for the dining room, returning moments later with a chair.

"I'll have to shoot holes in your roof," Dannell said, as he set down the chair and stepped onto its seat.

"You mean, *we* will," Faith answered. "To hell with the shingles!"

"Yes, ma'am."

But she let him go first, opening the trapdoor and pulling down the ladder that gave access to the attic. Faith imagined that the footsteps on her roof were louder, with the hatch open—or maybe they were simply drawing closer.

Going where?

She didn't know, and had no time to ponder it. There was a stranger walking on her house, who meant her mortal harm. That was enough for Faith to blast him off by any means available.

Dannell went up the ladder, struggled for a moment as

he swung his weight into the attic, rifle in one hand. Faith watched as his legs and feet vanished. She followed him without a moment's hesitation, only wishing that she'd worn the shirt and trousers that comprised her daily working uniform around the ranch, instead of an ungainly dress.

Too late for wardrobe changes now.

Grabbing the trapdoor's lip with her free hand, Faith scrambled up and through it in a swirl of skirt and petticoats, arriving just as gunfire thundered in the dusty attic space.

"Wandle, what's that noise?" asked Posey.

"I'll find out," Wandle replied. "You wait right here. Don't move a muscle, understand?"

"I want to come with you!"

"Keep still! The Danites hear you when you squeal."

Wandle felt instant guilt, but swallowed it, pinning her younger sister with a glare and pointed finger that she hoped would keep her down behind the sofa. They'd been lying there together when the shooting started, then stayed put when it had stopped as suddenly as it had begun.

Now there was something else. A noise . . .

Feeling a trifle foolish, even with the risk of being shot if she stood upright, Wandle crawled between the living room and kitchen, glancing backward frequently to make sure Posey didn't follow her. The mothers and her other siblings were distracted by their fear and by the silence after gunfire that suggested worse to come.

Her papa and the rancher lady had gone down this hall together, while the shooting from outside was still in progress, but neither had returned. Wandle felt momentary panic, fearing that she'd find them both sprawled dead in pools of blood, but how could that be? Gunmen firing blindly through the window shutters couldn't possibly kill two people that way.

Could they?

The wooden floor was hard on her palms and knees. Wandle supposed she would have bruises, but it hardly mattered. She and all her family could die at any moment. What was being black and blue compared to that?

And if Pa was killed already . . .

No! Don't even think it!

Creeping down the hallway, she was startled by the vision of a ladder dangling from the ceiling. Even more surprising was the sight of Faith Connover's skirt and left foot vanishing into that ceiling, through some kind of trapdoor.

Wandle's former home, outside of Alva, hadn't had an attic, but she understood the term and recognized what she was seeing. What she *couldn't* figure out was why the rancher lady would be crawling up into the attic now, when every gun and pair of eyes was needed to defend the house.

And where was Papa?

Before her mind could grapple with that question, Wandle heard the clomping sounds of footsteps, echoing from somewhere overhead. At first, she thought it must be Faith, or possibly her father, walking in the attic. Then, she realized the noises came from higher up.

Someone was on the roof!

It wasn't Marshal Jack. He'd gone out through the kitchen, somehow, underground from what she'd overheard. He wouldn't reach the roof by crawling through a tunnel. Any fool could see—

The Danites!

Wandle clapped a hand over her mouth, to keep from sobbing. If the killers had a man atop the house, with others covering the sides, there would be no escape. No hope.

Tears stung her eyes, and Wandle found it hard to breathe. She rose without a plan in mind, was reaching for the ladder, maybe thinking she could spend their last few minutes with her father, when more gunfire echoed through the house.

Louder this time, reverberating through the attic, coming

through the open trapdoor in the ceiling. And before her ears quit throbbing from the first shots, Wandle heard a voice raised in the living room.

"Look! Smoke!"

She would've sworn it was Moroni, even with the note of panic that she didn't recognize. More gunshots from the attic, but she turned and ran back toward the living room, arriving to find gray smoke spilling from the fireplace, billowing into the room.

"They've blocked the chimney," Draycen said. He crouched beside the fireplace with their father's shotgun, fanning at the clouds of smoke, but flames and choking fumes prevented him from looking up the chimney.

"Damn it all to Hell!"

The curse, coming from Draycen, startled Wandle June nearly as much as the attack itself. She had no time to think about it, though, as Posey ran to meet her, coughing, bleary-eyed, and threw small arms around her waist.

"Wandle!" she sobbed. "I'm choking!"

Wandle pulled her sister down, telling her, "Lay flat on the floor. Smoke rises to the ceiling, first. Stay calm. The house is *not* on fire. It's just smoke from the fireplace backing up."

"But—"

"No buts! Breathe, don't talk! And don't you dare stand up unless I say so!"

Slade knew the tool shed's door should be in front of him, no more than two long strides from where he stood . . . but what if he was wrong? What if one of the Danites was nearby and heard him blundering, rattling the implements that hung from pegs on three of the four walls?

He stood still for another aching, endless moment, eyes closed, picturing the shed's interior as he'd last seen it in full daylight. Slade couldn't remember *why* he'd gone into the shed and didn't care. It was the view that mattered to him at the moment.

When he had it in his mind and had reversed it to accommodate the fact that he'd been facing *inward* last time, toward the shed's rear wall, Slade saw the tools dangling in place. Off to his left, there should be shovels, rakes, and hoes. At his right hand, various hammers, saws, and other implements of carpentry. Behind him, axes, scythes, and other cutting tools.

He half turned, stretched out his left hand, and felt a curved blade brush his fingertips. A sickle. Moving cautiously along the line, fearful of making any noise, Slade found an ax and gripped its smooth handle, lifting it up and out to free it from its pegs.

A silent weapon, chosen for a moment when it might be suicide for Slade to fire a shot.

But now, both hands were full. He had to tuck his Winchester beneath his left arm, ax gripped in his right hand, as he took two cautious steps to reach the tool shed's door. Its simple outside latch had shown a tendency to drop, if a breeze shut the door while someone was standing inside, so Faith had drilled a hole and tied a leather thong around the outer bar, so no one could be trapped.

Slade found the thong and pulled it gently, fearing that the wood might scrape or squeak. It didn't, and a moment later he could feel the door move when he gave it a first, cautious shove. Two inches, to start, then farther when no one loomed up to attack him.

The flurry of gunshots had stopped, but what did it mean? Slade thought the firing hadn't lasted long enough for anyone to breach the house, but nagging doubts were unavoidable. He pictured Faith, wounded or cowering before gunmen, and fought the urge to rush blindly ahead, regardless of the risks involved.

I fail, she dies, Slade thought and took his time.

He stepped into the night, braced for a confrontation, finding none. Slade paused to ease the shed's door shut behind him to avoid it flapping, set the latch, and then moved on.

Hunting.

Slade couldn't place the source of gunfire that he'd heard seconds before he left the tunnel, but they'd stopped now, at least for the moment. The renewed silence had an eerie effect, raising the short hairs on Slade's nape, setting his teeth on edge.

It all came down to locating the Danites, now. He'd do no good for Faith or the Haglunds unless he could locate and take down the men who intended to kill them—and him. The sooner he got started, the better off they'd all be.

Even so, Slade stood beside the tool shed for another moment, looking toward the house. He breathed in gun smoke, heard the muffled sounds of frightened voices from inside, and saw a hunched form on the roof, etched in shadows cast by pale light from a quarter-moon. Someone was crouched beside the chimney, likely covering its flue to fill the house with smoke.

Slade couldn't reach the Danite on the roof except by shooting him. Before he took that step, he needed to discover where the others were. Another anxious moment showed him something—someone?—huddled near the chicken coop, some twenty yards off to his left.

Slade moved in that direction, planting each step carefully, afraid that scraping dirt or crunching gravel would betray him. When he'd halved the distance, he could smell the Danite's nervous sweat, made out the profile of his high-crowned hat, a moonbeam glinting on a rifle's barrel.

Closer.

When he still had fifteen feet to go, Slade paused and stooped to set his rifle on the ground. He needed both hands for the ax, although it went against his grain to leave the gun behind. An unexpected shot, just now, could be as fatal for the man who fired it as the one on the receiving end.

Three strides, each one in grim slow motion. Slade was

frightened to breathe, in case his target heard and turned to face him with his Winchester. His only edge in this show-down would be surprise—that, and the sharp blade of his ax.

At last, Slade stood behind the Danite, lungs aching for oxygen, ax raised about his head. He focused on the sniper's hat, allowed for the resistance it would offer and the air inside it, as he brought his weapon slashing down.

14

Tanner could see DeLaun Allred on the roof from his place near the barn. It was clear that he'd capped off the chimney, since smoke had stopped rising above it, but someone inside had marked DeLaun and they had been giving him Hell.

The first shots were muffled, from where Tanner stood, but he could hear them better when the cover fire slacked off to silence. Glancing up to track the sound, he watched De-Laun dancing on the ridgeline of the roof and realized bullets must be snapping at his heels.

Frustration seethed in Tanner, but there was nothing he could do about it. Smoking out the Haglunds was his best option, but it would take some time. He imagined a parlor or living room filling with wood smoke, the women and children beginning to panic before someone calls out to douse the fire or close the chimney damper. *Do something, for heaven's sake!*

He was counting on their inexperience with killing

confrontations—fear, confusion, fatal panic—to defeat them.
Every second spent inside the farmhouse from this moment
onward would be grating on their nerves, reminding them
that they were surrounded, that their enemies controlled the
world outside their fragile hiding place.

Tanner used those idle moments to reload his rifle, taking a chance with the process, since it required him to open
a loading sleeve at the muzzle end of the Henry's tube magazine. A gamble, yes, but no one burst out of the house during the minute while he was feeding rimfire cartridges into
the gun.

Up top, DeLaun had done his job and was retreating
toward the ladder planted at the northwest corner of the
house. He was halfway there when Tanner heard the muted
sound of two shots fired almost as one, inside the house.
DeLaun let out a yelp, grabbed for the left cheek of his
buttocks, then he was tumble-sliding down the long slope
of the roof, out of control.

Tanner could only stand and watch him plummet to
the solid, unforgiving ground below. His landing made a
grimace-worthy sound, and Tanner waited to see if DeLaun
was alive and conscious.

Aching moments passed before the fallen Danite stirred,
then struggled to all fours, testing his limbs like an elderly
hound roused from sleep against its will. When Tanner saw
that he could move, his focus shifted to nearby windows.
DeLaun wasn't in a blind spot anymore, although it might
be difficult to see him if he stayed low to the ground.

Tanner wished that he could bark out orders, but he
feared drawing attention to his injured man. The Haglunds
and their benefactors must know someone had fallen from
the roof. They couldn't have missed his bumping, rolling
passage, maybe heartened by his downfall, looking for a
chance to finish him.

DeLaun had managed to collect his wits, crawling along
the north wall of the house, dragging a left leg that refused

to participate. Tanner couldn't evaluate the wound from his position, and he was not equipped to treat a shattered hip or something similar, in any case. If DeLaun had been shot, the best thing he could do was stay out of the way until the battle was won, and then . . .

Then, what?

If he'd been ass-shot, Tanner guessed he couldn't mount or ride a horse. He certainly couldn't *walk*, and even if he'd tried, would only slow them down unbearably. Of course, there was still a chance he wouldn't survive his injury.

Particularly if he had a little help.

It pained Tanner to harbor such a thought, but he was responsible for the success of his appointed mission and for those selected to assist him in completing it. No individual could be allowed to sabotage that goal, either deliberately or by accident.

Against the odds, DeLaun reached the corner where the borrowed ladder stood, no longer needed, and continued crawling. Would he creep on through the night, until he finally ran out of steam and bled to death? Tanner decided to let him go and track him later, when the killing work was done.

He would have time to spare, then. More than ample to dispatch another soul.

Slade helped himself to the dead Danite's pistol and Winchester, leaving the ax where he'd dropped it, blade glistening red by starlight. He was surprised the killing hadn't turned his stomach, just a little, but he'd cut enough lives short that only the technique held any novelty.

And anyone who threatened Faith was lucky to receive a quick end, relatively clean.

Slade felt a little awkward, carrying a rifle in each hand, but he could always drop one if he had to use the other in a hurry, and he didn't feel like leaving firearms on the battlefield for other enemies to come along and use against him.

It crossed his mind, belatedly, that he could probably have stunned the Danite with the butt of his ax. But then what? Slade had no handcuffs or rope with which to bind a prisoner, and guarding one meant letting three more roam at will. He couldn't risk that, *wouldn't* risk it. Not with Faith and all the Haglunds counting on him to protect them.

One down. Three to go.

And one of them, it seemed, was presently retreating from the house, moving on a collision course with Slade.

At first, he thought the prowler was an animal. Low to the ground, lurching along on all fours like a crippled-up coyote, only bigger. Finally, faint moonlight helped him recognize another black-clad gunman, whose attempts to rise and walk were hampered by a game leg trailing in the dust.

Slade moved to intercept him, knelt to place himself eye level with the enemy, and set his captured rifle on the ground beside him, freeing both hands for his own Winchester.

When the struggling shooter was fifteen feet distant, Slade called to him softly but audibly, "That's far enough."

The Danite's head snapped up to face Slade, but his hat brim kept the moon's faint glow from picking out his features. That was fine with Slade, who watched the gunman's hands instead.

There was only silence from his opponent, other than the wheezing of his labored breath. The Danite had both hands pressed flat against the ground, an awkward pose for any kind of fast draw, but that didn't mean he would surrender without trying.

When he spoke at last, the other man said, "You should ride out, Marshal. Save yourself."

"That's not about to happen," Slade replied. "You're down by one already, fading fast."

Slade guessed the Danite must be glaring at him, but if so, the energy was wasted. His round face was nothing but a patch of shadow, underneath the high-crowned hat that seemed to be part of a standard uniform.

And when he made his move, it had a kind of sad determination to it, even though he must have known it was a futile gesture. Shoulders shifting to the left, letting that arm support his weight, the right hand swinging back to reach his holster.

All too little and too late.

Slade didn't have to aim the Winchester at that range. One squeeze of its trigger, and the flat crack of the shot echoed across Faith's property, rebounding from the house. Slade's bullet ripped into the Danite's shadow-hidden face and flipped him over on his back, legs twisted underneath him in a posture that would probably be painful, if the man had still been alive to feel it.

Two down, and he was halfway home.

Slade grabbed his second rifle, moving fast, in case the other Danites homed in on the sound of his gunshot. He wanted to confront them on his terms, if possible, without letting them flank him in a pincers movement.

But above all else, he had to take them down.

Dannell Haglund flinched when the gunshot rang out, then relaxed a bit when no bullet struck the farmhouse. He was standing at the bottom of the attic ladder, Wandle June beside him, keeping eyes averted as Faith Connover descended.

"Where did that come from?" Faith asked him, as she set foot on the floor.

Dannell could only shrug. "Outside somewhere."

"Maybe it's Marshal Jack!" said Wandle June.

Dannell thought he could see a shadow cross Faith's countenance as she heard that but knew he might have been mistaken, standing in the hall with only dim light showing from the living room.

Faith sniffed the air and said, "That's smoke!"

"They've blocked the chimney," Wandle told her. "Draycen's got the damper closed, but still . . ."

Dannell could hear his wives and children coughing, hacking in the smoke. He moved in that direction, knowing he should do something, uncertain what that *something* ought to be.

The first thought in his mind, herding the lot of them outside, would be a fatal error. There were two exits from the house—the front door and a side door from the kitchen—but a fool could see the Danites meant to smoke them out. Which meant they would be covering both doors, ready to fire when either one opened.

No.

But what was the alternative?

Faith's voice cut through Dannell's confusion. "Get everyone to the back of the house," she commanded. "We can shut the bedroom doors and put sheets down to keep the smoke out. Hurry!"

Dannell wasn't used to taking orders from a woman, but he did as he was told and gratefully. Returning to the smoky living room, he fanned the air with his hat, telling his family, "Come on! We're moving to the back, where there's clean air."

They followed him, as always, without question. Braylyn led the way, still carrying the pistol she had yet to fire, while Tennys trailed the children, making sure they all kept up to speed. Dannell went on to grab the big Sharps rifle from its place beside the front door, then turned back to find Faith watching him, a lady warrior standing guard.

He passed her, moving down the hallway, letting Faith bring up the rear. They'd left the attic ladder down—no point in raising it again while they were in the midst of fighting for their lives—and Faith remained beside it for a moment, covering Dannell's retreat.

"I doubt they'll try the doors yet," he suggested, pausing at the entrance to a bedroom where two of his wives and four children were waiting for him. The rest were peering through the doorway of a second room, next door.

"You're likely right," Faith said, "but when we don't come out, they're bound to risk it."

"I'll wait here, then," said Dannell. "You go on back."

"It's my home, Mr. Haglund," Faith replied, using a tone that brooked no challenge. "Your place is with those who need you."

"Well . . ."

"Go on, now," she insisted, still not facing him.

Unsure of what else he could say or do, Dannell retreated, closed one bedroom door after he gave its occupants a reassuring smile, then stepped into the second, pulled the door shut after him, and mouthed a silent prayer.

Zedek Welch was getting scared. He reckoned something had gone badly wrong with Tanner's plan, and now he couldn't find anyone to tell him it will be all right, that everything was still proceeding on its normal course.

And that would be a lie.

He'd seen DeLaun Allred drop from sight on the roof, dodging shots from the people inside. So far, Allred hadn't reappeared, and Welch couldn't decide if that was good news or bad. Had he been shot or fallen off to break his neck, or was he still in place and waiting for the fireplace smoke to drive their targets out from hiding?

Sometime after DeLaun's disappearing act, Zedek heard one more gunshot. That unnerved him, made him wonder if it was Tanner's signal for more firing at the house, but he delayed another moment and heard nothing more. His nervousness increased by the second, till Zedek felt like he wanted to jump out of his skin.

It would be easy, in the darkness and confusion, just to sneak away, retrieve his horse, and ride like fury, bound for parts unknown. He doubted that Tanner would be much inclined to search for him, and with a fair head start it didn't worry Welch, either way.

The thought of never going home to Utah, now, that was something else entirely. For he knew that if he ran now, he must keep on running. From the Prophet, from the church, and from his family.

At last, he set out looking for advice, making a slow, wide circuit of the house. Zedek kept hoping that the Haglunds and their lawman would come pouring out, let Welch and his brothers finish what they were bound to do, but he had no such luck.

Where were the others? By the time he rounded the north end of the house, Welch had seen no sign of DeLaun on the roof or lying on the ground below it. That was good news, at least, proving he hadn't been killed up high and hadn't tumbled to his death or crippling injury. But where had he gone?

Zedek moved toward the chicken coop where Tanner had stationed Hallace Pratt, before they started giving cover fire for DeLaun's big adventure on the farmhouse roof. With any luck, he'd find Pratt still in place—maybe with Tanner, too—and he could find out just exactly what is going on.

If not . . .

What would he do, if he'd been left alone somehow?

It's not that, Welch told himself. *It can't be.*

And he was right. Coming around the backside of the chicken coop, he spotted Pratt right away. Hallace was lying prone, facing the house. A shooter's posture. But . . .

What was that thing sprouting from his hat, as if it had taken root inside his skull? At first, DeLaun believed it is a trick of moonlight, some strange shadow, but a moment later he was close enough to nudge Pratt's boot and hiss his name.

"Hallace!"

No answer. And how could there be, when someone had

left an ax planted in Pratt's skull, handle pointed toward the stars?

"Sweet Jesus!"

Welch clapped a hand over his mouth, to spare himself from any further blasphemy, then spun away to vomit wretchedly. He'd seen much worse than this, had done worse, but the vision of a sometime friend cut down that way was literally more than he could stomach.

When the spasm passed, and he had overcome another urge to run, Welch spent several moments wondering who could have slaughtered Hallace. It couldn't be Allred or Tanner, unless one or both of them had gone insane. He wondered if the Haglunds had escaped, somehow, but saw no evidence suggesting it. They would be fleeing through the night with children screaming, if that was the case.

Another mystery.

Feeling exposed and vulnerable, Welch took another look at Hallace . . . and decided what must be done. Tanner would likely call it foolish, but they were getting whittled down with his plan and had nothing yet to show for it.

Holding his breath, biting his tongue against another gag reflex, Zedek wrapped his left hand around the curved haft of the ax. He gave a tug, disgusted by the grating sound it made, but couldn't budge it.

Cursing now, with no thought for his Savior, Welch put his rifle down and used both hands on the ax, bracing a foot on Hallace's right arm for leverage. Finally, after a monstrous heave accompanied by sucking sounds, the ax came free, blade dripping.

Feeling dead inside, Zedek scooped up his Winchester and left Pratt to the scavengers, setting a straight course for the side door of the farmhouse.

Faith heard a *thump* and cocked her head to listen for another. When it came, she almost flinched.

"There's someone beating on the door," said Wandle June, wide-eyed.

Which had to mean the kitchen door. Faith knew from prior experience that knocking on the front door should sound softer and more distant from the bedroom that she occupied with Braylyn and Vonelle, Wandle, and the two younger Haglund boys. Next door, Dannell and Draycen were on guard over Alema, Tennys, and the younger girls.

Faith weighed her options, made her choice. "Wait here," she told the others, hand already on the doorknob, while her right foot pushed aside the rolled-up sheets they'd used to stop smoke coming in beneath the door.

"No, wait!" cried Wandle June. "You can't go out there!"

"Someone's trying to break in," Faith said. "I have to stop them."

"But—"

"No buts. One of you put the sheets back, lock the door behind me, and don't open it again unless I speak to you by name."

"I'm coming with you," Braylyn Haglund said, the heavy Colt rock-steady in her hand.

"Your children need you here," Faith said. "It should be fine, if I stop lollygagging."

And with that, she left them, closed the bedroom door softly behind her, blinking in the hallway's smoky atmosphere. She had been right to pull them from the living room. The smoke had thinned as it passed through the house, leaving the dead fireplace, but it still stung her eyes and made Faith want to cough.

Fighting the urge, Faith made a beeline for the kitchen, where the pounding noise was loudest, echoing throughout the house with no other sounds to compete. Arriving at the kitchen entrance, she peered cautiously around the corner, teary-eyed from wood smoke, and flinched backward as an ax blade pierced the outer door.

Already there were half a dozen gashes in the tall door's upper panel, splinters of wood scattered across the floor inside. Faith's first impulse was to retreat and find a safer hiding place, but she could not allow intruders to invade her home.

Get closer.

She advanced on tiptoes, careful to avoid a squeaky floorboard near the stove, holding her rifle with the stock braced tight against her shoulder. She fought the need to flinch at each new blow against the door.

It's already ruined, so a few more holes won't hurt.

Next time the ax struck home, she fired, aiming above and slightly to the left of the exposed blade, gambling on the Danite being a right-handed man. Faith was rewarded with a grunt, and then a heavy weight was hurled against the door, scraping and sliding down its length.

She fired twice more, spacing her shots, and finally heard something—someone?—hit the ground outside. Faith ducked behind the cast-iron stove, expecting gunfire in return, but nothing happened.

One down?

She could only tell by opening the door, and Faith was not prepared to gamble that much. She would wait, instead, and damn the thinning smoke. No one would pass this way unless they killed her first.

And Faith was a survivor.

Amren Tanner crouched in darkness, waiting for the gunfire to resume. When nothing happened after three long minutes, he began to worry. There was still no sign of anyone emerging from the farmhouse, and he realized that his plan had failed.

It was time to find his men and try a new approach. Where smoke had failed, perhaps flames would succeed.

Tanner slipped back into the barn and found the lantern

where he'd left it, cooling just inside the door. He lifted it, shook the lamp beside his face, and heard kerosene sloshing around it its font. Half full, perhaps, and Tanner deemed it plenty to start a good fire.

He left the barn, dark lantern dangling from his left hand, the Henry clutched in his right, circling back toward the point where he'd last seen Hallace crouching by the chicken coop. From there, they would move on to fetch Zedek, then make their final move against the Haglunds and their ill-advised defenders.

As for DeLaun, well . . .

By dawn, the house would be in ashes, all of those within it slain. And long before a rescue party found them, Tanner's party—three or four, depending—would be long gone, riding toward their next stop, their next targets. They were shorthanded, but enough of them remained to acquit themselves with honor and complete their mission.

Maybe.

Or, if all else failed, to die in the attempt.

Tanner found Hallace moments later and thought at first, incredibly, that Pratt was sleeping at his post. A closer look revealed the truth and sent a fear jolt through his body.

Pratt was dead, but how? Tanner bent closer still, removed the flattened hat, and saw the ruins of a cloven skull. He couldn't decide which was more troubling in that instant: losing yet another member of his team or wondering exactly how and when the deed was done.

He stiffened, pivoted in a circle, braced for someone to come leaping at him from the darkness. Who? The lawman? Dannell Haglund? Someone else they'd missed among the rancher's hired men?

Tanner couldn't say, and he had no more time to waste. He had to locate Zedek and finish off their business here while two of them remained.

But, moments later, Tanner saw that he was too late. A

human form lay huddled near a side door to the farmhouse.
Dressed in black like him, it must have been Welch since
he'd seen Allred hobbling off into the night. There was no
point in calling out to his last soldier. Tanner had experience with corpses, and knew no living man could twist his
limbs that way and lie immobile in the dust for any length
of time.

"Goddamn you!" Tanner muttered, and forgot to ask his
Savior's pardon in that moment, as his hope ran out like
water swirling down a bathtub's drain. "Goddamn you all
to Hell!"

He fumbled matches from his pocket, dropping several,
retaining one. It was all he needed. Kneeling before the barn
lamp, Tanner plucked its chimney off and tossed it aside,
hearing it shatter on impact. He lit the wick, then dropped
the burning match. Picking up the lantern in his right hand,
he held the Henry rifle in his left.

Rising, making no further effort to conceal himself, he
set off toward the house.

Gunfire from the east side of the house had brought Slade
running back from the direction of the barn, where he'd
been hunting Danites in the shadows. It was Hell, knowing
there must be two gunmen at large somewhere around Faith's
home but being clueless as to any plans they might have made,
or even whether they would stick together. He'd found two of
them, more or less by accident, but Slade knew that the
odds in favor of continuing that streak were slim to none.

He again heard shooting, this time with a rifle. Worse,
the sound was muffled just enough to let Slade know that it
had issued from inside Faith's house.

If the Danites had broken in—

Slade reached the southeast corner of the farmhouse,
edged around it with his rifle leveled from the hip, and

saw the dark form of body sprawled outside the kitchen doorway. Black garb told him it was yet another Danite, evidently shot while trying to break through the door.

Which only left one still alive.

Slade didn't get his hopes up. Finding one man in the dark, with no place to begin his search, might prove more difficult than finding two.

Slade was about to go and check the latest casualty, make sure that he was in fact a corpse, when something drew his eyes off to the left. At first, he thought it might have been a firefly, but he could recall seeing no others since he'd left the tunnel.

What then? It was there and gone, but—

No! Where first a fleeting spark had shown, now there was steady light. Not strong, but clearly visible. And levitating now, from what he judged to be ground level, stopping when it got to shoulder height.

Slade had no fear of ghosts, wasn't convinced that they existed anywhere on Earth, and least of all in Faith Connover's barnyard. He was looking at some kind of lamp, held by a living man.

A man who was advancing toward the house.

Slade tracked him with the Winchester, afraid to move and make the Danite pitch his makeshift firebomb sooner than he planned. The other side of waiting, though, was an increased risk that a hasty pitch might reach the house and set the roof or wall afire.

Mouthing a silent curse, Slade moved to intercept the final hunter. When he stood between the lamp's glow and Faith's home, some thirty feet from where a dead man blocked the kitchen door, he called out to the lone survivor, "Stop right there! Turn up the lamp, then set it down. I need to see you drop your weapons."

The approaching figure stopped, but otherwise made no move to comply. A dry, rough voice replied, "The sinners must be purified by fire."

"Your 'purifying' days are over," Slade informed him. "This is where you make your last big choice."

"I have a duty to my Prophet and my God!"

"And you can tell the judge about it when we get to Enid. In the meantime—"

With a roar, the Danite charged. Slade saw his arm drawn back to hurl the lamp and took his shot. His slug ripped through the gunman's right shoulder, mangling the joint and forcing him to drop the lamp. It fell behind him, shattered, spraying fire across the Danite's back and legs.

The snarl of battle turned to screaming, as the tall man threw himself about, slapping at hungry flames, dropping his rifle in the process. Slade rushed forward, smacked him hard across the face with his Winchester's stock, then dropped beside the burning prostrate form and rolled it through the dirt, extinguishing all traces of the fire.

A snuffling grunt told him the man was still alive. Slade plucked a Colt and long knife from his belt, tossing them out of reach, then dragged the wounded Danite clear of any other flames.

"Jack!" someone called out behind him, and he knew Faith's voice at once. A moment later, she was kneeling in the dirt beside him, Winchester in hand, kissing his cheek before she turned her full attention to the singed and bloodied figure on the ground.

"Is he the last of them?" she asked.

"The very last," Slade said.

"He's breathing."

"Guess my aim was off, this time."

She kissed him once more, rising. "I'll go find some bandages," Faith said. Turning toward the house she continued, "I want this bastard fit to ride by morning."

15

"I must say, you surprise me, Jack."

Slade saw the bare suggestion of a smile on Judge Dennison's face, there and gone in a flash, almost before it could register.

"Why is that, sir?"

"Consider," Dennison replied. "You're under siege, two days of being harassed, stalked, and ambushed. You're responsible for—what? a dozen lives?—and cut off from anything resembling aid. You've killed two men, undoubtedly in self-defense, and still you manage to arrest the third."

"For all the good it's done," Slade answered, sounding out of sorts.

"Oh, it will do a *world* of good," Judge Dennison replied. "Granted, he isn't talking yet."

"And likely never will," Slade said. "The gibberish I got from him last night, I'd say he's either crazy or committed to go down alone."

In fact, aside from spouting scripture when it suited him, the Danite had said nothing. Slade had yet to learn his name.

"I've had a thought, concerning that," said Dennison. "It's possible our prisoner may help us without meaning to."

"Can't say I follow that."

"This case is what Hearsts and Pulitzers among us call *sensational*," said Dennison. "Assassinations with religious overtones, fanatic cultists, unsolved mysteries. I wouldn't be surprised if it attracted notice nationwide. In point of fact, I plan to guarantee it."

"How, sir?"

"I've already wired a couple of the major newspapers," Dennison said. "Does that upset you?"

"No. I'm just not clear on how it helps our case."

"We don't need any help with this one," Dennison replied. "I'll have your testimony and Miss Connover's. Presumably some of the Haglunds', too?"

"Yes, sir. I spoke to them about it."

"Well, then. There's no question that our prisoner will be convicted. As to the specific charge, we'll have some difficulty proving murder, since you foiled his efforts with the only living witnesses. Call it attempted murder, thirteen counts, and he'll get life."

"But still—"

"Meanwhile," said Dennison, "the press will make this case a cause célèbre from coast to coast. They read papers in Salt Lake City and environs, I believe."

"And when they do . . ."

"Someone, I think, will wish to guarantee our prisoner's continued silence. If he's hanged, their worries will be over. But a man confined for life may try to save himself. He may consider an official offer to reduce his sentence if he tells all and cooperates in prosecuting those who pulled his strings."

"Unless I read this fellow wrong," Slade said, "he won't fall for it."

"That's the beauty of my plan," Judge Dennison replied. "He doesn't have to fall for anything. I'll simply indicate that he's been offered leniency, perhaps suggest that he's *considering* a deal. It ought to do the trick."

"And when more Danites come to shut him up—"

"We bag them. Start the game again, if none of them will crack. Sooner or later, one will have a weakness. Then, we'll know the man or men behind this bloody business, and I'll see *them* in the dock."

"You'll be inviting trouble, sir."

"Inviting it to contain and destroy it," said Dennison. "I have a lower tolerance for zealots than I used to."

That was understandable given the judge's history, but Slade thought he saw a weakness in the plan.

"I'm thinking that if someone sends more Danites from out west, they may not make it by the time our boy's shipped off to Leavenworth."

This time, the judge *did* smile. "Justice is sure in my court, Jack," he said. "But it's not always swift. We have to let the poor man heal before he's tried. Then, even when he's been convicted, there's the matter of appeals to settle."

"Don't they normally go on to prison while that's in the works?" asked Slade.

"Indeed, they do. But this case isn't what I'd call a *normal* one, by any means. It may be under scrutiny by the Supreme Court of the land before it's over. I won't have it said that anyone was judged precipitously or imprisoned without due process of law."

Slade got it, now. The nameless Danite could be sitting in a cell downstairs for weeks or months, while Slade and the rest of Judge Dennison's marshals took turns watching out for his cohorts, waiting to grab anyone who came snooping around.

"I see," Slade said. "And what about the Haglunds?"

"Oh, they're free to go, as soon as we wrap up the trial. Meanwhile, we'll keep an eye on them, make sure they aren't harassed in any way or made into a spectacle."

Slade wondered where they'd go from here and decided he could ask them when he saw them next. But first, he had another stop to make.

"I'd like to see the prisoner," he said. "Make sure he's settling in."

"Of course," Judge Dennison agreed. "Maybe he'll have a change of heart and tell you what we need to know."

Slade doubted that, but nodded as he rose and left the judge's chambers, moving toward the stairs that served the cellblock in the courthouse basement.

Amren Tanner wasn't quite immune to pain, but faith in Jesus and the Prophet went a long way toward assuaging it. His shoulder ached, but from a distance, almost as if it he was feeling someone else's wound, by way of psychic processes. The burns on Tanner's back, buttocks, and legs were superficial, thanks to the quick action of his enemies. They'd saved his life—and all for what?

To hang him at their pleasure, he supposed.

And so be it.

He would die without saying another word, unless the urge to quote scripture enveloped him. On no account would he identify his fallen soldiers or incriminate the men who'd sent him on his final mission in the first place. They could rest assured on that score, though the heavens fall.

What troubled Tanner now was not his fate, but rather the appointed means of execution. Hanging did not suit him, as a true believer in the purity of blood atonement.

He had sinned, of course. All men were sinners from the moment of their birth, bearing the Curse of Eve, but Tanner's sin was worse. He did not think of killing heretics as a transgression, since he'd done it under orders from the men who spoke for God Almighty. But the failure to complete his final mission was a lapse for which he must atone.

And how?

His captors, naturally, had allowed him to retain no weapons. Even Tanner's belt had been removed, although if he'd desired to hang, he'd simply linger through the farce they call a trial and let the heathens do it for him. When they brought his meals, he had a spoon, but they retrieved it without letting him have time to grind a cutting edge on brick and mortar.

Determination was the key. Tanner had known that from an early age, schooled by his parents first, and then by Porter Rockwell for the task that would become his long life's work. No soldier of the Lord could last without commitment and determination to succeed—or, failing that, to expiate his failure at all costs.

There was no one to miss him, much less mourn his passing. Any feeling that his death occasioned, back at home, would likely be relief. Others would carry on the work that he had shouldered for so long, and likely do it just as well—or better, maybe with more subtlety.

Tanner would gladly leave them to it.

As for afterward, he had no fear of Hell, although a threat of falling into outer darkness still remained for those few humans who attained no kingdom of glory. That risk was remote, and Tanner was convinced he could avoid it altogether if he made a proper sacrifice.

How to begin?

The means were obvious. First, Tanner's left hand grappled with the bandage swaddling his wounded shoulder, working at the knots until they loosened, finally surrendering. The cloth was dark and damp with blood as he unwound it roughly, already previewing what would follow.

When his wound was bared, he offered up a silent prayer

for strength, and then attacked the stitches set in place to mend his flesh. Real pain assaulted him, then, but he was resolute, gouging with fingernails like ragged talons, breathing through clenched teeth while he dug and probed, rewarded with a pulse of hot, fresh blood.

Still wanting more, Tanner kept at it till the pain threatened to overwhelm his consciousness. At last, weakened but satisfied, he slumped back on the cot that was his small cell's only furniture. He shuddered, heard the drip-drip-drip of crimson life escaping, and was satisfied that he had done his best.

If only the damned heretics could give him time to die.

Slade was halfway down the curving staircase to the courthouse basement when he met one of the bailiffs, Ben Stone, coming up. The other man was clean-sheet pale, with just a hint of greenish tinge beneath the pallor, breathing hard, as if he'd run five miles instead of thirty feet.

"Marshal! I . . . he . . ."

"Calm down and say it, Ben."

Stone paused, bracing himself against the brick wall with an outstretched arm, and took two long, slow breaths. At length, he gasped, "Your prisoner . . ."

Slade didn't wait to hear the rest. He passed Stone, bolting down the stairs, taking them two and three at a time. There was a little stagger step when he hit bottom, then Slade got his balance back and ran full tilt along the gray, damp-smelling cellblock corridor to reach the Danite's cell.

It looked more like a slaughter pen inside. The nameless gunman lay half off his cot, head resting on the floor, glazed eyes wide open, staring back at Slade beyond the bars. Blood pooled beneath the drooping corpse, so much of it that Slade had trouble crediting that all of it came from a single body.

He didn't have Stone's keys, hadn't been thinking straight

enough to ask for them, and they'd be useless now, in any case. This was a job for Enid's coroner and undertaker. Slade could no more breathe new life into the prisoner than he could ride a horse to Mars.

He saw exactly how the man had done it, digging at the gunshot wound Slade had inflicted, mining it with gruesome fingertips despite the agony it must have caused him, until the flow of blood became a gusher that would surely finish him. How long had he lain unattended, while the spurting ebbed to seepage and his life ran out along with it?

What difference did it make?

Slade scowled. It seemed that he had killed the Danite after all, with just a little help. Another act of blood atonement.

No one would be coming for the Danite, now. There would be no further arrests, no trail to follow, nothing to indict the man or men who had dispatched him eastward—and who might, for all Slade knew, have other teams of killers in the field.

Suddenly weary, Slade retreated to the stairs, taking his time where Bailiff Stone had raced toward daylight moments earlier. There was no rush, nothing that he could do or say to change the fact that they had lost their one and only lead.

Case closed.

Slade saw it written plainly on Judge Dennison's face, as he reentered the jurist's private chambers. Once again, he passed Ben Stone, this time shamefaced, nothing to say.

"Ben's short a badge," Slade said.

"We're short a crucial prisoner," Judge Denison replied. "He died on Stone's watch, and from what I hear, died *slowly*. You confirm it?"

Slade could only nod and say, "It took a while."

"No indication he was helped along in any way?"

"No sir. None I could see."

"All right. So it's just negligence, not criminal conspiracy. I can't recoup the damage, but I've cut our loss as best I can. Stone's out."

"Somebody needs to tell the Haglunds."

"I can do that if you like," said Dennison. "They'll likely be relieved to skip the trial and get back on their way."

To where? Slade asked himself. And said, "I'll do it, sir. If you don't mind."

Dennison peered at Slade from underneath his busy eyebrows, then said, "As you wish. It seems I have more telegrams to send."

Stopping the various reporters he'd alerted to a great sensation in the making, Slade supposed. And would there also be a telegram to Utah Territory, asking Dennison's counterpart to check up on the Danites? If so, who would read it? What action, if any, would result?

Slade didn't want to think about that, now. It was beyond his jurisdiction, and he couldn't do a blessed thing about it. Not unless someone got nervous and decided he—or they—should send more Danites out to find Judge Dennison, silence his inquiries forever.

If that happened, Jack Slade would be waiting for them. That *was* something he could handle. And whatever god the hunters worshiped, they would need his help when that day came.

In spades.

"So, that's an end to it?" Dannell Haglund inquired.

"I'd say so," Slade replied.

"There'll be no trial."

"For that, we need a live defendant."

"And the Prophet suffers nothing."

"Not unless we find a witness who can name him and connect him to a crime. By which, I mean with *evidence*. Not hearsay, rumors, and the like."

"You saw his men in action," Dannell said.

"Yes, I did. But they're all dead now. What I *didn't* see was anyone behind them, giving orders, handing out the guns, whatever. I don't even know your so-called Prophet's name. You want to help me out with that, at least?"

Dannell considered it, then shook his head. "No point," he said. "Even if I could give you evidence enough for an indictment, it would just mean staying here, or going somewhere else to testify at trial. My family would still be targets."

Slade glanced toward the other Haglunds, grouped around the wagon they'd arrived in, making ready to begin their journey afresh. Wandle stared back at him, a vague longing expression on her pretty face.

"And aren't they targets now?" Slade asked. "Won't someone still be coming after you?"

"Perhaps," Dannell replied. "The first lot took the best part of ten years to sniff us out. Give us another ten, most of the children will be grown and out."

"They had to scour the country for you last time," Slade reminded him. "This time, they'll have a point of focus."

"And we won't be here. I'm thinking now, the Haglund name may vanish at the city limits. Look for me tomorrow, I'll be someone else."

"It's hard on children."

"They can take it," Dannell said. "They're what it's all about."

"Raising a family on the run?"

"No, Marshal. Raising godly souls to serve our Heavenly Father, on Earth and beyond, in the mansions of glory."

"You still believe, after all that's happened?" Slade asked.

"More than ever. The fact that I'm standing here breathing, with all of my loved ones alive, proves to me there's a God. And you might just be one of his angels."

Slade felt a blush warming his cheeks. He said, "I wouldn't mention that to anyone. They'll think you're crazy."

"*Crazier*, you mean to say?"

"What someone else believes isn't my business," Slade replied. "If you find solace in your creed, more power to you."

"Marshal, thank you for that. And for my family."

Dannell offered his hand, and Slade accepted. After that, their leave-taking included handshakes from the boys, stair-step progression from the eldest downward, then a round of awkward hugs and fleeting kisses from the women. Wandle June was last in line, throwing herself at Slade with force enough to stagger him and hanging on until her mother pried her loose.

"I love you, Marshal Jack!" she whispered fiercely, before she was pulled away.

Slade addressed the Haglunds as a group, careful to keep his eyes off Wandle June. "Before you know it," he advised, "you'll put all this behind you, like a nightmare that was scary once, but now you can't remember why." And facing Wandle then, he said, "It's best to leave some things behind."

Slade stood and watched them leave, some of the children waving all the way, until they passed from sight. Wandle waved once, and then did not look back.

All for the best.

Slade liked things simple, cut-and-dried. His job was like that, for the most part. He arrested felons, or they managed to escape, in which case they were someone else's problem. There were always wanted posters to remind him of the ones that got away, and maybe they'd be back sometime, to let him have a second chance.

Entanglements had always been Slade's bane. He'd been a drifter from his childhood to the day he'd gotten word of his brother's murder and had been forced to change. No, that was wrong. No one had *forced* him. It was more like he had been persuaded, then entangled by degrees, slowly, so

that he didn't mind. But having met the Haglunds, having
seen how much they suffered for their family and faith . . .

For Faith.

Slade reckoned that he had a choice to make. Where better to consider it than a saloon?

EPILOGUE

"So, that's the end of it?" Faith echoed Dannell Haglund's words.

"I think so," Slade replied. "I *hope* so, anyway."

Faith's parlor seemed a strange place to be sitting and discussing murder, but Slade felt at home there. He felt safe—which, in his current trade, might be a grave mistake.

"They won't send others out, to get even?" she asked.

Slade shrugged. "It's hard to figure what a pack of crazy men will do. Unless they change their style of dressing, though, we shouldn't have a problem spotting them."

"I'm glad the Haglunds are all right," Faith said. "I hope they find someplace where they can live in peace."

Better than resting in peace, Slade thought. But said, "I hope so, too."

Faith took his hand, adding, "But most of all, I'm glad that you're all right. You *are* all right, Jack, aren't you?"

"Absolutely. How are you?"

"Better. The judge sent out some men to help around the place, for now. I should be interviewing hands next week."

"Sorry about your other men."

"The sad part is that Handy was the only one of them with any family, as far as I can tell. I heard him talk about a brother, up in Philadelphia. Or maybe it was Pittsburgh."

"Are you looking for him?"

"I may try to put some kind of advertisement in the papers," Faith replied, "if I can think of anything to say. I couldn't even swear that 'Handy' was his given name."

"I know you'll do your best," Slade said. "You always do. About the other thing . . ."

"You mean the man I killed?"

"How are you bearing up?" Slade asked.

"I won't pretend it doesn't bother me," Faith said. "But he was an assassin, and he made the choice to do his business here, at my home. I'm not mourning him. Maybe a little for myself."

"My fault," Slade said. "It was a stupid thing for me to bring the Haglunds here. We should've kept on going straight to Enid in the first place."

"And been ambushed on the way? How would you feel right now, Jack, if the children or the women had been harmed?"

"We might have made it through okay," he said. "Your men would be alive right now."

"My man *is* still alive," Faith said, locking his eyes with hers.

"Did any of this shake your trust at all?" Slade asked.

"My trust in you? Not in the least."

"I guess I meant to say your *faith*."

"In what, Jack?"

"I'm not sure. Maybe in God? In family?"

"Why would you ask that?"

"All this killing in the name of a religion, when they're meant to give folks peace of mind," Slade said. "Targeting families for what they think or how they pray, when all they want to do is lead a quiet life, the way they choose."

"That isn't God's fault," Faith replied. "Always assuming that there *is* a god, somewhere. Men make the choices, take beliefs and twist them to their own mean, selfish ends. It's always been that way, since people started gathering in villages and towns, around the world. Men craving power— and some women, I suppose—take anything that's hopeful and pervert it. It takes other men, like you, to stop them if you can."

"You give me too much credit," Slade said.

"Not a bit of it. You've saved my life on more than one occasion, Mr. Slade. And likely saved my sanity, on top of it."

"There's something that I need to tell you, Faith," he said. "I've tried before but never seem to find the proper words."

"Sounds ominous," she said, trying to smile and not quite managing.

"It isn't easy for me, being who and what I am."

"I'm listening."

"We've been together for a while, now. Some might say through thick and thin. And the thing is . . ."

"What, Jack? What's the thing?"

Slade forced it out. "I love you, Faith. And I was wondering if . . . if . . ."

"If *what*?"

"If you would be my wife," the lawman said.